MW01205518

PAISLEY MOON

MILA HOLST

Langdon Street Press
212 3rd Avenue North, Suite 290
Minneapolis, MN 55401
612.455.2293
www.langdonstreetpress.com

ISBN - 978-1-934938-72-0
ISBN - 1-934938-72-6
LCCN - 2009937945

Cover Design and Typeset by Peter Honsberger

Printed in the United States of America

Dedication

I dedicate this to my family: my son Christian, my daughter Karen and son-in-law Steve, my grandson Karsten, and in memory of my son, Erik. Thanks to Karl in Munich, to Shirley, and to my family and friends for their loving support.

One

1968

Joseph walked across the small wooden stage of St. Matthew's parish hall. Tonight, the first Saturday in June, all else would be forgotten—the war in Vietnam, the hustle and bustle of politicking in and around Salinas. All that mattered was the dance, a fundraiser long planned by the tight-knit group.

"Ladies and gentlemen, on behalf of Saint Matthew's," Joseph Collins spoke into the microphone, stretching his arms to include the smiling ladies entering the stage, "we extend a warm welcome to you, our wonderful parishioners. These women have transformed our hall into a Hawaiian luau: Mary Ellen Bartlett, Bridget Vecchio, and my wife, Carolina Collins." He pronounced his wife's name in Spanish, "Cah-roh-*lee*-nah," softly rolling the *r*. "Father McCarthy," Joseph nodded to the parish priest, "will say the blessing." Everyone bowed their heads.

"In the name of the Father, and of the Son, and of the Holy Spirit. We humbly ask your blessing, Lord, for your brothers and sisters gathered here tonight." The elderly, slightly built Jesuit priest lowered his voice as he said, "We pray for the safety of our servicemen in Vietnam." He waited a few seconds before continuing with, "For the sake of our school, this fundraiser was deemed essential, and we thank all of our parishioners for the success we have here tonight."

"We have a surprise and the start of a new tradition," Mary Ellen announced. "The young woman who designed and created the scenery these past four years is hereby named queen for this special night. Carolina Sanchez Collins, please accept this crown and scepter as a token for all the work you have done for the parish."

Her mouth a perfect O, a small gasp escaping, and eyes wide, Carolina bent down to have the rhinestone-studded tiara pinned on her dark auburn hair.

"This is such a surprise! Thank you all for this honor," she said in her soft voice.

The orchestra played bars from the Beatles' *Yesterday*. Carolina nodded modestly as the crowd applauded.

"This will be the beginning of a tradition," Mary Ellen continued. "Who will be our queen as we look to the future? Carolina, will you and Joseph start the first dance?"

Joseph and Carolina stepped off the stage. "Joseph, did you know about this?" Carolina asked as she and Joseph glided smoothly to the dance music.

"No, hon, I didn't. I'm as surprised as you are," Joseph replied.

A lone, handsome man, standing in a shadow in a far corner, held up his punch glass in salute to the couple. Carolina was struck by his dark good looks.

He seemed to know Joseph, who nodded briefly at him.

"You don't look happy with the surprise. What's wrong, hon?" Joseph said, leading his wife around the dance floor.

"This crown reminds me of junior year in high school almost ten years ago. Most of us are certainly past prom age. They all had good intentions, but I feel a bit embarrassed."

"Oh—the year you were crowned most beautiful. And you are gorgeous, now more than ever," he whispered as he kissed her cheek.

"Carolina, the decorations look gorgeous! You, Mary Ellen, and Bridget have outdone yourselves again," Nancy Johnson's voice boomed as she twirled by with her teenaged son. Nancy's husband was deployed. She'd come home to Salinas with her youngest son to stay with her parents.

"Thank you, Nancy. I'm so glad it's turning out well. And I'm glad you joined us, Mikey," Carolina said, smiling at one of the handful of teenagers who didn't mind being at a dance with their parents.

"Let's get some punch, Caro," Joseph mumbled, steering her to the brightly decorated corner where his mother and sister chatted as they filled punch cups. Vince, Joseph's brother-in-law, nodded to Joseph and Carolina as he played saxophone in the orchestra made up of parishioners.

"Congratulations, Carolina. You make a lovely queen," Joseph's mother, Sofia, said as she embraced her daughter-in-law.

Tina, Joseph's sister, chimed in, "And they were so

right. All of this was your doing from the beginning. I'm so happy for you, Caro," she said, hugging her tightly. "Now, everyone will be eager to see who will get the honor next year. It's a great idea, whoever came up with it!"

"You younger women have made such a difference for our little church dances," Sophia Collins stated in her charming Italian accent.

"We need to get over to the supper line, Mom," Tina said.

"You two go ahead. I'll cover here. It's quiet for now," Carolina commented. "Mabel is set to help here when it gets busy."

Joseph nodded at Caro from where he'd joined a group of men. She lowered her large, dark brown eyes, hiding a moment of sadness despite her joy in anticipation of the evening ahead. She absentmindedly tugged at her skirt, feeling it ride smoothly on her slender hips. Her dark auburn hair hung to her shoulders in thick waves. She discreetly removed the tiara and set it on a table nearby.

Her thoughts shut out the music as she leaned against the corner wall, eyes closed, trying to block out negative thoughts. Not tonight, she thought. I want to enjoy this special evening that I've worked on so long. She shut out the turmoil of the last few months and smiled to herself. He loves me—he has a different way of showing it, she declared to herself as she thought about how she and Joseph had been married almost six years but had not made love in weeks. Carolina was afraid to think the worst—that he found someone else.

They met at the USO club in El Paso during her

senior year in high school. He'd asked her to dance and they'd been together ever since. She was a virgin on their wedding night. Her two older sisters, Anita and Marta, had put the fear of God into the two younger ones, Lisa and Carolina. The Sanchez girls did not break with tradition.

Joseph rarely drank, though he would occasionally meet a friend for a beer after work. He devoted many evenings to his recently widowed mother, Sofia. He managed the hardware store his father had founded. Carolina was aware the community considered Joseph an ideal husband and son. An Army medical discharge kept Joseph from further military service.

Sofia had taken to Carolina at once, welcoming the nineteen-year-old into the family. Carolina's quiet, down-to-earth, sweet nature made it easy for Joseph's small family to make Carolina feel at home so far away from her own. Joseph Senior and Sofia had made the trip to El Paso for the wedding and had been charmed by the warmth of the large Sanchez clan present in Grandmother Ana's spacious home and renowned gardens.

The patriarch Don Miguel Antonio Sanchez made sure the festivities in honor of his youngest daughter, by his account "the fairest of them all," were memorable. The extended family doted upon Carolina, and she took it all in stride. Miguel's devotion to his family was legendary in the neighborhood. When he courted Carolina, Joseph noted the closeness of the family and the girls' hero-worship of their father. Joe Senior saw that as well in the few days they were present for the wedding preparations and for the big day itself.

Because he was a tall man with a ruddy complexion and light brown hair, Miguel's demeanor gave him an aristocratic air. That was what Joe had thought the moment he met Miguel: that he was a Spanish aristocrat—a polite gentleman who made you feel at home at once. The Spanish idiom *Mi casa es su casa* (my home is your home) fit this man and his family perfectly. Carolina's mother, Esther, was the gracious hostess, making sure everything was in order.

Applause from the audience broke Carolina out of her reverie, bringing her back to the present and reality.

"Caro, the evening is turning out so well! I'll have some punch," Mary Ellen said, as she caught a glimpse of sadness in the beautiful young woman's eyes.

It was still dark out early Sunday morning as Carolina roused from heavy sleep with Joseph's body pressing against her. He smiled as her eyes fluttered open and he kissed her neck. Like the old days, she thought, as she surrendered to his caresses and responded to his quick, passionate lovemaking. She snuggled into him, feeling the warmth of his body still so close to hers, hopeful that her fears were unfounded. They soon fell asleep again.

Sunday was spent, as usual, at Sofia's, along with Tina and Vince and their toddler, Laurie. There was still daylight as Carolina and Joseph walked home, tired from a long, fun-filled Sunday, appetites satisfied by Sofia's delicious spaghetti. With Joseph's arm affectionately around her shoulder, Carolina fell into pace with him and placed her arm around his waist. She looked up at him, her hair bathed in the pale moonlight coming up behind her.

"There's your moon, Caro. This is the way I always think of you, with your profile against the moon, just like it was when we'd sit on your parents' porch."

Relishing their closeness, willing it to remain forever, she sighed. "Yes, I remember those first nights right after we met, when I told you how I love the paisley moon. See the patterns on the moon? Just like a paisley print."

He laughed softly at her words and squeezed her closer to him.

"The ladies' group of St. Matthews is proud to announce we have more than doubled last year's profits from the dance. We'll be able to donate to all our students—" Mary Ellen was startled as a woman's cries in the hall caused her to stop her speech abruptly.

The church secretary, Betty, rushed into the comfortable living room of the rectory used for their meetings, tears streaming down her face, shaking her hands as if in protest to what she had to say. The small group was stunned by the interruption.

"I just heard—I don't know where to begin—it's awful, just awful," Betty shrieked and stammered. "He's dead. It was just confirmed on the radio."

The women stared silently, trying to make sense of what Betty was saying.

"Who?" Mary Ellen asked as she went up to Betty and put her arms around her, trying to calm her. "Who, dear, who is dead?"

"Bobby Kennedy—I just heard it on the radio," Betty

said, sitting in one of the easy chairs. "Someone shot him in Los Angeles. He was walking through a hotel kitchen. A man shot him and he's dead." She placed her hands to her face and sobbed.

Mary Ellen placed a hand on Betty's shoulder and faced the ladies all gathered in a cluster around each other, tears in their eyes.

"This is terrible," a stunned Mary Ellen said, shaking her head.

Father walked in. They all looked at him, eyes wide in disbelief, not knowing what to make of the news.

"It's true," he said. "I just heard it myself. These are terrible times we are living in, but we have to be strong and keep our faith. I'll be making announcements at Mass this evening. We should be discussing the success of the dance and how much was raised, but this meeting will have to wait. For now, go on home to your families."

Carolina walked home, thinking of the unfortunate news and distracted from her personal uneasiness, but she pondered what had happened that morning with Joseph as she had been leaving for the meeting.

"If you get finished early with the meeting, meet me for lunch at Mom's," Joseph had said. His demeanor had seemed usual, Carolina thought. But a wry smile on his face puzzled her when she answered, "I doubt we'll be done much before one o'clock, so I don't think I'll be able to make it. Two other committees will be reporting later in the morning on their projects, and we all usually take longer than we'd planned. We'll have lunch with Father in the rectory."

She walked home slowly, a sick feeling in the pit

of her stomach growing stronger. What if I'm right? she thought. What if he is seeing someone? What will I do?

She gazed at her flowers and the shrubbery she lovingly tended. The rich, dark, moist soil was easy to till. She spent hours at the nursery picking out plants, choosing those she'd always longed for. There were hydrangeas in full bloom. Clusters of snapdragons in lovely colors proudly stood against the warm beige of the house. Roses splashed a profusion of color: pale pinks, yellows, deep reds, and her favorite, a rare watermelon hue.

She stopped and stared at Joseph's car parked all the way to the back of the driveway. The small single-stall garage with an added carport was hidden from the street. Joseph rarely came home during the day. She walked slowly to the back door, gripped the knob, and took a deep breath, pressing her lips together. She felt the knob turn easily in her hand. Her heart was pounding so hard and fast she could hear it. She swallowed hard. What if I have to separate from Joseph and even divorce? she wondered. Her thoughts were jumbled. What will I tell my family and my friends here? What will I do? She swallowed, and a bitter taste of bile told her she needed to relax before she could go on. She stood quietly just inside the kitchen, gently pressing the door behind her.

Voices inside the house startled Carolina. She gripped the knob harder and closed the door behind her. Instinctively, she sensed her placid life would soon change forever. After entering the small, neat kitchen, she took the few steps that placed her in the hall, and she stood facing the hall mirror, which gave her a partial view of the door to the bedroom. How many times had she and Joseph communicated with each other by looking into this mirror while she prepared breakfast and he finished getting ready for work? They'd laughed at the odd placement of the mirror by the former tenants, but had never taken it down.

Now there was another couple reflected in the mirror. She could see Joseph with his back toward her. He was bending down, handing something to someone out of view. His lover, she thought. It must be. Carolina wondered if she would recognize the woman. Was it someone she knew? A neighbor? She felt lightheaded and leaned against the wall to steady herself. Joseph laughed softly. Maybe it's nothing serious, she thought. Maybe it's just a fling and we can be happy together again. Maybe . . . She could feel the blood pounding in her ears.

A low male voice, not Joseph's, startled her. "You are as wonderful as ever, my Joseph. I can't get enough of you. You know how I've longed for you."

The two male figures were in clear view now. The other man, standing behind Joseph, reached around, buttoning Joseph's shirt, caressing his chest. She saw Joseph's arms stroking the other man's arms. The two laughed in their deep baritones. She could see the man behind Joseph as he kissed Joseph's neck, and Joseph turned around to face the man, returning the man's embrace and kiss. It was the stranger, the handsome man from the dance Saturday night.

Open-mouthed, eyes staring at a scene from another life, certainly not hers, Carolina gasped as the warmth of their embrace heightened. The two men turned toward her reflection at the sound. They did not separate at once. Joseph gently pushed the man's arms down, and then coolly asked, "Wasn't your meeting supposed to last past one o'clock?"

"It was." Carolina's voice was surprisingly calm. "But, because of what happened . . . we all came home . . ." she said, her voice trailing, with the word *home* barely audible. Her calmness surprised her. She was taking short, shallow breaths, and the slow, rising anger steadied her.

"I . . . I guess you're wondering what's going on, Caro. We . . . This is my friend . . . Tom and we . . ."

"You really don't have to explain yourself, Joseph. No. No, I don't wonder—not anymore." The pallor on her face was slowly dissipating.

In a daze, Carolina sat on the sofa, brushing Joseph's hand away as he reached for her. She picked up a cushion and held it to her breast, pressing it against her as she took slow, deep breaths. A thousand thoughts went through her mind. Everything fell into place. His increasing lack of interest in her the past few months was starting to make complete sense.

Joseph sat on the sofa, near Carolina, and buried his face in his hands, shaking his head side to side. He balled his hands into fists and made an effort to speak, trying to regain his composure. "Honey, you need to understand that . . ."

Tom stood in the hall, in the space Carolina had occupied moments earlier, hands on his hips, waiting for his lover to say something. Joseph looked at him for a long time, then shook his head slowly and motioned for Tom to step outside. Tom shrugged impatiently and pressed his fingers to his lips as if to blow Joseph a kiss, a hint of a smile breaking through on Joseph's grim face.

The moment she heard the door close, Carolina turned and faced Joseph. She was clutching the cushion tighter. In a low, deliberate voice she hissed, "How could you, Joseph? You've been living a lie with me all this time." Tears were rolling down her cheeks. She wiped them away angrily.

"Honey . . . Caro . . . please listen to me. I . . . I couldn't help myself. I've tried to stay away from . . . Tom. I do love you, I always have, and you're so beautiful and sweet and good to be with. Honey, please believe me. I didn't want you to find out. I wanted to keep this from you."

Joseph sat looking down at the floor, his hands pressed together. She looked at him and saw his tears. She gazed at him a long time and thought, I don't really know this man, my husband, a man I thought I loved and wanted to be married to forever.

Finally, in quiet, controlled anger, she spoke. "How could I have been so blind? How dare you do this to me, to us, to your family? Do they know, Joseph? Do your mother and Tina and Vince know?"

Joseph shook his head, which was bent down, his shoulders sagging. Somehow he did not appear as handsome as he had that morning. He seemed a total stranger to her. Carolina looked around the living room. How important everything had seemed to her before. She took in the furniture they'd shopped for and remembered deciding together on where to place the items they so carefully purchased. She thought of the plans they had spoken of just days ago, the Sunday after the big dance. How happy she had been! She shuddered as she recalled their last moment of love—it had not been as special as she had hoped, but at the time she felt connected to him and hopeful.

"Honey, we can work this out. I can promise you it won't happen again. I'll tell Tom he has to stay away. He doesn't live in town anymore. We can work things out."

"Joseph, don't insult me. Our marriage—if you can call it a marriage—is over."

"No, honey. Let's not do anything rash. I can promise you I'll stop it for good. It wasn't meant to be anything special. Caro, you must listen to me and give me a chance. I love you. I truly love you and want our marriage to continue and for us to have a good life together. We can be happy, like we were the first years. Remember how happy we were when we—"

"Joseph, stop," she said loudly, pushing his hand away from her arm. "You can't expect me to stay with you. Not now, not after what I saw today. I can never love you as I did. I wonder if I really loved you since I didn't know the truth about you."

"But, Caro . . . You know how happy we are here and how everyone thinks the world of you. My mom and Tina won't understand why you'd leave. Give yourself some time. You'll forgive me, I know you will."

Carolina threw down the cushion she was holding onto tightly and stood up. "Are you insane, Joseph? You think I can forgive what I saw today? I honestly think I could forgive you with another woman, but this

. . . this . . . other man?" Her voice was shrill.

She took deep breaths before she continued. "You want to stay married? Why, Joseph? For me to be your cover? I see why you were so thrilled I was a virgin when we married. I can't imagine it's normal to have as little sex as we —. You knew I'd never say anything or ask anyone about the subject. I'm the good wife who stays home, keeps a perfect house and sews, and is active in our church. How long were you going to carry on with your secret life? No, Joseph, at this moment I'm not sure what I'll do, but I will not stay in this marriage."

"Don't upset yourself so much. I had no intention of hurting you, ever. I am so sorry. Please forgive me. Whatever else you do, forgive me," Joseph said with his arms reaching out to her, his hands almost touching her hands. Reaching out, she held his hands but did not give in to his embrace. She held his eyes with hers, looking deeply into the hazel she had found so beguiling. He waited for her to speak.

"I will forgive you, Joseph," she said huskily, her voice composed, each word spoken slowly, deliberately, as she lightly held his hands, "but for now, you have to go. I will let you know how and when I will leave Salinas." She released his hands slowly, knowing this would be the last time they touched. She clenched her hands, willing herself to keep from crying, though it would be more out of sadness for the end of their marriage. Her love for him had changed forever.

Two

She locked the bedroom door behind herself and sat on the bed, but quickly realized the men had been together on the same bed. She gripped the corners of the sheets and pillowcases, bunched them up, and deposited them in the trash can in the bathroom. She placed fresh linens and a beige chenille bedspread on the bed. She was numb, emotionally exhausted, and full of uncertainty. Minutes may have passed before she heard the outer door close. She sighed deeply, looking around the bedroom. My bedroom, she thought, not ours. She couldn't believe what had happened, but she was relieved to know what had been wrong with them. She lay on the bed, staring up at the ceiling, thoughts racing through her mind.

She walked around the room, gently touching the photos of her family on the walls, avoiding smudging the glass. She smiled at their happy faces.

What in the world am I going to do? What will I tell them? I can't say that Joseph . . . No, I'll think of something. And where will I go? Back home?

She looked in the mirror and smoothed her hair. Her wry grin smiled back at her. "Most beautiful" indeed—

good thing no one can see me now, she reflected bitterly. Her wedding portrait, which had meant so much to her up until that morning, was staring at her along with portraits of her older sisters, Anita and Marta, with their thick, brown curly hair, and Lisa, her sister closest in age, older by five years, who was taller and thinner than the rest, with her black hair pulled back tightly from her face so the curls disappeared. Only *her* hair, Carolina's, was the color that had always attracted attention, the dark auburn that had caused her dismay at times, because it was different from everyone in her family, and not as curly as her sisters'.

She touched her parents' portrait: Her father, Miguel, standing tall, in his tuxedo for her wedding. A handsome man, here he looked like a movie star, like Cesar Romero, everyone had said. And Mamá, pretty and just as thin as when she was a young girl. Caro smiled as she admired the woman looking back at her. In this picture, I can touch my mother without her pulling away, she thought, and she looks back at me, directly at me.

She let the tears roll down her face. She walked around the room aimlessly, wondering what to do. She finally lay down in the bed, and soon slept soundly.

It was early morning, still dark, when hunger pangs awakened her. She touched Joseph's side of the bed and felt the empty space. Sitting bolt upright, she turned on the lamp and looked at herself in her clothes. She covered her face as the tears burst from her.

Why? How could he do this to me? She repeated the questions aloud to herself and sobbed until she was cried out. She removed her clothes and went into the shower, letting the wonderfully warm water cleanse her. In her bathrobe, she went to the kitchen and started coffee. It was four in the morning. She had not eaten since the morning before. The eggs she scrambled and bread she toasted were soon devoured. Sipping the coffee, she stared into space, willing herself to be strong, to find a solution to this unforeseen situation. She had no point of reference. Nothing like this had ever happened to anyone in her family or anyone she knew.

She put her hands together in prayer, like a child, and whispered her request, trusting an answer would present itself. She went out and got the newspaper, which was full of news about Robert Kennedy's shooting in Los Angeles. She began to read it but her mind kept wandering. Finally, as the dawn rose, she smiled as she thought of her aunts in Los Angeles.

She thought about how they had provided her with the refuge she needed when she was fifteen, that summer when she celebrated her fifteenth birthday so happily one day, only to discover the dreadful secret just days later. My aunts were my angels then, she thought. They will help me again. Of course! They will be my salvation again.

She dashed to their—her—bedroom, made the bed, and started going through the closet where she kept her sewing. The closet was full. There were dresses, pants, jackets, skirts: everything she had sewn over the past years. She would need boxes to store and transport her treasures. She gathered items to take with her and placed them in piles. She took down her paisley-moon print drapes and replaced them with the house's original floral curtains.

It was finally time to call Joseph. He answered at the store at once. He was always the first one there.

"Joseph, this is Caro. I will need five or six boxes, large ones. Please bring them as soon as you can. I'll tell you when you bring them what I have decided to do."

"Honey, are you going through with—?"

"Yes, it's settled," she interrupted. She would not give him a chance to go further. "I'll also need some cash, so you can be thinking about that as well."

"I'll come by later this morning, as soon as I can get away."

She replaced the receiver without another word. She called her aunt Margarita.

"Tía, this is Carolina. How are you, dear aunt?"

"*Mi hijita!* How nice to hear your voice."

"Auntie, would it be all right with you if I come down to visit with you for a while?"

"Oh, my dear child. What a question! It will be so good to see you again. You and your husband will be visiting?" she asked with a chuckle.

"No, Auntie, it's just me this time. I was hoping I could come down this weekend. I may need to stay with you for a while. There's some business I need to take care of and it may take some time," she said, trying to sound casual and biting her lip to keep from crying, happy that she had the presence of mind to think of her aunts. She changed the subject quickly as she felt her throat choke. "How is my aunt Mattie?"

"Oh, she's just fine. We've both had the usual colds and such, but other than that, we're both fine, thanks to God. I'm so glad you'll be here soon. You stay as long as you like, *mi hijita.* You know this is your home. I'll be expecting you. Give my love to Joseph and to his dear mother and the rest of the family."

"I will, Aunt Margaret. *Hasta muy pronto,* Tía."

That was the first step of her plan and certainly the easiest, she knew, but at least a start. Then she started thinking: I'm not sure my old car can make it safely to Los Angeles. There's really a lot more to think about. I've never been on a long trip on my own. I do have to manage, though. I have to make decisions for myself and prepare myself for life without Joseph.

There was a timid knock at the back door and Joseph popped his head in to announce his arrival. I guess he knows I'm serious, she thought.

"Where do you want the boxes, hon?"

"In the bedroom, Joseph. Thank you."

"Here's some money for you. Let me know if you need more. Will you let me know where you're going?"

"Yes. I'll be at my aunt's in Los Angeles."

"Oh, I should have guessed. They are such sweet ladies. I . . . became quite fond of them," Joseph stammered.

"Aunt Margaret sends you her regards, and to your mother as well. I'll stay with her until I decide what I'm going to do."

"May I call you there?"

Carolina hesitated before answering, "I guess so. Yes, it will be necessary for us to be in touch. It's best if you wait until I call you first. I haven't told my aunt what happened. I don't know what I will tell her."

"I understand. Caro, I know you don't want to me to say anything about what's happened. But . . . I do wish you wouldn't leave." He saw the determined look on her face.

"Joseph, it's best for us this way. You'll see it yourself soon. Make excuses for me to your family. Say my aunt called and I had to leave immediately. The same goes for any of the ladies from church. I really don't want to face anyone. I don't know that I could say goodbye without . . . Maybe someday I'll come back and . . ." She knew she would not return, not to him, not to this life.

"I need a better car to drive down to LA," Carolina said unwaveringly. She was surprised by how calm and strong she sounded and smiled at herself as she caught her reflection in the hall mirror.

"Of course, hon. I'll let you have mine. I wanted to buy you a newer car, remember? You were the one who said your old one was fine for what little you drove around town. I'll leave mine now and take yours, if that's OK."

"Yes, that will be fine. I'll leave you the phone number in case of emergency, but I do want you to wait until I call you. I plan to leave by the end of the week. In the meantime, please tell Sofia that I'm busy with the ladies' group. That should not raise any suspicion on her part, don't you think?"

Joseph looked at Carolina, seeing a different side of her. She sounded so strong and sure of what she was doing. Their married life had been one of him making all major decisions and Caro going along with much of what he said, though he respectfully always took her opinion into consideration.

He hesitated, waiting for her to say something else. When she did not, he cleared his throat and said shyly, "Will you call me before you leave or will you let me come over to help you?"

She looked around, knowing she would need help loading boxes and any furniture she may decide to take. "Yes, it would be nice of you to help. Thank you. I'll call you at the store and let you know when."

It had not occurred to Carolina that any signs of her packing and having a hauling truck in her driveway would arouse attention, and the last thing she wanted was to have to discuss anything with Joseph's family.

"Oh, Joseph, I'll have to take my own personal items and some furnishings. How will I get it all packed up without your mother finding out?"

"Yeah—well, I'll have to come in and help you the evening before to get it done. I'll do it myself Thursday night. Okay?"

"Yes, that will work out, I hope. I really don't want to cause your mother any worries. She'll have enough to think about when your truth comes out. I do wish it did not have to end this way, you know that," she said softly.

Joseph hung his head and shook it wordlessly. Finally, he spoke. "What can I say at this point? I'm going to do everything to keep it from my mother and sister. It would hurt them too much."

Early Friday morning, before dawn, Carolina was ready. Joseph's newer car was parked in the driveway with the hauling van attached. She had risen earlier than usual, eager to get on her way. Joseph had finished around midnight, working quietly and slowly, loading only through the back, so, they hoped, no one had noticed any activity. There were not as many boxes as Carolina had thought she would need.

I'll be at Tía Margarita's before seven tonight, she thought. She realized that she'd gone over and over what happened with Joseph so many times in her mind that she was exhausted thinking about him and his family. She knew that he'd have to explain everything to them on his own and was glad she wouldn't be in Salinas to face his mother and Tina.

She began the long drive. The next few hours would give her the distance she was seeking, almost desperately at this point. She had second thoughts many times while she packed the few household items she was keeping. She wondered if she could remain as strong as she was willing herself to be. Yet, the thought of Joseph with—. She could not bring herself to say his name, even to herself. That was enough to steady her resolve and move on.

As she pulled up to the curb in front of a neatly kept large home, Carolina saw her aunt looking out the window, waving at her, and soon running out the front door to welcome her. A tired Carolina beamed a smile in return, letting the warmth of the welcome reach deeply, thankful for the safe haven.

"My dear Caro, I'm so glad you've arrived safely. When will that dear husband of yours join you? You did not say why you were coming down on your own."

Carolina clung to her aunt, kissed her cheek, and said, "At times like these, family is more special than ever."

"Caro, you're trembling. What's wrong, *hija*?"

"Tía, let me rest a while and catch my breath. I drove all day. There is so much to tell . . ."

"Your aunt Mattie will be over any minute. She insisted on making her *caldillo* for you when I told her you were on your way."

"It's so good to be here again, though this visit will be quite different from last summer when Joseph and I ..." Her voice trailed. She stifled a sob as she clenched her fists.

"Here, let me get you something to drink. Would you like a glass of lemonade?"

"Lemonade will be perfect. May I please use your phone to call Lisa? You can listen while I tell her all that's happened. I know you'll all be shocked, dear aunt, but I may as well tell you and my family the truth right now. Joseph isn't with me. He . . . won't be with me anymore."

"Come to the kitchen, you can call from there. My, you've got me concerned about what's happened. Is Joseph all right? And I see you brought some belongings. Carolina, you're crying."

"I should have listened to Aunt Amelia when she told me to postpone my wedding. Don't look so surprised. Everyone knew I married Joseph to have the dream wedding I'd planned since I was ten. I thought we had an excellent marriage, at least at first. But I never dreamed . . ."

"Here's the phone. Call Lisa and tell her, if you're ready. You're safe with me. You can stay here as long as you need to. What in the world has that man done to upset you like this? It's a good thing he isn't here, or I'd give him the biggest scolding of his life for whatever he's done." She placed three glasses of lemonade on the table. Carolina drank almost half a glass at once.

"It's ringing. I hope she's home. You know how busy she stays with her projects. Lisa! I'm so glad you answered. Yes, it's me. I'm in Los Angeles with Tía Margarita. I just got here. I want to tell you . . ."

"Carolina, what's wrong?" Lisa replied. "Why are you crying? Has something happened to either you or Joseph? Tell me, the suspense is killing me."

"Lisa," she began, trying to control her sobs so she

could speak, "I don't know how I didn't see the truth about Joseph. I've suspected something was going on for several months, maybe even from the beginning." She had stopped crying. "I have to say in some way I'm relieved I don't have to stay with him. You and Tía Amelia were right. I shouldn't have married him so soon after my graduation. Well, it's over now."

Aunt Margaret stood up and placed her hands on Carolina's shoulders, bending down to kiss the top of her niece's head, smoothing her hair and letting tears drop down her own smooth cheek.

There were sounds at the front door and a bustling, taller, plumper version of Aunt Margaret appeared in the kitchen doorway. Aunt Mattie's presence filled the room. She was carrying a large pot. After placing it on the stove, the woman who appeared to be all kindness approached Carolina, bending down to hug the young woman. She had gently moved Margaret aside as she stood beside Carolina's chair and stroked her hair. The older women sat at either side of their niece at the round table in the corner as Margaret motioned to her sister to listen, intent on the conversation taking place. Carolina waved to her aunt Mattie and blew a kiss in her direction.

"I left this morning and took most of my prized possessions, though I hated to leave my home, my garden and flowers."

Carolina caught the puzzled look on Aunt Mattie's face as Aunt Margaret again motioned her sister to listen, this time with a sterner look on her face.

"I'm trying to tell everyone what happened to Joseph and me," Carolina said to Lisa and to her aunts, swallowing hard to stifle the sobs she was afraid would overcome her. She listened to her sister, many miles away in her hometown in West Texas, with her eyes shut, as her sister's voice came across the miles.

"Whatever has happened, you can tell me. I'm here for you," Lisa said in as peaceful a voice as she could muster.

Carolina regained her composure and said, "Yes, Lisa, I can talk about it now and even be angry at myself for being so gullible."

She paused a moment before continuing. "I imagined Joseph was involved with another woman. He had been more distant to me recently. Several days ago I came home early from the church club and . . . I walked into the bedroom and found him—and a man— together. I don't want to give you all the details—you can imagine. I thought I was going to pass out from the shock and I guess I almost did." She waited for the enormity of her news to become a reality to her sister and aunts. She could hear Lisa breathing on the other end, but for several seconds there was silence. The pallor of her aunts' faces reflected their surprise at hearing the appalling news.

Aunt Margaret leaned over and embraced Carolina. Now that she had the courage to tell her family, Caro wanted no more interruptions.

"It was hard for me to decide whether to tell you and my aunts the truth or to cover up somehow," Carolina said as she continued talking to Lisa. "As I drove down here, I made up my mind. I'm going to stay in Los Angeles for now, as long as Aunt Margaret will have me."

Margaret nodded vigorously as she heard this. She reached out and held Carolina's free hand in both of hers, patting her hand in a sign of assent and support. Mattie, on her other side, placed her hand on Carolina's shoulder, also nodding.

Carolina held the receiver away from her as Lisa's voice boomed the words she'd expected to hear. "My God, Caro, what an outrage for you. Oh, I wish I could be there with you. I can leave this weekend and spend some time with you."

"I'm all right for now, I guess," she said sadly. "It's all been a shock—I'll need some time to get over it. We had quite an argument that day, the first one ever, come to think of it. Joseph had never given me reason to be upset with him. What may be harder for him will be to explain my absence to his mother and sister. You know how close they are and how well we all got along. I just could not face them and make up a story for my leaving like I did."

The two older women gave each other knowing glances.

Lisa said, "It's so hard to believe someone who seemed so perfect for you . . . I'll have to tell our parents. You want me to, don't you?"

"Yes, I guess so, though it really should be me who breaks it to them. Dad will be so disappointed. Oh, Lisa. I've had such a time. Joseph actually expected me to stay with him after I knew the truth about him."

Aunt Mattie stood up and set about to heat the pot she had carried in. Ever the practical one of her siblings, Mattie wanted to have supper warmed and ready for them.

"He begged me to consider what the news would do to his beloved mother and sister but that only made me angrier. All these years we've been married, he's lied to me, and used me. I don't wish him any harm, but I won't live a lie for him. He even wanted us to have a baby! I can't bear to have to tell the family the sordid details. Dad is so fond of Joseph, like everyone else."

"Don't worry about anybody over here. You take care of yourself and get on with your life. I'll see about getting time off."

"You really don't need to do that, though I appreciate it very much and know you'll always be there for me. I'll be fine. I'll spend some time here until I decide what I'm going to do. I drove all day and the exhaustion just hit me."

"I'll call you tomorrow, or you call me if you want to talk. Give my love to Aunt Margaret and Aunt Mattie and all my love to you."

"Give everyone my love, Lisa."

Carolina set the phone back on the table, out of the way. She glanced apprehensively at her aunts, her father's sisters.

"My goodness, Carolina! What a terrible experience for you. I have to say I would never have dreamed that of Joseph. The two of you seemed to be so perfect together." Margaret shook her head as she spoke.

"The family has never had to face anything quite like this. Or, if there has been, it's certainly been kept quiet. Perhaps that is the best thing to do, *querida*. Before everyone starts talking about what's happened, you may consider a quieter resolution." Of course Mattie would have such a suggestion.

"*Si*, Caro. Think about it before you break up your marriage."

Carolina looked up at her aunts, seeing the strong similarity to her beloved father. The two women, though not as tall as Miguel, had the same fair complexion and light hazel eyes, their masses of hair now glistening white. They had settled in Los Angeles as young brides, raised their families, and were such dear, loving women. Carolina smiled warmly at them, feeling their love for her. I am so blessed to have them, she thought. But it won't be easy getting them out of their old mindset. Of course, no one will want any scandal rising out of my marriage—and divorce, which surely will happen, she admitted to herself.

Aunt Mattie served three bowls of her renowned stew and placed them on the table, and all three ate heartily, their voices low as they talked about Carolina's situation.

"What are your plans, Carolina dear? You know you can also stay with me as long as you like, but of course, you'll want to move on with your life. Have you given thought to what you might want to do?" Mattie asked.

"It's a bit soon to be thinking along those lines, Mattie. Give the girl some time to think and decide later on."

"Caro," Margaret continued, turning to her niece, "you're exhausted and need your rest. We'll talk tomorrow about what you'll do in the days to come. You're a wonderful young woman. You have us—your family—and there's a world waiting for you. After you've rested, you'll see why the Lord may have brought you here at this time in your life."

"Aunt Mattie and Auntie Margaret, you always cheer me up. I'm so glad I have the two of you." Carolina hugged them both tightly.

A different scene was playing out in El Paso, in

Carolina's parents' home.

"Dad, I need to talk to you now, just the two of us."

"Lisa! I didn't know you were home. Come, sit down and talk to me. You've been so busy lately. How is everything going with my little girl?"

Lisa chuckled at her dad's words. She leaned down and kissed his cheek, sitting close enough to reach across to grasp his hands. His mere presence comforted her, as it had all her life. She accepted his direct look into her eyes. He waited patiently for her to speak.

"Dad."

She thought she had the right words to break the news to him. What could seem to be a simple problem to anyone else or to another family was not so for the Sanchez family. Her father led by example. In the neighborhood, it was largely accepted that whatever the Sanchez family did was the model to follow.

"I talked to Carolina. She's visiting Aunt Margaret and Aunt Mattie," Lisa said, and her voice sounded as strong and confident as she willed it.

"How nice! How long will they be staying this time? It's so good of Caro and Joseph to visit my sisters."

"Well, it's not quite as you think." She hesitated and looked around the cozy living room, tastefully decorated. All around were photographs of members of the family. Each photograph told a story. Each showed the love shared by all of them. How was she going to burst this bubble? The principle that their family followed the rules, lived good lives, and through any adversity relied on the strength they had always shared was a tenet unbearable to break, from her point of view. The invisible thread that bound them to each other and to the faith they proclaimed was discernible in this room.

"Carolina is visiting by herself. Actually, she's going to stay with them for a while. She's not sure how long. She's even considering getting a job and supporting herself."

"What are you talking about, Lisa? What do you mean she's by herself? Where is Joseph? Has something happened to him? Tell me!" The urgency in his voice did not surprise Lisa. Of course her father would be upset and fear the worst.

"No, nothing's happened to either of them. They're fine. She . . . wants to give herself time to be on her own for a while. It's really not that bad, Dad, to work and support oneself."

"That's your privilege to feel that way, and you have fulfilled your choice of having a career. But Carolina? She always wanted to be married, and she has a wonderful husband. What else is going on? What are you not telling me? Have they separated?"

"Well, yes. Yes, they've separated and will try to live apart for a while, at least. You know how young people are. They want to give themselves time to be apart for a while. Maybe things will work out. I . . . I hope they will."

Don Miguel was silent for several seconds, staring straight ahead, reflecting on what he had just been told.

"I don't know what to say, or what to think. This has never happened in our family before. Why, there has never been a divorce, not as long as any of us can remember. Not in the Sanchez family, or on your mother's side. No, there's never been a divorce and I hope there never will be. It's unthinkable," he said, raising his voice.

They heard the back door open and Esther's "Hello" rang out.

"Mom's back," Lisa said. "Don't say anything yet, please. I don't want to get everyone upset and a lot of talk going around about Caro. Okay?"

"This will stay between us for now. As soon as you hear anything, please tell me."

Lisa nodded in agreement.

Three

"You've always been an early riser. I remember fondly that summer you spent with me, after your *quinceañera*. You'd get up at sunrise, have coffee with your uncle Fernando and me, and then you would sew all morning before your cousins came over," Margaret said to Carolina.

"That was one of the happiest summer vacations here with you and my aunt Mattie and all my cousins."

"Yet, I recall how sad you were when you first arrived, Caro. I've always respected your privacy, but even now, I can't imagine what had occurred in your life to sadden you so."

"That was ten years ago. Here I am again, seeking refuge with you, this time for a totally different reason. I wish I could tell you what happened so long ago, but I have to say it wasn't important. You know how silly and emotional a fifteen-year-old girl can be, Auntie." The young woman said this with a shrug, hoping to seem convincing. This certainly was not the time to dredge up old wounds.

The sound of the front door opening and Aunt Mattie's bubbly "*Buenos días*" reached the pair in the kitchen. "I knew you'd both be up by now. There's someone I want you to meet, Carolina, one of our dear neighbors. I've asked her to come over before she goes on to her shop."

The women walked into the living room where most of Carolina's belongings were neatly stacked against the far wall. The small moving van was not in front.

"The van is parked in the back, in the alleyway," Margaret said, answering the obvious question Carolina was about to ask.

"When did you bring in my things?" Carolina was surprised to see her belongings in her aunt's living room.

"The young man next door kindly volunteered when he saw Mattie and me struggling to bring in your sewing machine late last night."

A tall, heavy-set blond woman stood in the doorway and knocked.

"Come in, dear Greta. This is our niece, Carolina."

"Good morning, ladies. Carolina, your aunts have told me so much about you. It's a pleasure to meet you at last."

Carolina graciously accepted Greta's outstretched hand and returned the warm, strong handshake, immediately detecting a slight German accent in her greeting.

"Your aunt tells me you sew. I'm interested in seeing your work," Greta said, not wasting any time.

"I see my aunts have placed most of my pieces here on the sofa and on the dining table. These are the pieces I've been working on recently. This one isn't quite finished, as you can see," Carolina said, holding a tan skirt. She touched the dresses and skirts gently, softly, lovingly. "Most of the items I designed myself," she said in a firm, yet soft voice. She held up her favorite, a lavender paisley dress, "and some I fashioned out of combining what I saw in magazines."

Greta picked up the paisley dress, holding it close to her and turning it toward the light to view the detail, carefully running her fingers down the seams. Her expression was serious as she looked wordlessly, closely, first at one, then another article of clothing, holding a pant suit up and studying the zippers, the button holes, scrutinizing the facings on the blouses. Carolina and her aunts stood by in anticipation as Greta took her time with each piece.

Finally, she spoke, her voice clear, strong, businesslike. "I must say this is excellent workmanship. Have you studied professionally? Your seams are perfect, these hems are almost invisible. I'm impressed by the styling. I recognize some of the patterns. But I also see your original designs."

"Thank you. I . . . have mostly worked on my own, as long as I can remember. I can't say I've studied sewing other than the high school classes that were available. But that was years ago. I learned from my aunts at home when I was a child. I've sewn just about every day the past few years."

"I can see you enjoy your trade. Your talent is obvious. My shop is small. My clientele prefers the personalized work I do, and I have stayed busy since I opened my shop three years ago. I do have a partner who I must admit is not the easiest person to get along with," Greta said with a grin. "But she is as demanding in her work as I am, if not more. That is the secret to our success. I am just now considering hiring an assistant and would like to offer you that position, if you will accept it. You can find out for yourself if we can work together. You'll have the opportunity to carry out your own ideas."

Carolina looked at the small group gathered in her aunt's living room amid her possessions, not believing what she was hearing. She nodded silently, her beaming smile speaking for her.

"I'll be talking to you later, perhaps this evening if that will work for you. Can you come by for supper? Let me know when I get home, around five. A pleasant day to you, ladies," she nodded to the older women. She waved goodbye as she let herself out the front door.

Putting her arm around her niece's waist, Margaret said, "You see, Carolina. You already have a job offer in something you love to do. Greta needs an assistant and you appear almost at her doorstep. I say this was meant to be."

Carolina hugged first one aunt, then the other. "Aunt Margaret, Aunt Mattie, my life is already taking a better direction."

Questions about the woman, the shop, and what would be expected of her ran through her mind. This would be her first job, and the thought of it pleased Carolina. She couldn't wait until that evening when she and Greta would meet again. "In the meantime," she said to her aunts, "I have so much to do. First, I'll settle into the guest room." She smiled as she picked up the clothing and began carrying it to the room. "It's good to have something to keep my mind off—my problem. I guess I have to let him know I made it here safely." She looked at her aunts, who nodded in unison. "I also want to help you with the housework, Aunt Margaret." Both aunts put an arm around Carolina.

Her phone call to Joseph was brief, lasting less than a minute. She gave him only the bare details that she was safe at her aunt's home and would be in touch "in a few days or more." She hated that she choked up after she hung up and was glad for the chance to escape to her room. She focused on the anger she felt as she relived, only for the seconds it took, the sight of Joseph with—his lover. She forced herself to say the words "his lover" aloud in her room. Briefly, she thought back on her friends in Salinas, mostly church ladies she worked with, people she had been with only days before, doing work she had enjoyed as she felt useful in being of service, at least in a small way. I'll miss all that, she thought, as if it were in a distant past.

For her meeting with Greta, she wore one of the pantsuits she had recently made. She and Greta ate a light supper. They were both eager to get down to business.

"Mattie told me briefly how you came to be in Los Angeles and you may need a few days to get organized. As soon as you are ready, I'll be expecting you. You can ride in with me."

"That is so kind of you. I'll be ready in a day or so. I can't wait to get sewing again, and in a shop! I'll do my very best for you. You'll see, Greta. Thank you for this opportunity."

"I've been busier than usual. We've gotten some orders recently that have taken longer than expected. You and I will work together. My business associate, Connie, prefers to do all her own work."

The next day Carolina quickly and cheerfully set

about to organize the dresses and skirts and pantsuits that were so much in vogue, humming to herself while her aunts busied themselves with cooking dinner, to which Greta was invited. Carolina hurried with her chores so she could help her aunts. Delicious aromas filled the house throughout the day.

Lisa called around lunchtime. "I'm not surprised things are already working out well for you, Caro. Leave it to Aunt Mattie to find the right connections for you. She's as energetic as ever, isn't she?"

"My aunts and I are cooking up something fantastic for supper tonight, and I've been busy settling into the guest room and putting my things away, also. Lisa, it's my first real job. You know how Joseph never wanted me to work. I feel like I've awakened to the real world and can't wait to get started."

"That's the spirit! I can hear the optimism in your voice already. Caro, I started to tell Dad what happened, but he didn't take too well to the news you and Joseph separated. I didn't have the heart to tell him the whole story. He and I decided not to say anything to the rest of the family yet. He's hoping you'll get back together 'where they belong,'" she said, attempting to imitate their father's gruff voice.

"I guess in time everything will come out. I really don't see me getting back with Joseph. It should be me breaking the news to my parents. This shouldn't be your problem."

"Let me see how he is these next few days. I'll call you and let you know." They quickly hung up, both aware they were avoiding a situation that was not quickly going to change.

By dinnertime, the dining table was set with Aunt

Margaret's good china. After Greta arrived, the four women settled in to enjoy the Mexican fare so lovingly prepared.

"This is my favorite, Mattie," Greta said. "*Caldo de res* has always reminded me a little of a dish my mother prepared in Munich, though not quite as spicy. I've grown to love the chile seasonings so widely used here, and don't think I could eat without it now."

"How long have you lived in Los Angeles, Greta?" Carolina asked.

"I've been here since 1958. I fell in love with everything in Los Angeles—the sunshine, the traffic, the beach, the quick pace, and my husband William [she pronounced it Villiam], who passed away just over three years ago in an accident. He was the one who encouraged me to open my shop. I was like you, sewing all the time, and I'd sell a few pieces, just for fun."

"Oh, I'm so sorry about your loss, Greta."

"It's okay now. I take life one day at a time. I have my good friends and my wonderful neighbors, Mattie and Margaret. This is home for me. I love it here and visit my family now and then. We keep in touch by phone, though not as often as we all would like, I'm sure."

"I'm ready to start working tomorrow, Greta. I can't wait."

Carolina rode with Greta on her first day of work. She could not explain the instant affinity she felt with the woman.

"Well, here we are. This is the Couture Shoppe. I was lucky to find this space for sale. All the buildings on this block are old, charming, and quaint, almost like time stood still."

They entered through the back door into a neat, orderly workshop.

"You see how I have set up the material, by type and colors. And over here, William put in the lighting, over the machines. I've always had the extra two sewing machines. There's also room to grow," she said, motioning around the spacious rooms.

"This cozy waiting area with books and magazines for customers to choose from looks comfortable. And the fitting rooms are practical. You have a lovely shop," Carolina commented.

"I'm glad you like it. From what I saw of your work, I think I have made a very good choice in taking you on as my assistant. There's Connie coming in now. I've told her only a little about you. She's a reserved type of woman. Don't be surprised if she's unusually quiet. That's just her way."

The attractive, slender, dark-haired woman politely accepted Carolina's handshake, but her expression was sullen.

"Let me show you around, Caro. Connie likes to get to her work at once. We won't disturb her routine," Greta said cheerfully, hoping Carolina would not be discouraged by Connie's somber mood.

The first day flew as the two women worked diligently on the various projects before them.

"Your work is even better than I first thought, Carolina. You have a natural talent, I can see, for fine workmanship. My customers will be pleased with your work."

Carolina felt at ease at once with the work expected

of her. It was everything she had expected and more. She completed two outfits Greta had been working on. "This is what I had hoped," Greta said, holding up the piece she had started and Carolina had finished. "We'll make an excellent team."

Connie looked up from her machine, a grim expression on her face. Greta and Carolina exchanged glances as they noted the resentment on Connie's face. Greta shrugged and ignored Connie, taking Carolina's arm as they both walked into the storage room to pick up the material a customer had chosen. On the drive home, Caro brought up the subject she had until now not dared mention.

"Do you think Connie resents my working with you? Or what do you think it is, Greta? I don't want to upset your partner."

"You shouldn't worry about it. Connie came to me, recommended by one of my clients, shortly after I opened, and also, she is not a partner, as such. The building is mine, thanks to William's idea to go into business. I respect Connie's privacy so I won't mention more about her. She's really not that bad, just quiet and moody. But what I do with my side of the business is strictly my decision. You're my assistant and you mustn't let anyone interfere with that."

"I don't want to cause any problems."

She called Joseph a few days later to let him know everything was well. He again begged her to reconsider and asked if she would return to him. The sound of his voice sent chills through her. I must still care for him, she thought with a shudder.

"Joseph, you know by now that we cannot remain

married. Please understand." She was serene, and not at all as angry as she expected to feel. "I'll let you know what my next step will be."

Greta asked Carolina to have coffee with her the next morning rather than get directly to their project. "We have some time before Connie gets here, and she may not come in today."

"Yesterday she actually was almost pleasant to me and told me she's trying out for a play, so she's rehearsing her dancing. Maybe she'll warm up to me," Carolina said.

"Don't count on it, Carolina, and don't take it to heart," Greta replied.

Carolina was downcast while drinking the coffee. She looked at Greta and spoke. "I called my husband last night. I still can't believe the turn my life has taken. I'm glad you've given me this opportunity to work."

"I understand you've been through a shock from what little I've picked up."

Tears came to Carolina's eyes. She dabbed at them irritably. "I'm angrier at myself for being so naïve and not seeing what was probably in front of me. I lived with a man I believed I loved almost six years, and the last two or three we were more roommates than a married couple. That should have told me something, but I was more intent on my comfortable life than confronting him." Much as she tried, Carolina could not hold back tears. She was immediately embarrassed and turned away, dabbing her eyes with a napkin.

Greta placed a hand on Carolina's shoulder.

"It wouldn't have been any easier for you either way. It's a harsh fact to accept. Another woman, okay, but not another man. Though I am not judgmental, as you may have noticed, I do think everyone should be true to themselves and to those lives they touch. He should never have married you, Schatzie. It was not your fault. The man used you to cover his true nature. It's also understandable he would do that for his mother and sister and society."

Carolina looked up from her coffee in response to the name Greta called her and the truth she spoke.

As if reading Carolina's thoughts, Greta stated, "Schatzie is a name much like honey, or sweetie. Somehow it came natural to me to call you a German nickname. I hope you don't mind."

A big smile appeared on Carolina's face. "I like it— it makes me feel at home here with you. I hope you aren't disappointed in taking me on to work with you. I assure you I will be able to do my best."

Greta's hearty chuckle broke the tension. "I can't tell you how many times I've given in to the tears bottled up inside me. Losing William was one of the toughest moments I've had to survive. It's good to let your sorrow out and then get back to living. You're going to be fine, Schatzie, I just know it. We're going to be good friends, you and I, and the best working partners."

One afternoon Carolina was alone in the shop. She looked up at the gentleman who stood in the doorway and nodded a deep-voiced hello to her. Their eyes met and held. Later she would remember how her heart skipped a beat, how glad she was to be seated or her knees would have buckled. He was older, she thought possibly ten years older, and tall and slender, with dark brown hair on a high forehead and deep blue eyes, elegant good looks.

"Hello," he said again, returning her smile. "I'm Jack Morten."

She stood and walked up to him. He took her hand gently. His blue eyes held her gaze. She led him to the sofa where they both sat and looked at each other for a few moments.

"Greta will be back soon, Mr. Morten. Or are you Connie's client? I'll be happy to . . ."

"There's no hurry. I'll sit here and wait. I don't believe I know you."

"I'm Carolina, Greta's assistant."

"*Encantado,* Señorita Carolina," Jack said in perfect Spanish. *"Mucho gusto de conocerla."*

"I'm pleased to meet you, too. You speak Spanish quite well."

"I've studied it and use it in my business now and then. It's such a beautiful language, I speak it any chance I get. How long have you been working here?"

"It's been a few weeks, though it seems longer to me."

"I've been getting my shirts custom-made here by Greta since she opened her shop. I knew her husband."

Jack sat back on the sofa, relaxing against the high back. He had not taken his eyes off Carolina, and she hadn't taken hers off him.

"May I get you something to drink while you wait, Mr. Morten?"

"Please, call me Jack. And, yes, I'd love some iced tea, thank you."

Carolina felt Jack's eyes on her as she walked to the back. She walked back slowly, placed the two glasses on the table, and waited for Jack to speak. She didn't trust herself to say anything. He might hear the exhilaration in her voice.

"I'm glad to see Greta's business has grown enough for her to hire someone to help her." His voice was deep and low. He sat so that they almost faced each other on the sofa. "Are you from Los Angeles?"

"No," she said, looking down before raising her long-lashed brown eyes up at him, happily noting the admiration she hoped to see. Her smile broadened. "I moved here from Salinas. What about you?"

"This is my home. I own a construction company. Not very large, just enough to keep me and my crew busy and yet build a high-quality product, houses mostly, and a commercial project now and then. I've just been to Australia for a month. I mixed business and a vacation."

"I hope you and Mrs. Morten enjoyed yourselves," Carolina said, her heart racing faster than ever. She had not seen a ring on his finger, but that would not be a sure sign either way. Surely he'll notice my hands shaking, she thought, grasping them tightly.

"There's no Mrs. Morten, Carolina. We've been divorced about three years."

Carolina purposely held her smile and nodded demurely, sipping her tea.

"And you, Carolina, you're such a beautiful woman. You must have a boyfriend, or are you married?"

Carolina held her gaze down, away from Jack, averting her eyes, fearing he would see her white lie and especially her excitement, a giddiness she felt deep inside. She set the glass down and said softly, "No. No, neither."

They lost track of time while chatting amiably. Carolina listened to Jack tell of his business ventures. He spoke in a quiet, unassuming manner. She answered his questions, hoping not to sound too eager when she casually answered, feeling his constant gaze on her face. She guessed him to be in his mid-thirties, and was surprised when he told her he was forty-six.

From the back of the shop, Greta's voice reached the couple sitting on the sofa. She placed the packages she was carrying on the counter.

"Hello, Jack! You finally got back from your trip. Ah, I see you have met my assistant, my most capable assistant, I must say."

"Greta, it's good to see you again." Jack stood up to embrace Greta. "Here, I brought you a souvenir. I thought you might enjoy this," Jack said, handing Greta a small gift-wrapped box he had in his briefcase.

"It's so thoughtful of you, Jack. You always think of me on your trips." She opened the box to reveal a small, exquisitely carved relic. "Thank you! What a beautiful koala bear."

Carolina stepped away and returned to her machine, putting away the completed garment. Jack and Greta walked to the back to look at the material set aside for him.

"Yes, this is perfect, Greta. You know the colors and style I like."

"Stay and have a glass of wine with us, Jack. Tell us about your trip. We have time, don't we, Caro?"

"I'm afraid I already took up much of Carolina's time telling her about my trip and my business."

"Well, your return calls for a celebration."

Greta brought out one of her finer wines, one she

thought Jack would enjoy, and offered both Carolina and Jack some lunch meats and German bread she kept for such occasions. Jack and Greta sat on the sofa, with Carolina facing them both from the easy chair angled against the side wall.

"I've kept you both way past your closing time, and I'd like to invite you lovely ladies for dinner," Jack said, smiling at both.

Greta replied quickly, saying, "I'd love to, Jack, but I've already made plans for this evening."

Jack leaned toward Carolina and, reaching for her hand and then gently holding it, said, "Don't disappoint me and say you have plans, Carolina. I would be honored to have you join me for dinner."

"I have known Jack for some years now. I can say he is a true gentleman. Schatzie, you should accept his invitation," Greta remarked.

Jack and Carolina were gazing at each other's eyes. "Say yes, Carolina. I'd love to get to know you," Jack almost whispered.

Carolina nodded, modestly lowering her eyes, remembering how her sisters had preached modesty to her so many years ago when she had been but a young teenage girl.

Carolina called her aunt to let her know she would be late getting home. Greta waved goodbye as Jack sped off with Carolina in the early dusk.

They sat in a corner booth of a fine restaurant. Jack instinctively knew not to rush Carolina or ask too many personal questions. Carolina, too, sat back and let Jack speak, listening to his deep voice, taking in every detail about his face. His head of full, dark brown, wavy hair and his high forehead gave him a distinguished air, she thought. His slender, muscular build she found most attractive. His dark blue eyes seemed to penetrate anything he looked at. Now and then she would look at his hands and wonder how their touch would feel against her flesh. She hoped he didn't hear her soft gasp as a chill went through her at the thought of him touching her. She could already imagine his lips on hers.

He moved in closer, slowly, until he could reach her hands, and he took first one, then the other, until he had them both in his, firmly.

"Carolina, I don't want to frighten you by what I am going to say. I have never felt as I do right now, with you, and I hope you will accept me as a beau, as old-fashioned as that sounds. I'm older than you, and I've been married and have children, but from the moment I saw you, I knew I would want to be with you, get to know you."

"Yes, I agree this is happening so suddenly. But, I'm not frightened. I feel safe with you. We'll have to take our time, though."

"Yes, of course. Maybe I sound like a teenager, but I never felt as happy as I do right now, with you."

They ate their dinner slowly, talking about their lives in general. Jack was so easy to talk to, Carolina forgot all about her misery with Joseph, briefly telling Jack what she had experienced only a few weeks ago. She had to admit to him that she was, indeed, a married woman.

"I'm sorry I didn't tell you earlier. It seems like what happened was ages ago. I was so hurt and humiliated. I didn't think I'd ever be able to talk about it, certainly not to another man."

"It must have been terrible for you. I hope you can put it out of your mind for now. I understand why you would not mention—what happened. Let's enjoy this evening. I have not dated anyone since my ex-wife and I separated. I wasn't ready and wasn't even looking for anyone."

Carolina looked into Jack's eyes. They bore into hers. A sense of security she never had before encompassed her. He asked her to dance. The sensuous Trio Los Panchos and Edyie Gorme were playing Besame Mucho by piped-in music.

How perfectly ironic, Jack thought as he listened to one of his favorite singers, a Jewish woman who spoke and sang in perfect Spanish, as Carolina's body comfortably nestled in the booth, at a safe distance from him. Safe for the moment, he thought. She mustn't get too close to me—yet.

Jack held Carolina's arm as they left the restaurant, the electricity rushing between them. In the car on the way home, both were silent, knowing they should not rush into this romance. They quietly sat in the car down the street from Aunt Margaret's house, where hopefully she would not see them. Jack took Carolina's hand in his and brushed her fingertips with his lips as they said goodnight.

Carolina went in the house and peeked into her aunt's dimly lit bedroom. "*Buenas noches*, Tía," she whispered when she saw her aunt's eyes were open.

"I hope you had a good time, *mi hijita*," Aunt Margaret murmured.

Carolina nodded as she softly whispered good night. As she closed the door to her bedroom, she decided she had just had the best time of her life—so far. Lying in bed, Carolina closed her eyes and smiled as she thought of Jack. I can't believe how I feel, she thought, touching the fingertips he had kissed moments ago. She realized that she wanted the night to fly so she could see him again. She could still see him standing in the door as he walked in the shop, and she said to herself, I knew at that moment I would love—. Oh, I hope I'm not wrong again. Not this time.

The next morning, rising earlier than usual, Carolina prepared breakfast for her aunt, eager to get the day going so she could see Jack again.

She waited for Greta, fondly reminiscing over the evening spent with Jack, going over every detail, enjoying the anticipation of the day ahead of her.

Greta was respectful of Carolina's privacy and did not ask for details, but she could see Carolina's glow for herself.

"Greta, Jack was even more wonderful than I imagined. He is so easy to talk to."

Around ten, a young man entered the shop with a florist's box that Carolina opened to find a single gardenia, the sweet scent filling the room; she placed it next to her machine. A sealed envelope was attached. Carolina read the brief note Jack had written.

For a beautiful woman—

Carolina, you mentioned your love of flowers. Let this be a token of what I hope will blossom between us.

Jack

Carolina sighed deeply, her heart racing, and tucked the note into her purse. Greta came in then and saw the flower, commenting, "I had a feeling he would be the romantic type," and putting a warm hand on Carolina's shoulder. "I'm happy for you, Schatzie."

They both looked over at Connie, wondering what she might contribute to the conversation. Connie managed a tight grin with her lips pursed. Carolina had remained polite and kind to Connie. Whatever problems Connie had, she was keeping them close to herself.

Greta rarely spoke about her own life and never asked questions delving into Carolina's private life. They often worked in comfortable silence, each concentrating on the project at hand. For Carolina, gratitude was uppermost in her sentiment toward this kindly woman ten years her senior.

The California sun had taken its toll on Greta's fair skin, so it was apparent to Carolina that Greta spent many hours outdoors. Greta occasionally accepted a dinner invitation to Aunt Margaret's or Mattie's, otherwise, as soon as Carolina was dropped off, Greta would disappear for the evening.

"The age difference does not matter, does it?" Greta mentioned, referring to Jack and Carolina. "My first husband in Germany was my age and he was an immature fool. After the first two years he left me for a slightly older woman. My William was fifteen years older than me and we had as perfect a marriage as any woman would want. We never had a bad moment between us."

"I didn't know you had been married before, other than William."

"I don't talk much about it; sometimes I even forget it happened."

Later that day, Jack arrived at the shop a few minutes before closing time. Carolina's beaming smile announced her joy at seeing him. He looked at her, and said, "You are even more beautiful than I remembered. I asked myself this morning if possibly I dreamed we met. But you are real! How was your day, Carolina?" He leaned down toward her and held her hand.

"It's been a great day! How nice to see you again. Thank you for my beautiful flower."

"Well, Jack, you and my young assistant," Greta's voice called out from the back room, "have excellent taste," she said as she walked into the area, carrying a shirt for Jack. "I hope this is what you had in mind."

"It's perfect, Greta. I've never gotten a shirt from you I didn't like. Now, young lady, I would very much like to invite you to join me this evening. What would you like to do? Dinner again? And a movie? Or how about someplace we can dance?"

"Jack, I'd love to, but I'm not dressed for going out. We've had a busy day."

They had a casual dinner and went to a movie. They sat in the car outside Aunt Margaret's house again. Carolina's head was spinning from the quick pace of their relationship.

"What are you thinking, Carolina?" Jack asked softly, holding her hand in his. "Is this all a bit fast for you?"

"It would seem that way, wouldn't it? Yet I feel so comfortable with you. I do think we need to discuss the fact that I'm very much married."

"Yes, I thought of that all day. What are your plans? How will you handle your situation? I am being open and honest with you. I've never met a woman who made me feel like you do, and I won't sit back and let you get away from me."

"I know my marriage is over. There's no doubt of

that. Everything has happened so quickly with you. I want to be fair to you, Jack."

"The marriage situation must be difficult for you. Let me get my attorney to handle whatever needs to be done. There will have to be a divorce or annulment eventually."

"I have to talk to my family about this. No one has ever been divorced in my family and I can't imagine how . . ."

"Let's not allow this to get in the way of what is beginning for us. Be happy with me and enjoy the evenings we spend together."

Jack gently held her face with both his hands, his fingers caressing her lightly. He pressed his lips to hers and she opened hers to receive his kiss. He did not dare kiss her as hungrily as he wanted to. That would come later; it had to. She felt herself melting into his embrace, his arms enfolding her completely.

The stirring deep inside was a new sensation for her. She didn't remember ever feeling this for Joseph. She forced herself to stop thinking of Joseph.

She moved her lips back enough to speak. Their lips almost touching, she murmured, "I have to say goodnight now."

Again, for the second night in a row, Carolina slumbered with a smile on her face, a new smile. This one was from her heart. This is what it feels like to fall in love, she repeated to herself as she fell into a peaceful sleep.

The next day, Jack planned a romantic picnic, having made all arrangements as a surprise for Carolina. Jack had enlisted the help of his vice president and close friend, Don Hanson.

"I've never seen you like this, Jack. I'm almost jealous to see you behaving like a teenager. I hope you're not mistaken this time," Don said.

"No, not this time. She's everything I've ever wanted without knowing she was what I needed. Aside from her obvious beauty, she's sweet, and caring and naïve."

"The age difference isn't an issue with either of you? She's what—twenty-five? Jack, I'm your best friend, and I'd hate to see you suffer again as you did through your divorce. You know, when Jane left you and the children, it was rough for you. You're lucky your parents are so helpful and able to help out with Aaron and Melissa."

Jack looked at his business partner and confidant without answering.

"And there's the other issue. She's Catholic, isn't she? Does she know about you?"

"Don, I appreciate your concern and admit I had a pretty rough time the first few months, but mostly out of shock that Jane would leave our children. I saw then how much we had grown apart. I won't let myself get into such a situation again. And, no, the subject hasn't come up. I'm going to wait a while before I tell her."

"Well, you just met this young woman. Give yourself time to get to know her. Go easy, Jack," his friend said, patting him lightly on the back, shaking his head in disapproval.

"Wait till you meet her. You'll understand."

Four

"Carolina! I'm so glad to catch you at home. How are you? And how are your aunts coming along?"

"Sofia! How is everyone doing?" Carolina's heart sank as she heard Joseph's mother's cheerful voice.

"We're fine, thank you. I asked Joseph for your aunt's number. It's been so long now. How is your aunt? Is she well enough for you to come home?"

"She's better, better than we'd all expected. It's just that I—well, I need to spend more time with my family. They have so much that needs to be done, and I'm the closest one here. Aunt Margaret's daughters have left town, as you know, and there's really no one else to help them. I just don't know when . . ."

"Caro, it's kind of you, I do understand, but you'll get back as soon as possible?"

She tried desperately to think of a way to stall her mother-in-law.

"My aunt's calling me. I'm sorry. I'll have to get in touch with Joseph later. Thank you so much for calling." She hung up quickly, aware of how rude she must seem to Sofia at this moment.

In Salinas, Sofia knew something was not right with Carolina's long absence. She would have a serious talk with Joseph.

Later that evening, when Sofia asked Joseph about Carolina being gone, he replied, "I think she was not as happy as she seemed to be, Mom. I couldn't talk her into staying with me. Maybe she needs a little more time, but I really doubt she'll come back to me." Joseph hoped his mother would believe him. He was tired of hiding the truth from all who asked about Carolina's sudden departure. "I'm not going to ask her again," he tersely said as he hugged his mother.

After talking to Sofia, Carolina hurriedly changed her clothes, because Jack was on his way. Her happiness bubbled, thinking of how their relationship was blooming. She had not yet told her aunts anything about her boyfriend out of respect for them. Knowing they would object to her dating before any dissolution of her marriage, she avoided the subject. It seemed the simplest thing to do for the present. She scrawled a note to her aunt and dashed down to Greta's house to wait for Jack.

The next morning Margaret was quieter than usual when Carolina approached her.

"Tía, I'll probably be out this evening. Don't expect me for supper."

"Carolina, come, sit by me a minute." Aunt Margaret looked solemn. "You're a grown woman. I love and respect you and know you have been through a bad time. But you should know what you're doing is not right. It's too soon for you to become involved with another man. You are not even legally separated."

Carolina stood frozen. She had no idea how much

her aunt knew of her romance.

"I've seen you in the car with your friend. I know he waits for you down the street. Caro, mi hijita, please think about what you're doing. Who is this man, anyway? What will your parents say that we know about this relationship and watch you break every rule sacred to us? Your dear father will never forgive me, or Mattie." She was wringing a handkerchief as she said this, a pained expression on her usually calm face. "We haven't said anything to Miguel yet. We don't think it is right for us to tell him. If you decide to go through with a divorce, and have your friend, you must inform your parents yourself."

After her long speech, Margaret covered her face with the hankie in her hands, wiped her face, placed her hands in her lap, and looked up at her niece. Caro looked at the clock. Seven-thirty. She would not meet Greta for another twenty minutes. She had to respond to her aunt's concerns.

She sat beside Margaret, picked up her aunt's hands in her own, and said in a firm voice, "I'm sorry I've upset you, and I really wish I had time to talk to you about it right now. I promised Greta I'd be ready early today. We have a project we need to get started on. Tía, for now I'll tell you it's not as bad as it seems to you. Jack is the most wonderful man I've ever known. We'll talk about it tonight, when I get home. Okay? We'll talk then. Please don't be angry with me. Don't be upset," she said as she kissed Margaret on the cheek, hurriedly grabbed her purse, and dashed out the door, hoping Greta wouldn't be upset that she showed up early.

On the ride in, Caro was quiet, thinking about what her aunt had said. She knew Aunt Margaret was right.

Everything she said was true. But there is no way I am giving up Jack, she thought determinedly.

"What's the matter, Schatzie? You seem so preoccupied this morning, as well as being ready rather early," Greta said with a laugh, trying to make light of the situation. Caro grinned and shook her head. They arrived at the shop before she had a chance to answer.

Connie had not been in the shop the day before. There were days she did not make it in, but as she worked solely on her own projects for her exclusive customers, this was not a problem. All Carolina knew about Connie was her name, Constance Jones, and that a man dropped her off and picked her up almost every workday. Connie had finally warmed to Carolina's kindness and at least was not as surly as the first few days. Carolina's first impression had been that Connie may be resentful of Greta having an assistant, or that Carolina herself would take over any of Connie's clients. Greta had assured Carolina that was not the case when one day Carolina finally asked her about it.

"No, Connie's just trying to work without calling attention to herself. It doesn't have anything to do with us working together, I can tell you that. Someday she may open up to you and tell you her story. I've promised her not to say anything to anyone," had been Greta's cryptic explanation.

Now that Carolina was well established in the shop, Greta would leave occasionally to run errands, meet with clients in their homes for fittings, or do whatever she deemed necessary, which meant that, on the days Connie wasn't there, Carolina was sometimes alone in the shop. That was the case that morning. She was busy sewing, pondering Aunt Margaret's words, wondering what in the world she was going to say to her, knowing she would eventually have to face up to all that had been said that morning.

Jack's usual morning phone call appeased her. The mere sound of his deep voice filled her with joyous anticipation. Jack made her feel special—prettier, smarter, and more alive than ever. When they spoke, she forgot everything and everyone else.

That afternoon, still alone, Carolina got up to receive a customer, a woman who walked in and stood at the counter. "I'm Priscilla Eaves. Here's my card," the woman said tersely. It had her name, address, and several phone numbers. "I'm looking for this woman," she said, showing Carolina a sheet with three snapshots paper-clipped to it. The first showed a slender blond woman, waist-length hair coiled to one shoulder; another showed the same woman in a formal gown; and the third, slightly out of focus, had the woman in shorts and ballet shoes showing off beautiful legs, a dancer's legs, with a stage background. Carolina stared at what had to be pictures of a slightly younger, fair-haired Connie Jones! A blond Connie, not the one she worked with almost on a daily basis.

She looked up to see Priscilla was looking directly at her, obviously studying her face to catch a sign of recognition. Carolina shook her head silently. Priscilla said, "This is Catherine Jeffries. Her family is searching for her. We're looking into all shops of this kind, as she has been known to work as a seamstress at times. May I leave my card, and if you should come in contact with her, please call. It's urgent," the woman said in a monotone. She nodded, turned, and walked out the door.

Carolina sat on the sofa, sorting her thoughts on what had just transpired. Minutes later, Greta walked in through the back, as usual, set down the notebook where she kept the orders pending, and said, "That iced tea looks great to me. I'll come join you."

As she sat beside Carolina, she said, "What happened? Have you seen a ghost?"

"Greta, a most unusual thing just happened. I wish you had been here. A woman came in—here's her card. Apparently she's a detective of some kind. She showed me some pictures of someone who looks like Connie, only this woman has, or had, long blond hair. She was about five or six years younger. She said her family is looking for her."

"Oh! Did you say anything?" Greta could not conceal her concern.

"No. No, I didn't. I really had no idea what to say. It was a total surprise. Do you know what it's all about? Is it Connie?"

Greta hesitated before speaking. "I've told you I can't tell you anything about Connie. She asked me not to say anything, so I won't. But she should know that someone is looking for her. I have a phone number for her and I feel I have to let her know. I'm going to have to tell her about this woman."

Finding the number in her address book, Greta dialed and waited for the response. Finally, after many rings, Connie answered. Greta said, "It's me, Greta. Are you coming in tomorrow? Oh, I see. Well, you need to know that someone came here looking for . . . Yes, that's right, just this afternoon, a few minutes ago while I was out. Carolina was here alone."

Carolina was watching the expression on Greta's

face, trying to catch a hint of whatever the women were hiding. Surely it's nothing criminal, she thought. She chided herself for even considering it.

"No, she didn't say anything. But there's no telling if the investigator caught anything on Caro's face. No, she has no idea."

After a few more OKs and some no's, Greta hung up. She stared at the wall for several moments before joining Carolina on the sofa again. She finished the glass of tea, faced Caro, and calmly said, "Connie won't be coming back for a while. Luckily, all her work was done and she's going to call her customers to give them her new address and phone number. As far as we're concerned, Connie Jones—or Catherine Jeffries— is gone, and we don't know where she went."

Oh, my, thought Carolina. It must be something criminal. And here I am in the middle of it. She managed a half smile, attempted to shrug off her unease, and hoped she presented a façade of sophistication.

"It's not at all what you're thinking, not anything criminal," Greta said. "It is a family situation. I would tell you, but there's my promise—as soon as things clear up, I'll tell you."

"How did you know what I was thinking?"

"I can read you like a book, as the saying goes. You looked like you were ready to run back home to your family. I assure you, it's nothing that would affect us, or the shop. I promise. Now, let's get on home!"

"Put the report where Jack will never think of looking when you've read it through. He mustn't find out we've had this woman investigated." Rose's hands shook as she held the papers her husband gave her. "Arnold, I do wish he'd never met her. It doesn't seem there is anything really dark and serious about her, though, just from the first pages I've read."

"We can't give up. She's got to be up to something. Why else would a young, beautiful Latina woman want to date an older man she just met? She must know about the money. She's still married, not even legally separated. Seems she left this husband of hers so unexpectedly no one in Salinas was able to shed any light. Of course, our Mr. Smith hasn't reported back on the husband, Joseph Collins. He's been to the hardware store the family owns, but nothing's turned up."

"I do so hope Jack will get over this infatuation. That would resolve things for us, wouldn't it? What have you heard from Don?"

"Rose, he's as concerned for Jack as we are. But Don knows nothing about our Mr. Smith or that we've initiated this, er, little investigation of ours. There's too much of a risk it would slip out to Jack. We'll have to keep quiet until we get something substantial on this woman, Carolina. There's nothing at all on her family in El Paso. They're highly esteemed, and of course, as we expected, they're a Catholic family. But then, why would she be separating from her husband if she's as 'good' as Jack makes her out to be?"

"I just don't understand how he could become so involv-ed with anyone in such a short time," Rose sighed, shaking her head.

"Let me read this report. I have to see if there's any news at all that could possibly convince Jack to stay away from her or even give us leverage to pay her off, if necessary." After several seconds Arnold exclaimed, "I wonder what this is all about. The woman she works for, or with, as Jack says, has a bit of history herself. Our man Smith is good. He dug this up all the way from Germany. Oh, did you see this? Did you see there's an investigator searching for the other woman who works at the shop with them?"

"Yes—I talked it over briefly with Mr. Smith. I don't think it's anything serious enough to cause Carolina any problems. All in all, I don't like any of it. I hope Jack wakes up and gets over his infatuation before something serious happens. We may have to trust Jack's judgment. He's been so happy these past few weeks, certainly happier than I've ever seen him," Rose chuckled.

"I'm also considering the fact we may have to accept this woman if Jack has his heart set on her."

Rose reached up to caress her husband's cheek. "We haven't met her—maybe she is everything he's making her out to be."

"Darling, we may have to accept her," Arnold said with a shrug.

Five

They drove in silence for a while. Jack had gone over in his mind how he would approach Carolina with the surprise he'd planned for her. First, he was not sure she would accept. Second, he had to respect the fact that she may not be ready for a physical relationship with him. He'd never met anyone quite like her. They had "dated" for some weeks now. He always thought of the word in quotes—"dated"—which to him meant something teenagers did; certainly no one his age dated.

Carolina and he had kissed, and he'd held her close enough that he knew she had been aware of his desire for her. He would discreetly push her away when it became awkward for him, and when desire for her nearly overcame him, he would press his fingernails into his palms. He was not sure how much longer he could do this. Yet, he respected her so much and understood her plight. She had left her marriage almost against her will. She had not been prepared for such a man as Jack, which was apparent to him. *Good thing I'm so patient,* he told himself often.

"Jack, you're so quiet. Is everything OK?" she asked timidly, reaching over to hold his free hand, a shy smile on her face.

He took his eyes off the road long enough to gaze into her face, her gorgeous face, he thought, smiling back at her. He released his hand to caress her face briefly, and picked up her hand to touch her fingertips to his lips. "No, my love. Everything is fine. I'm taking you somewhere special. It's a place I've wanted to show you. I want to be sure it will be to your liking. My mind is preoccupied with that. We're almost there."

He pulled up to a plush condominium complex set back from the street. Trees obscured the buildings from the street. "Here we are."

He led her to a front door next to a garage. Neat flower beds lined the impeccable walkway. Mature shrubs were strategically placed so each unit had complete privacy. Jack opened the front door with a key and led her in, holding her hand. She scanned the sparsely furnished apartment. An entry led to the living room to the right; to the left was a hallway leading to a bedroom. The wide, spacious entry led to a kitchen on the right past the living room.

"This is so nice, Jack. Is it yours?" She was puzzled. She knew Jack lived with his parents and his children. He had never mentioned having his own place.

"It is now. Look around and see how you like it. I'd like your opinion of it."

What little furniture was in the apartment was of a quality Carolina did not expect to see in a furnished apartment. She walked into the kitchen. It was light and airy with a large window overlooking masses of mature bushes. None of the other units were visible from that window. There was a small utility room past the kitchen. She walked to the bedroom and saw a king-sized bed and a triple dresser. No clothes were in the ample closet.

"It's really a beautiful apartment, Jack. You were lucky to find one in such a location. The trees and shrubs and flowers would be enough to make me want to live here. It's superb."

"Come sit here by me," he said as he led her to the sofa and, putting his arms around her, held her close to him. She sank into his embrace, closing her eyes, feeling his warmth, and wanting to stay with him like this, always.

They kissed a long, deep, passionate kiss. She held his face with her hands and kissed his cheeks, then his forehead. He held her close against him, knowing he could not hold back now.

Finally, he pushed her back so he could look into her eyes. "Caro, this apartment is for you, for us. I'm hoping you'll accept it. We can't go on like this. I need you and want you with me, totally, completely. You know I love you. At least think about it before you answer, my love."

She managed to move out of his embrace, stood up, pulled him up toward her, kissed him lightly, and whispered in his ear, "Yes. Yes to everything."

Later, much later, she would think of something to say to her aunts, explain why she would move out of a house that was home to her. Later she would explain to her family why she had to be with this man, now, despite her upbringing and the fact she was not free to be with him. Now all she wanted was to feel him, kiss him, know his body, and see his nakedness. As their arms and hands explored each other's bodies, all she could think of was the love she felt for Jack. And the love she felt from him. Nothing else mattered.

Later, lying naked next to him, she kissed his closed eyes. He fluttered them open, smiled, looked at her with longing, and made love to her again.

After showering together—oh, the excitement she felt showering with Jack—she had no doubt she was making the right decision. She had never experienced such pure pleasure, and the elation was visible on her face. Jack saw the change in her and delighted as well in her openness. She had blossomed before his eyes and under his touch like one of her prized flowers.

"Caro, my love, you are exquisite. You make me feel young all over. What we've been through before was worthwhile now that we have each other."

Carolina hugged him tightly, her eyes wide open, not daring to believe all that had happened was true. She timidly touched his member, delighting in the freedom of being able to do so. He held her close, allowing her hand to remain where it was. He kissed her.

"Nothing will keep us from being together, Caro. I swear to you. If I could marry you tonight I would. I know it's hard for you to accept what I am offering you, and I respect you and love you the more for it. We may have a hard time ahead of us until you can be free. I'll make it as easy and smooth for you as I possibly can."

"I loved you the moment I saw you. That's why I came to Los Angeles when I did. To meet you."

"I want you to have this apartment. You'll get a car, of course. This will be our place. Will you accept it?"

"Yes, I will. We'll be very happy here. I'll find a way

to ease away from my family, hard as that will be for me. I'm a woman now. My choice is to be with the man I love. We'll work things out."

Six

"Miguel, *mi amor*, you remind me so much of Carolina, the way you love the full moon. Would you like your supper out here? We can eat out on the patio like we did when the girls were still our babies," Esther said in her soft voice. She knew how preoccupied he was, worrying about Caro, their youngest, his favorite.

"That's a good idea, Esther." He helped Esther set the patio table. "Our girls have been independent of us for many years now, but I can't help thinking about them, and how they might solve their problems. I've never been one to intrude into their lives."

The resonance of his deep voice stirred Esther after all these years. She looked at him with love in her eyes, grateful for the years God had given them together— her shameful secret a forbidden memory—and she thanked God for their four daughters.

"For others, an impending divorce may not seem as disastrous as it does to us. I certainly understand Carolina's unhappiness at finding out the truth about Joseph. I can imagine how difficult this has been for Caro. And equally difficult for Lisa to break the news to us." Esther looked at Miguel before she continued. "I suppose we are isolated in many ways, mi amor. To us, marriage will always be sacred, a union to be blessed with children, to last forever. Are we wrong?"

"No, Esther, we're not. We cannot sit in judgment of Joseph, though. That would be wrong. Oh, I can't imagine what dear Caro went through. I am so glad she is with my sisters. They are a source of security to her. They always have been."

Miguel Antonio Sanchez, devoted husband and father, held in highest esteem by his family, a true patriarch, beloved by his daughters, smiled up at the heavens and took in the beauty of the dark blue sky and bright stars and said a prayer to God: Keep my daughter Carolina safe in your hands, protect her from all harm. He smiled at Esther and reached for her hand as he had done all his married life.

In his mind and heart he could still hear his daughters' youthful laughter as he called them in from their backyard. He was a hard worker and earned a good living, but he knew without Mamá Ana's financial assistance early in their marriage he would not have been able to afford this large house nestled among well-kept middle class homes.

His role in life had been determined the moment he laid eyes on Esther, a beautiful, shy fifteen-year-old, when a cousin invited him to a grand wedding celebration in Chihuahua City in Mexico, just a few hours south of El Paso. He had continued visiting the lovely young lady, her huge, long-lashed brown eyes in a perfect oval face mesmerizing the impressionable twenty-year-old for a year until her family accepted his marriage proposal. Mamá Ana warmly welcomed him as her son-in-law on the condition she would accompany her oldest daughter to her new home in a new land. She promptly sold most of her land holdings to move to El Paso with her younger daughters Mariana and Amelia. It was 1929. The wealthy, attractive widow Ana Aranda was proud to have her daughter marry an American citizen. She insisted, however, she be allowed to provide whatever it took to have a house fitting their social standing in Chihuahua. They would have visitors, surely, from their hometown, and it would not do for the Aranda family to have anything but the best, as she could well afford. Miguel, of course, resisted, saying he would be able to provide for his wife and future family, but in the end Mamá Ana won out, as she would for the rest of her life, with her sweetness, charm, and unrelenting resolve.

He could still hear the echo of his daughters' voices telling him how much they loved sitting at his feet listening to him retell their family's history. Esther had acclimated to her new home and country, facilitated by her mother and sisters moving in two blocks away in an even bigger house.

Grandmother Ana's house soon became the focal point for the growing family. Anita and Marta were born by the time the Sanchez couple celebrated their third anniversary in Doña Ana's lush garden. Mariana was eventually wooed by a classmate, Bill Stone. They wed as soon as Mariana graduated from high school. Amelia followed her sister's example, accepting a proposal by the handsome young man next door, Eduardo, a year after she had completed her schooling.

Miguel was especially proud to tell of how his

own family had come to this part of the country many generations removed. The Sanchez clan was among the first to settle in the lower valley that gave birth to the sprawling, sunny, dusty city it now was, the unique flavor of a border community evident in the culture they all enjoyed.

Days after Jack surprised her with the apartment, Carolina had called Lisa, hoping to catch her alone. Carolina blurted out her latest news, speaking quickly and being as brief as possible, avoiding the scolding and questioning she was sure Lisa would provide.

"I've met the most wonderful man and I can't keep it to myself any longer. He's older but absolutely the right man for me. He's a businessman here in LA, a friend and client where I work. I've never been as happy as I am now. I know you'll find the right time to tell our parents."

She hung up without giving Lisa the opportunity to ask more than the minimum of questions.

Shortly after Carolina's call, Lisa found her father alone, though she would have preferred to tell her parents together. She clenched her fists, partly for courage to tell her father and partly in anger, still reeling at Carolina's escapade.

"Papá, now she has met someone else, and in no time at all she has moved in with this older man," Lisa said. She paused as she saw the stricken look on his face. "Yes, you heard right. He's twenty-one years older," she said, her voice shrill as she paced back and forth. "I haven't had a good night's sleep since she told me her news."

"I know you mean well, but I don't think any of

us have a right to dictate who she can date or make an issue of how old this man happens to be. You girls know my philosophy. So far, it's worked well. We do our best, always. We trust in God, always. I trust Caro knows what she's doing. I'll tell your mother. She may as well know as soon as possible."

"She's still a married woman. She'll be the first in the family to get a divorce. I have a hard time even saying the horrible word. I don't see how you can be so calm."

"It's closer to work, Auntie. You'd be amazed at how inexpensive it is. Greta's friends run the apartment complex and I was able to get a really good deal." Carolina hated lying to her aunt, but she could not bring herself to tell her she would be living with Jack. Never mind she was twenty-six years old, with a job of her own. She should be able to make decisions without asking anyone's permission.

"I'll still come by here often. We can call each other anytime. I will move out this weekend."

She went into the bedroom to continue packing, breathing rapidly, caught up in the excitement of asserting herself. Her thoughts were interrupted by a gentle knock on the door as her aunt entered the room.

"Caro, I don't want you to be upset with me. Of course, I understand you're an adult and need to be on your own. I respect you as the grown woman you are. I want the best for you, that's all. I don't want you to make another mistake with your new gentleman."

She hugged her aunt, tears rolling down her cheeks. "I know I'm doing the right thing this time. These are tears of happiness."

Seven

The Couture Shoppe was busier than usual. Carolina made time to move into the apartment quickly, hanging her clothes and setting out her toiletries. Jack would be traveling north on business, so she took advantage of her spare time to decorate with artwork they'd chosen together and make their new home a cozy haven. He was slowly bringing in his possessions, enough for a few days at a time. His children would remain in his parents' home. He intended to spend some evenings at his parents', though he had not yet discussed this with Carolina. Jack was confident Carolina would agree with his plans.

"I'm glad to have some time with you, Greta," Carolina said after work one day. "We're all so busy. We haven't caught up with each other's news."

"We have so much going on here in the shop, it's hard to relax and enjoy a glass of wine like we did just a few weeks ago."

"I won't rush home today," she said, accepting a glass from Greta. "Jack won't be back until the end of the week. He's getting a contract with a company out of San Francisco. We can relax and enjoy a chance to talk."

"You said your parents finally know what happened with—your husband." Greta had noted Carolina rarely mentioned Joseph by name. "That must have been hard for them to accept. From what you've said about your family, they live by the book. I love these American sayings," she said with a chuckle, hoping to lighten the mood of the theme she inadvertently brought up. She lifted her wine glass. "*Prosit!* To us, to our wonderful friendship!"

Carolina nodded, holding up her glass, smiling at her friend. She began speaking softly, her low voice almost inaudible at times. Greta moved in closer but out of Carolina's direct sight, instinctively providing the privacy her friend needed.

"It happened the summer I turned fifteen. My *quinceañera* was a huge success. It's such a beautiful celebration for a girl's fifteenth birthday—a Mass, and then a dance, with as many as fifteen girls and boys, and a fancy dinner. I wore the traditional long, white dress. My cousins came from California and were part of the group. A few days later, my cousins and I were staying at Grandma Ana's house. I woke up with a horrible migraine, and to escape the noisy crowd, made my way to my own house, just two blocks away, without anyone noticing. As I had hoped, no one was home. I went to the darkest bedroom and had been asleep some time when I awoke to the sound of my mother crying. I heard a man's voice, though not Papá's." Carolina uttered the last word in a whisper and stopped speaking for a while as she sipped the wine slowly, lost in her thoughts.

Greta sat motionless, waiting for her friend to continue. Though the sun was still out, the room was growing dark without any light on.

"I managed to crack the door enough to make out the people in the living room. A man was holding my mother by her shoulders as she sobbed quietly now. His deep voice startled me as he said, 'I never dreamed you carried my child. I would have made every effort to convince you to stay with me.' They spoke softly and quickly, and sometimes I couldn't hear them clearly as they moved about in the room. I caught myself from gasping when I heard her tell him 'how hard it has been having your child without your knowledge.'"

"He said, 'I just learned of her existence—in my heart I already love her, because of my love for you, Esther, and because she is my own.' I thought I would faint. I can still her hear voice saying, 'Roberto, there are days I can't bear the thought of what we did. It was wrong, you know that. We were wrong to give in to our love.'"

Carolina spoke as in a trance and continued. "Then I heard the man say, 'I know that. But when I think of how much I've loved you, I think of those months we had together, and I'm grateful for that. Please, Esther, let me have photographs of Carolina to take with me.' I'll never forget his words."

"I saw my mother take the stack of pictures on the dining table. There were so many from my birthday party. She picked three or four for him. Then she took some from the many albums and handed them to him. He held her close a long time. They stood there weeping together. It was heartbreaking even for me, though I was so angry I wanted to scream at them. He whispered something to her and soon they both left, first him, then my mother seconds later.

"I ran to the bathroom and was sick to my stomach. I pounded on the tile floor and then sat on the floor of the bedroom, rocking myself as I cried. My dear beloved Papá was not my Papá! How could I overcome such an ugly, horrible truth? How had such a thing happened? My parents were never separated, as far as I knew. They always seemed so happy together. He's the kindest, most loving man, the wonderful type of father you read about, that you see on TV and in movies. He was the one who sat with us and told us stories in bed, tucking us in and giving us advice on everything."

Carolina sat quietly, sipping her wine, looking straight ahead, tears rolling down her face. Greta waited patiently, tears on her face also, sipping her wine, and finally getting up to light the lamp, giving the room a soft glow. She locked the front door and returned to the sofa.

"Can you imagine what I had to live with? I pleaded with my parents to let me go stay with my aunts by myself. After a couple of days they relented and sent me back with my aunts and cousins returning to LA. Three of them were Margaret's and Mattie's daughters who had come for my grand celebration."

The shrill ring of the telephone startled them. Greta answered, saying a noncommittal "Yes" and "No" several times, and then a quick "I'll call you this evening." She gave no explanation about the phone call. She had just returned to the sofa when the phone rang again.

"I'll have to call you later," she said into the telephone without waiting to hear who was calling, thinking it was the same person. She was silent a moment as she realized it was someone else. Then she said, "Oh, sorry, Connie." She listened intently for what Carolina thought was a long time. Finally, Greta spoke.

"It couldn't be helped. How could anyone have known you don't want to be found? I've kept your secret all this time and have helped you as much as I believe I can. We'll have to be more careful."

Again, Greta listened to Connie for some time.

"Sure, come by tomorrow and we'll talk about it."

She placed the receiver down gently and remained at the counter, apparently collecting her thoughts. "Now, dear Caro, you can tell me how you managed that day you found out the truth. You were a mere fifteen!"

"I couldn't even look at my mother that day," Caro continued her story, now more in control of her emotions. The unexpected phone calls had eased the tension she'd felt building up as she told her tale.

"At least that explained my mother's attitude toward me. Greta, she was cold and distant to me, always. I noticed a difference in the way she spoke to my sisters, the way she gave them her complete attention. I had never been able to understand why, at least from the time I was old enough to figure out there was something not right. It's hard to explain. She was—is—an excellent mother, but she always ignored me. I've never told anyone my secret. It was so hard to keep it from my sister Lisa, but I can never tell her. Or anyone else in the family."

"Schatzie, you know you can trust me. I'll keep your secret—forever." Greta placed a hand gently on Caro's shoulder. Finally, Caro wiped her face with her hands, a crooked smile on her face.

"Jack wants to go meet my family in El Paso. I'm not ready for that. He must never find out my secret. No one must ever know. That other man—Robert—lives here in Los Angeles. There's several Robert Russells in the phone book. I've never known which one he is."

"You've never seen him again?"

"No. His mother has a little grocery store in my old neighborhood. I don't know how I managed to never return there after that summer. Or when I went with my friends, I always stayed outside. I vaguely remember her—his mother. It also explains my unusual hair color," she said with a lighthearted laugh. She smiled as she looked at Greta. It felt good to finally share the burden she carried. "I'm keeping you from whatever you have to do. Let's close up this place."

"You were honest with me and now I have to share my story with you. It will only take a few minutes, Schatzie." Greta quickly rinsed the wine glasses and set the wine bottles out of the way. "Come, listen to me before I change my mind," she said with her usual hearty chuckle.

"The person who called me," she spoke quickly as they sat on the sofa, angled so they could face each other, with Greta making a mental note to get the area redone, "is my lover, as Americans say. His name is Paul. But—he's married. His wife is an invalid," she spoke quickly, "and as he won't divorce her, we have our secret life."

"I guess it's understandable all the way around. Where is his wife, if I may ask?"

"It's been a few months that he gave in and finally had to place her in a nursing home. It was very hard for

Paul. He's kind and gentle and patient. We met at the grocery store. It struck me as odd that he had baby food jars and baby cereal in his cart. He saw me staring at it and I apologized when he caught me. He laughed and said, 'Of course you'd never expect an old fool like me to have a baby. It's for my wife who's an invalid, and this works quite well for her.'

"I was so touched by this that I told him how wonderful for a man to take care of his wife like that. He saw my cart had one of everything. I was buying a small T-bone steak, two small potatoes, and a tomato. I even had one each of the fruit I was getting. I told him I had lost my husband about a year earlier. He asked me to have coffee with him in the deli section and we did. We lost track of time and we agreed to meet again at the store. We met for several weeks before desire hit us. It hit us pretty strong," Greta said with a laugh. "We met at a motel that night and we've been seeing each other ever since. It's been the most rewarding relationship I've ever had, other than my William. He asks nothing of me and I ask nothing of him. I really don't want to marry again. He goes to visit Alice several times a week. He's retired from the military and invested wisely as a young man. He bought a small apartment complex that he fixed up and he lives quite comfortably."

Greta stood up abruptly, and stated, "That was enough of my story for tonight. I want to tell you I appreciate your confidence in me, Schatzie. I trust you as completely as you trust me. Let's get on home and enjoy the rest of the evening."

Eight

❦

"Connie Jones is my name now," she had told Greta over the phone when the job she was desperately seeking was within her reach.

"I used to be called Catherine Jeffries, but 'Cathy' certainly doesn't suit me, does it?" the tall, slender blond asked Greta as they spoke together in person that first time. Greta had given Connie the opportunity to prove herself as a seamstress and it had worked out.

In Catherine's mind, a woman with a sweet name like Cathy would be a perfect wife and mother. No, "Connie" suited her, she thought. And it was the ideal name for a famous dancer, as she dreamt of being from the time she discovered dancing in the small, northern Arizona town where she had been the prettiest girl, the tall, thin blond the wild boys ran after. Even as the poor child she had been, she always played up her cool blond beauty and married the handsome guy who proposed, never mind he was just as poor as she.

Now, in the darkness of her heart, at times a scrap of memory of the sons she left behind crept out. Did they remember her? They were so little when she calmly walked away from them—did they ever wonder what happened to her?

Greta had listed to Connie's story with stoicism.

"Nick turned out to be a great father to the boys, born one and a half years apart. From the start he spent more time with them than I could, or would; I never figured out which. He read to them at night, he'd say prayers with them, tucking them in after I said goodnight to Tommy and Billy."

She loved them in her own way. Maybe she had never been meant to be a mother. When she met Greta, she somehow found the nerve to tell her most of her story, though never all of it. No, there were many things "Cathy" would never tell and would just as soon forget. Like the grandfather who raised her and the things he would do to her while she pretended to be asleep. With her own mother gone most of the time, she had no one to turn to, no one she dared tell.

"I just up and left—I had to. I couldn't stay one more day in that little town with Nick and me and the boys going nowhere."

When she saw Greta was not going to judge her, she continued her story.

"One of the men who took a liking to me in Vegas said I'd have to learn proper English and he set me up for classes. Now and then I'll slip and some old words will come out, but mostly I concentrate on the right grammar."

Her mind was always on something else, dancing mostly. Not a day went by without her practicing dance steps. She knew she was good at it, the same as her expertise in sewing. "At least I got that from Momma, before she went off for good."

Nick would compliment her on how neat she kept their small apartment over the grocery store where he worked. She had sewn slipcovers and pillowcases and flowered curtains for the two bedrooms and tiny kitchen, though the windows looked out to the back and all she could see were the trash containers and desert cactus. She kept the curtains closed and lived in her dream world for the most part.

"I finally packed my suitcase one day Nick had taken the boys to his mother's house, and with the bit of cash I managed to save, left town on the bus. He must have found the note I left on the kitchen table that night. I told him not to come looking for me and that it was best this way.

"In no time at all I got a job dancing in a club, not on the strip, but I knew it would be a matter of time before I'd find something better. I never forgot what I was after. Hollywood—movies, even. That's still my goal."

A raven-haired Connie soon established herself as a seamstress, her clientele gratified with her finely detailed work. On the rare occasions she smiled and chatted openly, she told Greta she was the only woman she had ever trusted completely. Greta never told Connie that from the beginning, Greta sensed Connie was a lost soul, lost in the sorrows she had endured in her childhood.

Nine

Carolina poured coffee as she and Greta sat comfortably in an alcove where they could see someone enter the shop.

"This streusel is delicious, Gretchen," Carolina said to Greta. "You could as well have opened a bakery." Carolina had adopted some of Greta's German words, delighting in her friend's nickname.

"Ah, Schatzie, I know it's your favorite—how did you guess I actually considered that instead? I would be getting up a lot earlier if I baked every day. And I would most likely be a lot heavier."

Greta resisted the second piece she was about to take and instead took a second cup of coffee.

"Caro, I had a lovely life in my beautiful Munich. I was the third of five children, the oldest of the girls. Poppa was a banker, quite successful. Mutter, that's German for mother, cooked and kept an immaculate house. We Neubergs first lived in Frankfurt during the war, but our family home was in Munich. It's my turn to tell you my story—how I came to Los Angeles—and about my family." Her tone was almost serious.

"Mrs. Rand is coming in this afternoon to pick up her dress. We don't have any appointments pending, so we have time for a comfortable chat,"

Carolina said.

"We were a boisterous family," Greta continued, "each of us two years apart. My two older brothers played well with us, but my sisters and I were inseparable. We'd walk around arm in arm, the three of us. The war came and we managed to survive. That's when we returned to Grandmother's big house in Munich; Poppa thought it was safer. He became ill and died soon after the war. I was rather ordinary looking, the strong, sensible one, or so it seemed. My younger sisters were the pretty ones. One summer I surprised everyone by eloping with the butcher's son, from the neighborhood.

"The first years were happy ones. I had a little girl, Monika, after a year of marriage—"

Carolina could not hide a look of surprise. She held her hand to her mouth but refrained from commenting. Greta continued as if she had not seen the shock on her friend's face.

"I came home from work one day and found Horst waiting outside our apartment. He told me quite calmly he found someone else, an older woman—well, only two or three years older—and he was on his way out with a suitcase. That same night I went to my mother's house with two-year-old Monika and moved back in. I was unhappy, of course, but even the next day, I knew it was meant to be. My dream was to come to America, especially after the war. I'd seen movies and could only imagine how wonderful it would be to live here.

"I told my mother a few weeks later that I was saving my money and would be making the trip to California, at first with the pretext that it would be a vacation and I would return. I knew I would not. Mutti said, 'If you leave, you cannot take Monika. She stays with me.' I think she knew what I was planning. She was devoted to Monika."

The telephone rang. Carolina rushed to answer, speaking briefly. "Yes, everything is ready for you. I'll be here when you come by for the final fitting."

Greta poured fresh coffee. They sat back and savored the delicious brew before Greta continued.

"I arrived in Los Angeles on a warm summer day and found myself in paradise. It was just like the movies. Only better! I walked on the beach. I loved the feel of the sand on my bare feet. The cool, foggy air was perfect for me. I had enough to live on the first couple of months without worrying about employment. I made friends with people on the beach. I met the man I would marry, the love of my life. William McLean was wonderful to me from the very beginning. He had a good job, as I told you before, and we married soon after we met. He was everything I had dreamed of—strong, kind, sweet—and he loved me. He arranged everything for me to stay here. I became a citizen as soon as I could. The 1960s were good to us.

"I used to write home all the time, telling them all about Southern California and how it truly is a magic place. I asked Mother to send Monika, but she always said no; the girl was now so attached to her, they could not be apart. It was hard for me, of course, but so far away that in time I got used to having only the photographs they sent.

"I was always either sewing or baking. Will convinced me to open this shop. Will loved it, said it was perfect for me. When he passed away I almost went back to Germany. Two of my steady clientele talked me out of it. Jack is one of them. They said, 'Go, visit your family, and then come back if you belong here.' That's what I did. This is home. I mourned my Will, but I've settled into the life I have now. I'm content with Paul. We need each other in our lives."

Greta leaned back in her chair, eyes closed, exhausted from reliving what she had put in the past. A tear rolled down her cheek. Carolina reached over and held her hand.

Carolina was silent, waiting for Greta to comment on what she had just related. "I suppose you're surprised I had not mentioned Monika. She's a big part of my life—it's so hard to imagine our lives together, though. Of course I love her. But I was a young woman when I came here, eager to get on with a life I had longed for deep inside me always. I knew I was angry, and why I left so quickly was because Horst had gone out of my life so . . . suddenly. My life was turned around. Monika has always been safe with Helga—my Mutter—and now, after so many years, we're all settled into our comfortable spaces."

"Greta, you don't have to explain your motives to me. I'm your friend, and I will be, no matter what. Just as you have been a friend to me from the first day we met."

"I've been surprised myself—how easily you and

I became friends! I have sensed a bond with you that is difficult to explain."

"Me, too," Carolina said. "It's hard for me to believe how my life has changed. Just a few months ago I was so unhappy with Joseph. At least now I see how unhappy and closed in I was. I thought I wanted to be with him forever. Now that I am with Jack and have my work here, I feel fulfilled, and so alive. I've shocked my family and maybe even hurt some of them, but I have to be true to myself. I would not have met him if I had not been here, in this shop, doing what I love."

"You are creative, Caro. You had to experience the joys of creating. And here in my shop, no one judges you or expects you to be something or someone you are not. Paul knows everything. He and I are soul mates, as he puts it. He cannot leave a wife who cannot defend herself—I wouldn't expect him to. I have a part of my family so far away they may as well be on the moon. Sure, we talk on the phone every week. Monika is going through some teen problems. My sister Karin and my mother keep me up to date. Maybe next summer I can make a quick trip. I've invited Monika to visit here, but she's got a boyfriend, and someone would have to accompany her. It's not as easy as it would seem to be."

Caro nodded silently.

Ten

❦

"Does this dress look OK? Or should I wear the pale yellow? I don't want to wear anything too extreme the first time I meet your parents and your children. Oh, Jack, what if they don't . . ."

"You really have nothing to be nervous about. They're just as ordinary as anyone you know. I've told them about our wonderful romance and they can't wait to meet you." Jack stepped out to the hall for a moment.

"I have something for you, something that reminds me of our first night in the apartment. You looked at the moon and told me how happy you were. I had the date engraved on it." He unhooked the clasp of the silver crescent-moon pendant to place it around Carolina's neck.

"Jack, I love it! It's so original."

He reached over and squeezed her hand on the drive over to his parents' home, reassuring her. He had never seen her so tense. Though he loved his parents and was devoted to them, he acknowledged their unusual fussiness when it came to their only son and whoever was in his life. His hope was that Carolina's sweet nature would easily and quickly win them over. Her uneasiness was contagious, and by the time they arrived, he was just as nervous, if not more.

"Mom, Dad, Carolina Sanchez is soon to be my fiancée. I am very proud to introduce you to each other. Caro, my parents Rose and Arnold have heard a lot about you."

"Welcome, welcome, Carolina. Am I pronouncing it right? I've been practicing all day. Rose has been so excited to meet you and so have I. My goodness, Jack, you were right. You are beautiful, Carolina," Arnold gushed.

Carolina pressed her lips together in a tight smile, willing herself to get over the tension she had been under all day. Jack's parents certainly were polite, and their welcome seemed sincere. She felt embarrassed to have doubted Jack and leaned forward to accept Jack's father's hug. Mrs. Morten encircled Carolina's waist with her arm.

"She's been beside herself all day, waiting for you and hoping whatever she cooked would be to your liking," Arnold shared. "Come in, make yourself at home. This, of course, was also Jack's home until he moved into some apartment recently. But I guess you know about that."

"I'm very happy to meet you both. I've been happily looking forward to this all day." Carolina hoped her white lie did not show.

As they were led down the wide hall to the dining room, Caro could not help but notice photographs of the family. She saw one of Jack in his younger years.

She longed to stop and look but felt she would have to wait until the right moment.

"I'll show you around the house after dinner. I know Jack must be hungry, aren't you, Jack? This is his usual suppertime. Of course, on a Friday we have our traditional kosher meal. Jack, would you light the Shabbat candle?"

Jack hoped his total and utter surprise at what his mother had just said was not obvious, for he would never offend his parents under any circumstances. He wondered what in the world had happened since he last saw them. They rarely followed the ancient traditions. Why now?

"Of course, Mother," he said as he went to the sideboard, where an elegant lighting match was ready for him.

Rose stepped into the kitchen and quickly returned with a tray, set it on the table, and went out to get the remaining platters. Arnold served Carolina, making small talk, gazing at her as he did.

"How long have you been in Los Angeles, Carolina?"

Carolina answered the usual polite questions, tasting the food and smiling at her hosts, making herself feel the hospitality the Mortens were eager to display. She noticed Jack seemed a bit distracted, as if his thoughts were elsewhere.

"Have you been busier than usual, Jack? You seem lost in thought," his mother commented, noting it as well.

"No, Mother. I was just thinking about Melissa and Aaron. I haven't seen them this past week. I thought they might drop by and say hello and meet Carolina."

"Well, they decided to give you both a little more time with Arnold and me before they meet Carolina. That was quite adult of them, don't you think? Carolina, you know Jack's children live here with us, don't you? They went to spend the night with friends. They were invited to Shabbat services first, and then they'll be at the club for dinner."

Now Jack could not hold back his surprise. He could not recall his children ever being invited to Friday evening services.

Jack stood up to help remove the dishes, insisting his father and Carolina remain seated and chat some more. He could see Carolina had made a favorable impression on the older gentleman, who had not taken his eyes off the young woman. Jack glanced back as Carolina's ravishing smile lit up the room.

As soon as mother and son were in the kitchen, Jack asked in a calm, low voice, out of earshot of the dining room, "Mother, what were you talking about? We haven't carried out any of the old traditions in years. And when did the kids start going to services?"

"Well, Jack, it's about time we did! Mel and Aaron were happy to go. You should have seen them."

"I imagine they were, but . . ."

"Now, you just help me carry the dessert plates like the good son you've always been." The petite woman pulled him down so she could reach up and kiss his cheek. "That's my good boy."

"I was wondering," Arnold began in a somber tone back in the dining room, "if Jack told you the story of our family name. It has a history, you know. The

Morgensterns were a proud and prominent banking family in the old country. We've had paintings of some of them restored. Jack was named after his great-grandfather Jacob. He'll have to tell you the complete story some time, also why the name was shortened to what it is today."

Jack ushered them all into the living room, hoping to distract Arnold. Jack reached over and held Carolina's hand, their hands resting on the sofa between them. Her adoring smile at Jack was not lost on anyone in the room.

"Carolina, do tell us about your family, dear. They're quite far away, aren't they? In West Texas, from what I understand. What business is your father in, my dear?"

"Mother, I told you before. Carolina's parents aren't in any business. Her father works for the railroad and her mother is a homemaker. They're honest, solid, down-to-earth people who produced the woman I'm in love with. I guess you forgot."

"Mother didn't mean any harm, Jack. We simply want to converse with your lovely . . . fiancée and get to know her. Do you come from a large family? I do believe Latinos usually do."

Carolina's merry laughter rang out. "Yes, I guess we do. I have three wonderful sisters, older than me; two of them are married. My other sister is a teacher, devoted to her profession. And there are many aunts, uncles, and cousins. We don't need to invite anyone to our gatherings to have a festive occasion. The family alone is more than enough. I have several aunts and cousins here in Los Angeles. I am proud to say I come from a large, wonderful family."

Jack beamed at Carolina and squeezed her hand. That should hold his parents, he thought, at least for a while.

"We're sure they are, of course they are wonderful. We hope we get to meet them soon." Rose and Arnold nodded in unison as Arnold spoke. He had managed to save face for the moment. But he continued, "We hope they don't mind having a Jewish son-in-law. You are Catholic, aren't you?" Carolina nodded slowly. "Ah, yes, you are. Well, that should not be an obstacle when you're in love."

Carolina held her head high as she looked at Jack while Arnold spoke. She clutched his fingers as she nodded her head when Arnold asked his question. Jack recognized the questioning look in her eyes, aware she must be taken aback by the unexpected revelation.

The seconds passed as all eyes were on Carolina. Her smile had not faltered. Finally she spoke in a firm voice. "Of course not. I would not let that be an obstacle, as you call it. We'll work things out, won't we, Jack?" she said with a determined squaring of her jaw. In those few seconds, she saw that Jack's parents were attempting to create the very obstacle they just mentioned. Everything fell into place. They were not in favor of her and Jack's union, despite their seeming kindness to her. Jack also sensed what had happened and felt protective toward his beloved. Yet, he was torn within. He knew he would have problems with his parents as long as he was with Carolina.

Jack subtly changed the subject, discussing his latest

business venture, knowing that would easily divert the two determined people sitting in front of him. How could he have misjudged his parents so completely? His thoughts were tumbling, even though he was able to steer the conversation away from the previous topic.

"I have an early appointment. So, we must say goodnight and thank you for a lovely dinner, Mother."

"Yes," Carolina said as she stood up with Jack and accepted his proffered arm. "I have so much to do. Saturday morning is my time to catch up and spend time with my aunts. You know, we Latinos love to spend time with our families." Her cool smile spoke volumes.

Soon they were at the front door, Jack kissing his mother goodnight and shaking his father's hand, and Carolina again thanking both Rose and Arnold. They were finally outside, headed to the car. Jack held the door open for Carolina, holding her arm as she slid in. He felt her arm stiffen in his hold.

They drove in silence. During the ride Carolina either looked straight ahead or out the window, away from Jack. She was tense and did not hide it.

"I guess you're wondering when I was going to tell you. I really didn't think it was that important."

"Not important?" Carolina asked after she had remained silent a long time, causing Jack to wonder when she would reply. "How could something that huge not be important? Jack, I just wonder why you didn't tell me. Did you think I wouldn't stay with you?"

"That did cross my mind. You're not angry?"

"No, I could never be angry with you. I just wish

you had told me yourself. This is clearly quite important to your parents. They object to me, don't they? Your mother is lovely, so petite and pretty, and your father, well, he's quite a gentleman. He made me feel so at ease—until the remarks about your being Jewish, and me a Catholic."

In the apartment, she snuggled in his arms, their feet up on the ottoman. Jack held her close and kissed her cheek lightly. She turned her face to him so their lips could meet.

"I love you, Jack, the way you are, everything about you. Nothing else is important to me. You're everything to me."

"I won't let anything come between us, Caro. You're the love of my life. I'm sorry I didn't tell you before. I guess I kept putting it off, hoping it would just go away and never be a problem." He kissed her passionately.

As she was falling asleep, she finally gave in to the thoughts that had risen earlier. How would her family accept this man in her life? She had been blithe about the issue earlier that evening, but she knew it would be an unexpected shock for her parents and the rest of the family for Carolina to marry a Jewish man. As far as she knew, no one in her family had ever been anything but Catholic. Well, she decided as she was drifting off, snuggled against Jack and relishing the lovemaking she so luxuriated in with him, we'll just have to see what happens. I'm not giving him up. She placed her hand on Jack's arm that was wrapped around her, a smile on her face.

Eleven

The doorbell rang early in the evening. Carolina peered through the peephole and was surprised to see Jack's face behind a camellia bush.

"I wasn't expecting you until tomorrow night! And what a beautiful plant," she said as she stepped aside to let him in.

"Let me place the pot just inside the door for now. I can't wait to tell you the news! You know how I've been going north on business. Well, it's partly true. I did have an excellent opportunity to look into some contacts for building around the Salinas area, and we'll be getting started with that in the coming months."

He caught the startled look on her face as he mentioned Salinas. He knew how fond she had been of the city despite the outcome of her marriage.

"Now, don't look like that. Everything's fine. I've been meeting with an attorney and it's all taken care of. I waited to tell you when I had the good news. Your marriage will be annulled in a short time. The attorney managed to convince … Joseph," he hesitated saying the name, "that this was the best way to go. The report I have is that he and his family accepted the finality of dissolving the marriage. As soon as everything is ready, you and I can be married."

She was relieved at not having to go through whatever she would have done on her own. I wouldn't have known where to begin, she thought.

"I—I don't know what to say. Was it a terribly difficult thing to do? Oh, Jack, I never suspected what you were doing on your trips. I'm so relieved—and grateful."

"It really did turn out to be a good thing for me to scout around up north. I've found areas ready for development that I'll either do directly myself, or at least get in on the financial end."

"That's wonderful, Jack. What a great solution you came up with. An annulment! Oh, but what about the church?"

"Sam Cohen, my attorney, is taking care of the legal paperwork," Jack said, referring to the pending legal separation. "But as far as the church, it's not that easy. That's more complicated and may take much longer, even years. So, I don't know if you want to proceed with that, because then we can't get married for a long time. I don't want to pressure you, but I would like us to get married as soon as possible." His voice was soft and low, the voice that made her melt with desire for him.

She hugged him. "We'll get married as soon as whatever has to happen happens." She laughed happily as she looked into his eyes and saw his joy.

He began to set the table for them, looking over at her, smiling as he silently said a prayer of thanks for the turn his life had taken the day he stepped into the Couture Shoppe and met Carolina.

"It's almost closing time, Greta. I wondered if you'd make it back before I leave with Jack," Carolina remarked late in the afternoon a few days later.

"I know you wonder where I've been all day," Greta said breathlessly. "Here, please help me with these bottles. I'm so excited I'm afraid I'll drop them. Jack should be here any minute, right? I want to tell you both together."

"Yes, he's on his way. I've never seen you so excited." Greta's enthusiasm was catching, and Carolina's smile was almost as big as Greta's.

"Oh, good, there's Jack. I can't wait much longer to tell you. Help me open the champagne and pour it, Schatzie."

"What's the occasion? The two of you look radiant, and of course as beautiful as ever," Jack said, leaning over to kiss Caro and hug Greta. Jack removed his sport coat and set it on the sofa.

"One of our clients, Mrs. Meyer, has recommended our Couture Shoppe to do all the costuming for a new dinner theater opening up. It's a fabulous opportunity for us. It means a lot more work for the two of us, Caro. We definitely have to hire an assistant or two."

"That is great news, Greta. Have you gotten legal advice regarding the contract?" Jack's expression showed his interest.

"I knew you would ask about that, Jack. That's where I've been all day. Mrs. Meyer, who isn't directly involved—it's her neighbor who asked her who had made the dresses for her daughter's wedding—and her brother-in-law, Harvey Carper, are funding the theater. I brought the contract for you to look at. I trust your judgment, Jack."

"Would you like to have my attorney look at it?"

"I trust you to do whatever you believe is best."

Greta turned to Carolina, cleared her throat, and in what she hoped sounded like a solemn business voice asked her, "Would you like to become my partner officially, Caro? I probably should have asked you privately, but I'm too eager to offer you the opportunity now. You've been with me long enough for me to know your work and your commitment to the shop. It's fair that you have a share in what should be a good investment. If you want to talk it over with Jack, I understand."

Carolina nodded silently at hearing Greta's words.

Jack spoke at once. "You're a born businesswoman, Greta. You've been successful with a shop you started on your own raw talent and built it up in a short time. If this contract turns out to be as fair as I think it is, it will be a huge boom for your business." Jack said as he turned the pages of the legal document. "As for your offer to Carolina, there is no reason for her to hold off on becoming a partner. She'll be my wife soon, and though she won't need to work, I know how much this means to her. I'll be glad to provide the financial backing. It's an excellent investment."

Greta poured the champagne and proclaimed: "A toast to the future of the Couture Shoppe, to my partner Carolina, to Jack, and to . . ." Laughter rang out as they each lifted a glass and sipped the delectable sparkling wine.

Greta interviewed several applicants for assistant positions in the following days before deciding on two women in their twenties who demonstrated the qualities she and Carolina agreed were necessary. Carolina felt comfortable accepting Jack's offer, knowing it was a matter of time before she would be Mrs. Morten. A deal was made where Carolina would have 49 percent of the business. The money invested would allow for the necessary expansion the extra work entailed. A quick remodeling was soon started by Jack's company.

The shop was bustling as never before. Greta and Caro found that making the costumes for the plays was as much fun as their regular work. Caro turned out to be the more innovative one and would either draw up patterns herself or search through books to capture ideas for the period pieces.

Getting home later than usual one evening, she was greeted at the door by Jack.

"Hi, hon," she said. "Sorry I'm so late, but we had a deadline for the theater that we just barely made in time. There was a change . . . What is that smile on your face? You look like you're up to something!"

"Here, sit down, put your feet up on the ottoman. Let me take your shoes off." He propped the pillow behind her the way he knew she liked. They kissed softly as he held her in his arms, her head tucked into his neck. She closed her eyes in bliss. I think I love him more each day, she thought.

"I do have news for you, Miss Carolina Sanchez. Your annulment became final today. Everything is settled. You are a free woman, free to be my wife as soon as you agree to a date."

Carolina was speechless. Her grin became wider as he spoke the words. "That is wonderful, Jack. I'll have to let my family know. Oh, I'm so happy."

"First, we are going to have an engagement party as soon as possible, and then start planning a wedding. I'll leave that up to you to choose as big or small a wedding as you'd like, though personally a small, intimate celebration would be more appropriate."

Carolina was nodding and smiling, suddenly wanting to get up and shout to the world that she was free and would soon be Mrs. Jack Morten.

"I'll call my family in El Paso tomorrow. I have to think about how I'm going to tell them, and maybe by tomorrow I'll know when we will marry. My aunts here suspect we're seriously considering marriage, as I talk to them about you every time I call them or go see them, and they finally admitted I was right about you."

"Yes, let's decide right now! We can get everything organized. We'll have a simple ceremony by a friend, a justice of the peace, and how's a small banquet room at my parents' club sound to you? That should hold the people we'll invite: my friend and vice president, Don Hanson, and his wife; my family including my children; your aunts and cousins; Greta; Lisa; and whoever else can make it from El Paso."

"Yes, just a few close family and friends, and I'll make my dress, and just my sister and Greta as my matron of honor. Oh, Jack, it's so exciting."

Their nightly lovemaking was as intense as ever, perhaps more so this time. She had a hard time falling asleep for the first time in a long time. Her mind was awhirl with joy at all the plans she would have to make in the coming days. Jack also had tossed and turned before falling asleep.

The next day she arrived early to the shop, glad to find she was alone, and quickly dialed her home in El Paso. She had never mentioned to anyone in her family the fact that Jack and his family were Jewish. Eventually I'll have to tell them, but not now, she told herself. She didn't want anything to spoil their happiness. Lisa's cheerful voice gave her the warm, loving feeling she had come to expect.

"Sis, I knew that would be you calling at this hour! How's everything? What's going on in your life?"

"I want you to be the first to know. I'm a free woman again. Jack was able to get an annulment worked out for me. And—we are officially going to get engaged this weekend with a little party. I hope you can make it, but I know it's very short notice. Here's the most important part, Lisa. I hope you and my family will be able to come to our wedding."

There was a brief moment of silence before Lisa respond-ed. "I'm happy for you, Caro. Truly I am, even though I seem to be the old-fashioned one of all of us and didn't approve—well, I won't go into that now. I did tell mom and dad about you and Jack, though. They're both happy for you. I'm sure they'll want to hear all about your planned wedding."

Lisa's tone of voice did not match what she had just said. In fact, Carolina thought she sounded unhappy, but she was determined to let nothing spoil her joy at the way things were turning out with Jack.

"Jack and I had dinner with our aunties not that

long ago. They absolutely loved him. He was his usual charming self. They have gotten over their old-fashioned taboo about my dating him."

"What matters now," said Lisa, trying to match her sister's elation, "is that you will be in a good and true marriage with the man you love. But will you marry in the church? I know it takes a long time to complete an annulment through the church. Did you get to meet his children? You mentioned that was pending a week or so ago."

"It went great! Aaron and Melissa are so easy to talk to—at least they were with me that evening. We took them to dinner. They picked the place, a pizza parlor with a jukebox. Melissa and I immediately hit it off. Aaron was a bit quiet at first but soon forgot his shyness, which is the way I interpreted it. By the end of the evening, I even got Melissa's measurements in the ladies room so I can whip up a dress for her. I'll think of something special to do for Aaron so he won't feel left out."

"I'm so glad. Teenagers can be hard to read sometimes. What about the church wedding?"

"Lisa, we don't want to wait. It's going to be a civil ceremony. It's going to be a small, simple wedding. I really want you to be my maid of honor if you can make it. You can let me know later. We haven't set the date yet, but possibly in a few weeks or a little over a month. I know you'll love him when you get to know him, and his children, too. I look forward to spending time with the kids."

"Yes, of course I'll love him like my own brother, the same as I love my other brothers-in-law."

"How are your projects coming along?"

"My latest is working with young girls who get pregnant and drop out of school. I've started a program where they can continue with school, even get special training so they can work and be self-sufficient. There's also the pregnancy prevention I've worked on the past couple of years. I get so engrossed in my work I don't have much time for anything else. But Rick is still around, ever the patient guy. He's heading a program working on keeping teenaged boys from dropping out of school. We make a great team!"

"Yes, you always have. I know I've nagged you before, but why don't you two get married and be a team for life? He'd make a wonderful husband."

"You know my sentiments on the subject. No marriage for me. I have to be able to go my own way if I so choose."

After saying goodbye to Lisa, Carolina made a quick phone call to her aunts to give them the news and update them on the family in Texas.

"I'm glad we're together to hear you're engaged, Querida. We all send you and Jack our blessings."

As Carolina was replacing the receiver, she saw Greta walking in, laden with sketchbooks and material.

"*Gruss Gott*, Schatzie! What a beautiful morning." Greta often greeted her friend in the customary Bavarian manner.

"Gruss Gott and good morning to you, Greta." Carolina ran over to help place the items on the counter.

"Thanks. I hope you have some coffee ready. We have a lot to work on today. I have the sketches for the new costumes already. It's to be a renaissance theme—

something I've always wanted to do."

"I love renaissance style and have tons of ideas for costumes. It will be such a delight to work on that style."

"Barbara at the theater told me they've been working on the play for almost a year and have the music ready as well. All they need is for us to show them the sketches and work them in with what they already have. It's going to be such fun for us to create!"

They flipped through the drawings, commenting on how they would cut the material to get the right sheen on the festive patterns.

They took their coffee cups and sat down in the small office behind the kitchen, part of the remodeled portion. They closed the door behind them. "Greta, I want to ask you to be my matron of honor for my wedding, most probably within the next month or so, as soon as we can get the details worked out. As of yesterday, I am free to marry Jack."

Greta placed her cup down and walked around the desk to where Carolina was sitting. With outstretched arms, she waited for Carolina to stand. They embraced warmly. "I am so happy for you, Schatzie. I know this is what you both have been waiting for, and finally it's all coming true for you. It's too early in the day for champagne. We'll have to do that later."

"Jack wants to have a small engagement party this weekend. I know it's short notice. I was hoping you would ask Paul to accompany you. Surely he can make an exception."

"That's very sweet of you to think of him. It's

about time he meets the people I've been talking about. Let's get to work now. We have a lot to do the next few days. I hope it won't be too much for you also planning the wedding. And your dress! Ach, you have to start work on your dress as soon as possible."

When Greta got nervous or excited, her German accent became more pronounced. It had gotten heavier as the women conversed about Carolina's upcoming wedding. Both knew it was due to the excitement of the news and laughed. They set about to complete one or two of the pieces needed for the play, aware of the tight schedule.

"I have a bit of a worry, Greta," Carolina said shyly later that afternoon. Greta turned to look at her friend, a puzzled look on her face. "I am late this month. I never have been before."

They looked at each other a while, their faces both reflecting the thoughts racing in their heads. "I suppose it could be related to the recent stress of the extra work, Schatzie."

"It's just a few days so I'll wait and see. I haven't mentioned anything to Jack yet."

Greta nodded silently. Each had a worried frown on her face. They went on working. By the end of the day each had completed a costume in purples and reds, the sleeves extra wide, hanging at the ends. They were pleased with the finished products.

The following Saturday, the caterer placed the elaborate centerpiece on Rose and Arnold's highly polished mahogany dining table. The stately house appeared grander than usual, as Jack had spared no expense in decorations. Arnold stood with his arm around Rose, both with a resigned, forced smile. They looked at each other and shrugged. Aaron and Melissa were walking down the stairs, laughing at the joke they were sharing.

"Don't the two of you look superb? You'll make your father proud. That's a beautiful dress, Melissa. The pale turquoise suits you," Rose said.

"My Dad's fiancée made it for me. She surprised me with it."

The doorbell rang and Jack and Carolina walked in. "We wanted to be sure we'd be here before any of our guests arrived," Jack said, with a grin from ear to ear.

Melissa inclined her head toward Carolina and gave her a light kiss on the cheek. "We're happy for you and Dad, Carolina."

Carolina noticed Melissa pronounced her name correctly, rolling the *r*. Aaron's tall, lanky figure was outlined by the candlelight from the still-dim dining room. Jack put a protective arm around his daughter and another around Carolina as he said, "I'm happy to have my children and my future wife getting along so well."

Chimes rang out. One of the hired staff opened the door. "There's my family," Carolina said as she broke away and went forward to greet the relatives who had been able to attend. They all hugged, and Carolina led them to where Jack and his parents were standing.

"Mr. and Mrs. Morten, these are my dear aunts, Margaret Casarez and Mattie Torres. This is my cousin, Angelica Torres, Mattie's daughter. I'm so glad you all could make it. I want you to meet his parents, Rose and Arnold Morten, and Jack's children, Melissa and Aaron."

Carolina's aunts and cousin hugged Jack warmly and then turned to his parents. "We're happy to meet your family, Jack," Mattie pronounced with the smile that lit up any room she was in. Jack returned the warm embraces, murmuring his greetings in Spanish to Carolina's family. The senior Mortens nodded and smiled warmly at Carolina's family, making polite comments of welcome. The guests were led into the living room where Carolina noted there were extra chairs, in elegant brocades matching the other pieces, providing comfortable seating for all the guests.

Jack joined the small group, eager to spend time again with Carolina's family, recalling the lovely time he had when he met Carolina's delightful aunts at dinner at Margaret's. An easy conversation soon was flowing. Aaron and Melissa joined in as the punch was served. Jack's vice president and close friend, Don Hanson, and his wife Eva arrived, both eager to get acquainted with Carolina and her family, knowing how important this was for Jack's sake.

Carolina excused herself, Jack close behind her, as she heard Greta's voice in the entry foyer. As they stood next to Jack's parents, ready to welcome their last guests, Rose muttered below her breath, "Oh, the one with the married lover!" Though obviously stunned at what she had just heard, Carolina leaned forward to embrace her friend and warmly welcomed Paul. Caro glanced over at Jack, wondering if he had heard what his mother had so unexpectedly uttered. Carolina had briefly mentioned Greta's relationship with Paul, and she thought perhaps she had misunderstood what she had heard. Maybe Rose meant something else. She caught Jack's eye and saw at once that he had heard and wondered about the comment. She was able to read the embarrassment on Jack's face. He leaned over to Caro, kissed her cheek, and ever so softly whispered, "I'll talk to you about this later. I'm so sorry, my darling. Bear with me."

Her look told him everything he needed. They stood looking at each other, silently communicating that nothing would come between them.

Rose had her back to the couple. Arnold caught the look between Jack and Carolina. At the moment he was torn between his love for his wife and his only son. He had heard Rose's comment and realized she had not been aware of being heard and that it meant Jack would discover their secret endeavor in checking on Carolina and those connected to her. How else would he be able to explain Rose's intimate knowledge of someone they had never met?

Arnold took Rose by the hand and led her away from the foyer with the pretext of looking in on the caterer in the kitchen. Jack stepped aside, avoiding direct eye contact with his parents, his mind whirling in wonder at how they had information on Carolina's closest friend. As he warmly shook hands with Paul, his free arm around Carolina, he made polite remarks to everyone around him and quickly deduced the only plausible answer.

"Paul, I'm happy to meet you. I look forward to getting to know you." Carolina smiled broadly beside

Jack and hugged Paul spontaneously.

At six feet four inches, Paul was easily the tallest in the room. His tanned, weathered face, sandy hair, and ruddy complexion showed his love of the outdoors. His firm handshake with calloused hands spoke volumes to Jack. His relaxed smile indicated he had not heard anything spoken out of turn, much to Jack and Carolina's relief.

Determined to enjoy the evening with his fiancée and their guests despite whatever his parents were up to, Jack made sure those gathered in the living room were comfortable and had been offered drinks and snacks. Soon they all would be seated in the dining room. He could see across the hall to the sumptuous food being carried and placed on the table. Jack moved place cards swiftly, changing his and Carolina's seating from the original plan. The guests were summoned to the dining room. As Jack's father moved toward the head of the table as originally planned, Jack took his arm and steered him to the middle, where he and Rose would be seated next to each other.

Arnold Morten looked at his son, noted the stern determination and firm set of his jaw, and knew he and Rose had been found out. He assumed correctly that Jack had no way of knowing how they had gotten the information on Carolina's friend, but that it would become evident in no time at all. Arnold became pale at the thought of any discord between himself and his son. They had never had so much as a cross word between them. Arnold knew he and Rose had gone too far and wished at that moment they had never pursued their horrible prying project. He slumped in his chair as he thought of the consequences of their deeds, took out his handkerchief, and wiped his sweating brow.

Jack leaned in toward him, concerned for his aging father's health.

"What's wrong, Dad? You're trembling. Here, have a sip of water." He held the glass of ice water to his father's lips, hoping the whole situation would not blow up into something serious. The guests were taking their places and murmuring about Arnold Morten's health.

"It's nothing, I'm fine. I'll just sit here and rest. The water feels good. Please, don't worry about me."

"Dad, there's no need for you to be upset. Whatever happened . . . It doesn't matter. We'll forget about it for now, OK? Here's Mother now. Don't let her see you upset. She's not aware of . . . what happened. Mom, come sit here by Dad. I prefer that you two sit together. I'll lead the toast from the head of the table." Jack's warm tone to his parents set everyone at ease. He could not bear to hurt or upset his parents.

Jack held the chair for his mother and eased it in gently as she placed her hand on Arnold's, a wan smile on her lips. She looks so small and frail, Jack thought. Her mind has not been as sharp as it used to be. His heart cringed at the idea that his mother's mind was deteriorating. He made a mental note to have her assessed by a physician as soon as possible. He placed a loving hand on her shoulder after he pushed in her chair. She lifted her head up to her son, an adoring look on her face.

Roast beef and platters of chicken in puff pastries were soon the center of attention on the elegant china. The vegetables on glass plates were delectable in exquisite sterling baskets.

Champagne was poured. Jack held up his crystal glass with one hand while his other hand held Carolina's. A hush came over those seated around the table. He waited until all the guests were silent, and their faces turned toward him.

"My dear parents, children, Carolina's family, and friends—I am proud to announce that Carolina Sanchez has accepted my proposal of marriage. We will become man and wife in the very near future. I am blessed to have found the love of my life when and where I least expected."

The guests raised their glasses and declared congratulations.

After dinner, when all had gathered again in the living room, Jack, seated next to Carolina on the small settee, asked her if she could be ready for the wedding in four weeks. He asked if that would be enough time for her to make her dress.

"Yes, I already have an idea of the style. I'll get started on it right away."

Jack stood up, got everyone's attention, and announced the date of the wedding. "We'll probably not send out invitations since all of you gathered here will be our only guests again, unless your family in El Paso can make it, Caro," he said. "It will be at the country club down the road. How does three in the afternoon sound to you, my love?"

Carolina nodded with a joyous, dazzling smile.

Twelve

"I've sent one of the men to pick up your sister at the airport. He'll drop her off at your cousin's house. I'll be at my parents."

"Until tomorrow, my love," Caro said and kissed Jack goodnight on the eve of their wedding. She went into the bedroom where Greta was closely scrutinizing Carolina's wedding dress as she hung it in the closet.

"I'm honored I'll be the one helping you, Schatzie, but I'm surprised Lisa won't be coming over here to the apartment to be with you," Greta said as she fluffed out her own dress hanging on a hook on the bedroom door.

"She's getting in very late. Oh, Greta, I haven't been able to think of anything else, but what with the work for the theater, designing and making my dress, and the other situation with Jack's parents—I am still late. I do believe I'm pregnant. I'm surprised Jack hasn't noticed. You know how I love my coffee. Well, the mere thought of it makes me nauseous. I don't have morning sickness as such, but certain odors just don't agree with me. My breasts are puffier and tender. I haven't gained any weight yet, thank God, because I'd have to alter the dress."

Greta hung Carolina's dress in the closet and sat on the chair next to the bed, looking at Carolina, who turned to her. Both were silent a while. Finally, Carolina spoke.

"Jack found out his parents hired a private detective to check on me, my family, and my friends. In my opinion they were worried that I was out to 'get' their son. It was painful for Jack—he loves his parents. They've always been close. One thing, though, his mother seems to be getting more forgetful and doesn't trust people as she used to. I thought Jack made more out of their snooping than was necessary. I know there's nothing for me to hide. But in their checking, they found out about Paul being married. They didn't get all the information and background. As you and I had already agreed, I had told Jack about it, and he said he doesn't blame either one of you. In fact, he liked Paul and would like us to get together for dinner when we get back from our honeymoon."

Greta had been shaking her head in disbelief. "Well, this is California. Most people don't get shocked about anything. That's one thing I noticed when I got to know some people here."

"Apparently the Mortens are very protective of their son. They were afraid he was getting in with some gold digger. I didn't even know how successful his business was for a long time. I'm going to continue to work as long as I can. When I have the baby, I'll find someone to help with her so I can work as much as possible."

"Her? You already know?" Greta's hearty laugh

filled the apartment.

"I don't know. That slipped out. It doesn't matter what I have as long as the baby is healthy."

"Oh, I just thought of something! Weren't they upset because I'm from Germany? Jack and I had our discussions about that when I first met him. I was a child in Germany when the terrible Holocaust happened. Quite frankly, I heard about it after it happened, as a big ugly secret. I was mortified that it happened, and I could not believe there could be such cruel people in the world. Jack and I made our peace about the Holocaust over many glasses of wine when he would come into my shop in the evening."

"He spoke with his parents a few days after the engagement dinner. He told me he would not hurt them for anything in the world, but he had to stop them from going on with their search. That's when he found out everything they had done. Also, Jack told me he arranged for his attorney to make it easy for Joseph to agree to a quick annulment with a gift of money and the danger of his truth coming out to his family. He wouldn't tell me how much he paid, and his parents were not able to pry into the details. I guess other people's lives are always the most interesting. When Jack was telling me all this I was afraid they had discovered my own little secret. But, apparently not. He didn't say a word about it and I think he would have."

Greta saw the worried look on her friend's face.

"Schatzie, I know how that would hurt you, if the truth came out about your father and mother. But it's not your fault. Try not to let it bother you at this time in your life. You are marrying a wonderful man, a man who truly loves you, and it seems like before you know it you'll have a child of your own. Let this happiness bring you the joy you've been seeking."

"Yes, you're right, Greta. I'm only going to think of our beautiful time together, Jack and me. Now, goodnight, dear friend. I'll see you about one o'clock tomorrow afternoon."

The morning was clear and cool. It promised to be a perfect day for a perfect wedding. Carolina showered and drove herself to the hairdresser, who was close by. She tried on her light lavender gown upon arriving home, making sure for the tenth time it would fit perfectly. I am obsessing on perfection, she thought. The phone rang. It was her sister.

"Lisa! How's everything going?"

"My dear little sister, I am so sorry I'm not there to help you. I want to come over right now. I'll get one of our cousins to take me. Is that okay? I just wish I could have gotten in earlier last night."

"Sure, you can come over now. That would be wonderful, to have a few minutes with you while I'm getting ready."

Greta was soon at Carolina's apartment door, earlier than planned. "You hair looks so pretty, up in a twist like that. You have great hair color. It's unusual, but it suits you," she told Carolina.

"Let's sit and chat a minute or so. My sister is on her way over. She's bringing Aunt Mattie's *caldillo*. We'll have that for lunch. It won't be too heavy before the wedding. Oh, Greta, I'm so excited. Today is finally the day I've been dreaming of—again. This time it's a better dream, and hopefully with a true 'happily ever after' to it!"

After a short time the doorbell rang, and Lisa was standing at Carolina's front door with a box holding the pot of Mexican stew. Caro took it from her and set it on the stove. Lisa dashed out to get the rest of her personal belongings. As she placed them on Carolina's bed, the sisters embraced lovingly.

"It's so good to see you, my little pet. I wish the others could have made it. But you know Mamá, it's all we can do to get her to the other side of town, much less take a trip to California," Lisa said. She turned to Greta, hugged her as well, and said, "I'm happy to meet you. I've heard so much about you from Caro. I'm glad she has such a great friend in you."

"I'm pleased to meet you, too. I feel like I know the family, hearing about all of you from Caro. This is a great day for us to meet."

"Come on, you two. Let's eat. I'm famished now and don't want to be stuffed at three o'clock." Carolina was soon serving the hot caldillo, ladling it into deep bowls.

The women were dressed in their finery, makeup on, hair done up. After eating, they helped the bride with her gown.

"This is so beautiful, Caro," Lisa said as her fingers glided lightly over the organza dress. "You designed it yourself, didn't you? It has your touch. The pale lavender looks wonderful on you. And how did you manage to get the beads on with all you have to do?"

"It took me the most time to find this color material. I didn't want anything too frilly. This V collar accentuates my longish neck and full bustline. I had to cheat and have one of our assistants work on this beading."

"Not just because you're my sister and I've always loved your sewing, but this is stunning! It's so simple yet elegant, and the pale color works well with your skin tone and hair. You do have a flair for style; you always have. Oh, and you made the veil to match, with the beading along the top to fit like a delicate tiara. It almost makes me want to get married just to have something so stylish to wear!"

Their merry laughter filled the room. "If that's all it takes to get you to change your mind about getting married, I'll design something totally fabulous for you."

"You get the groom, we'll provide the dress," Greta chirped in between the laughter.

The limousine and driver Jack had hired promptly arrived at the apartment. The ladies were dropped off at a side entrance of the club for privacy. A bouquet of camellias was on the dresser, along with two smaller bouquets of tiny, pale peach roses for Lisa and Greta.

"I wasn't sure Lisa would be able to be here. This works out well for me to have my two dearest friends— one, my own sister—as bridesmaids," Carolina commented.

The women walked out into the small foyer outside the private banquet room, out of view of the general public. A quartet was playing in a corner. The guests were seated on chairs set up to form an aisle. Jack stood straight and tall next to the judge. Don was standing to his left. The wedding march began, and the handful of invitees stood up, facing the door.

Lisa walked in slowly, smiling, nodding to her

cousin and aunts. Greta counted to ten before she, too, walked to her place. She beamed as if the ceremony were her own accomplishment. Then she realized that in a way, it was. She brought them together and had been supportive of her dear friends from the beginning.

Carolina saw Jack standing, waiting for her, and thought, I've never felt so happy. The love I feel for this man is so much more than I ever dreamed. This wedding will seal and complete our love.

She walked slowly, each step taking her closer to him. He reached out to her with his right hand as she approached him. He held her hand in his and they stood facing each other, their eyes and smiles speaking their love for each other. At some point the judge began his recitation. Each answered when they were prompted, and in a few minutes first Carolina, then Jack, said "I do!" They kissed, and there was a soft round of applause. The musicians played the classical piece louder as the couple walked together toward the back of the room.

Immediately, the chairs were moved around to the sides of the room where the tables had been placed against the walls. Across from the quartet, waiters were bringing in trays of food. Punch was provided for Jack's children and those guests not drinking wine or champagne. Carolina's family milled around her, offering their congratulations. Aaron and Melissa hugged the bride to form a trio.

"I hope you and Dad will be as happy as you are today for a long time," Melissa said with tears welling up in her eyes.

Aaron nodded in agreement with his sister, a happy

grin on his face as he said, "I wish you both the best. I've been practicing saying that."

The newlyweds briefly stood in line as the guests offered their congratulations. Carolina moved away from the small groups of people and let her thoughts wander. I'll have to tell Jack as soon as possible about my pregnancy, she thought. I'm feeling just a little more tired than usual.

She sat at a table in the middle of the room against a wall where she had a good view of everything going on. She saw Jack standing and chatting with her aunts. She saw Lisa make her way to greet Jack's parents, who were each holding a glass of punch. Lisa's knack for being able to engage anyone in easy conversation was being demonstrated as she listened intently to whatever Arnold Morten was telling her. They looked over at Carolina and lifted their glasses toward her in a toast. She nodded back at them and held up a glass of wine that was on the table. She held it to her lips but did not drink. The Mortens and Lisa resumed their conversation.

Carolina's glance continued around the room, and she was delighted to see everyone comfortably chatting and glad to have the chance to replenish her energy. Jack was still chatting with her cousin and aunts. He waved her over, but she remained seated and motioned with her hand she would be there shortly. She turned her head back in the direction of her sister and the Mortens and was surprised to see a strange expression on Lisa's face. She was no longer smiling and in fact appeared puzzled and angry as she slowly looked from the Mortens to Jack and then to Carolina. Carolina wondered what could have happened in the few seconds she had looked away from that small group that had so changed her sister's attitude. At one point Lisa placed her hands on her hips, took a deep breath, and glared at the couple. Lisa relaxed her stance and stood back from the Mortens, apparently said something emphatic as she pointed her index finger at them, and walked away.

The Mortens stood looking at each other. Arnold bent down to whisper something to his wife, steered her out toward the foyer, and stepped out of Carolina's vision. She saw Lisa walk purposefully toward her aunts, who were still talking to Jack. Lisa nodded to Jack and leaned down to say something to Aunt Mattie. Jack moved away, aware Lisa wanted to speak privately with her family.

Jack turned and took a step toward Carolina, but at that moment Don approached Jack and took him by the arm, steering him over to where Eva was sitting. Carolina's attention was caught by the sensation of her family's gaze upon her. She turned her head and was astonished to see her sister, her aunts, and her cousin staring at her, but not as they had before. Now they looked angry or upset or—. She could not imagine what was going on.

She got up and walked over to where Jack was seated with Don and Eva. He stood up and put his arm around her waist, holding her close to him, and kissed her on the cheek. She tucked her head into his shoulder, feeling the warmth and security she was now so used to. "How's my lovely bride?" he asked. "You looked so comfortable sitting over there. I know you needed some rest. You've been working much too hard, my dear. It's time you cut back your long hours."

Greta and Paul joined the bride and groom, each with a plate of hors d'oeuvres. A light conversation ensued among the couples. Don and Eva took the opportunity to get up and walk over to select their servings of food.

Carolina glanced casually to see her family also going up to the buffet. She continued to be puzzled by what she had witnessed, and knowing that the Mortens had previously attempted to find fault with her, she dreaded whatever may be happening. She and Jack were now husband and wife and completely happy. Nothing else mattered, as far as she was concerned. I'll tell him about the baby tonight, she thought with excitement.

As her family sat down to begin their meal, she saw Greta approach them and take a seat at the table. Greta had her back to Carolina, but Carolina could see her sister's expression as Greta spoke. Lisa clenched her lips and started to say something. Greta held her hand palm outward as if to stop Lisa from saying anything. Lisa looked over toward Carolina, catching her sister's eyes on her, saw the puzzled look on her face, and clenched her lips again. Carolina could see her aunts, Lisa, and her cousin Angelica listening intently to Greta, who stood up, said "Okay?" in a slightly louder tone, and then walked away, out to the hall. Carolina could tell by the way Greta held her back stiffly that something serious had just been discussed.

She decided that whatever it was, she was not going to let it spoil this beautiful and perfect day. She smiled up at Jack and held his arm close to her. He kissed the top of her head and whispered, "I love you." They looked at each other, oblivious of everyone and everything else going on about them. They would start their married life as contented and loving as they had been from the moment they met.

Greta had been seated at a table out of Carolina's vision, but she had observed the same sequence of events, with Lisa talking to the Mortens. The couple's animated chatting with Carolina's older sister had piqued Greta's interest, for she was fully aware of what had transpired just weeks ago. Greta rightly had guessed the Mortens had made some commentary to Lisa to cause her to jump at their bait. As Carolina's aunts served themselves in the buffet line, Greta had drawn in close to them and overheard the comment, "We never dreamed he was Jewish. What will our brother say to that?"

As soon as Margaret, Mattie, Angelica, and Lisa were seated, Greta seated herself at the same table, her back to Carolina. Conversation had stopped abruptly as Greta joined them. Lisa clenched her lips and commented, "What will I tell the family back home? She should at least have told us so it wouldn't have been such a shock."

Greta responded, "Why should she tell you about their private life? And why would you want to spoil this day for her? Can't you accept their love for each other? And as long as it doesn't matter to her, why should it matter to you he is Jewish? He's an excellent man in every way. She's never been as happy as she is now. Don't ruin the day for them. Okay?"

Greta had said the last word a little stronger than

she had intended. The last thing she wanted was for her friend to have her wedding day spoiled, especially by her own family. She was furious with them and with the Mortens, and she wished she could tell them all off, but not here and now. She had forced herself to walk out to the lobby and went straight to the ladies room, hoping to calm down enough so no one would notice, though she doubted she was completely successful. Coming out, she saw the Mortens standing down the hall, his arm around her. They looked old and fragile, and she wanted to go talk to them but held back. No sense in getting them riled up, she thought. They'll come around as time passes and they see how happy Jack and Carolina are, and when the baby comes—let's just wait and see what happens then.

"Well, this is certainly quite different from what we expected, isn't it, Tías and Angelica? I have to admit Greta is right, and we mustn't spoil Carolina's big day. But—I am shocked that she has accepted marrying a man of the Jewish faith. I can't imagine what Papá and Mamá will say. Of course I will have to tell them sooner or later." Lisa's voice was calm, aware of how easily she could mar her sister's wedding.

"Ay, mi hijita, this is something I never expected. I will sit here and smile and not say one word against my dear niece," commented Margaret.

"Mamá," Angelica spoke with the voice of reason, "with all due respect to you and the rest of the family, I really don't see how this can be so terrible. Her husband seems to be an excellent man who obviously loves Caro. He's an honest businessman who'll provide well for her. She seems extremely happy in her own little world now. I just don't see why you're making such a big scandal of this. I don't see why our family—all of the family on both sides—will make such a fuss."

"Angelica, you don't understand. You're Carolina's age and you're not even dating, so you can't see what impact this will have on the family. But we have been Catholic for generations. There has never been as much as a divorce before. Now Carolina gets divorced and then marries a man of the Jewish faith. *Por Diós*, how can you say you don't understand why we're upset? But we must be polite. We cannot let this ruin her wedding day. Let's put on our smiles and keep up appearances. Our family has never given in to any sort of scandal. We've managed to keep—whatever has happened— quiet and not give anyone reason to bring gossip about us." Margaret kept a smile on her face as she spoke.

"Tía Margarita, you're right, as always. I don't think anyone has noticed anything other than Greta. Jack's parents obviously are not pleased with this union, either, but we must not give in to them and let them see we're upset. Ignore them for now, and we'll figure out how the rest of the family handles this. Thank goodness my parents are far away and won't know for a while, at least," Lisa said, her exasperation difficult to hide. "Let's put on a good front for now."

Thirteen

"We can't stay out here much longer without attracting Jack's attention. Are you ready to go in there now?"

"I suppose so. Oh, I just don't know. I'm afraid we've ruined things for Jack and he'll be angry with us. We have to admit this woman Carolina seems to be as sweet and kind as he's told us all along. There have been days I've regretted making a problem out of his choice of a marriage partner."

"Now, now, Rose. Don't upset yourself. You had good intentions. What if she had turned out to be all wrong for him? We would all be thanking each other to find that out in good time. As it is, she's turned out to be a lovely woman. Melissa and Aaron have come to care for her already. Look how disappointed we were with Jack's first wife, leaving him and the children and running off to South America, or wherever she went. He knows we've had his best interests at heart. Don't fret yourself any longer. Let's go in and be pleasant and get something to eat. The food smells delicious from here. Let's go, sweetheart."

Rose held onto Arnold's arm and let him guide her in, a big smile on her face, hoping it was not noticeable that she was making such an effort with it. She nodded politely to Carolina's family seated at the table closest to the door and then nodded over to that German woman, apparently a close friend of Jack's. Rose saw that the German woman had brought her gentleman friend with her and Jack and Carolina were seated at the table with them. Jack noticed Rose nodding to the guests and showed his approval by nodding and waving to his parents.

Arnold went over to the buffet to pick out what the two of them would have for dinner. Jack appeared right behind him. Arnold was relieved to see Jack did not appear to be upset. In fact, he seemed rather happy with the way things had turned out.

"Dad, I'll take you around to talk to the guests after you've had supper. Carolina is tired and we had agreed this little get-together would only last a couple of hours."

"Whatever you say, son. It's turned out quite well. 'Don't do anything too grandiose,' you said. Your mother and I were outside getting a breath of fresh air. She hasn't been feeling well and I don't want her tired out."

Jack sat at his parents' table for a few minutes. He was well aware of his mother's objections to this marriage but felt they would both come to love Carolina when they got to know her. He had noticed Lisa's abrupt change in demeanor after she had spoken with his parents, and he could only deduce his mother had made some inflammatory statement. He was determined to have the afternoon go smoothly for his and Carolina's sake.

"I can see Carolina's family is about ready to leave," Jack said. He stood up and walked over to their table, helping Aunt Margaret up from her place.

"I am so glad you were with us tonight, and I hope you will do us the honor of being our guests at our home as soon as we move in. You are the first ones to know about the house. Carolina doesn't know yet, but I have been preparing a house for us. I'll tell her tonight."

"How sweet of you to tell us, Jack! Why don't you tell her now so we can see the look of surprise on her face?"

"That's a good idea, Aunt Margaret—I'll do that. It's not quite ready, but I suppose I could tell her now as her wedding gift."

Jack walked over to where Carolina was seated with Greta and Paul. He took her hand and she stood next to him, safe in his embrace. He held up his glass of champagne to get everyone's attention.

"Thank you all for being here with Carolina and me this afternoon for our wedding." Everyone applauded and smiled at each other.

"I was saving this as a surprise for Carolina, but her Aunt Margaret thought it a good idea that I tell her now. Caro," he said, his hand caressing her cheek, "I have a house for us. It's not quite ready—it needs a few finishing touches—but by the middle of next week we should be able to move in. It's the pale yellow brick one with the huge trees and the landscaping you liked so much on the way to my parents'. I knew you'd love the garden. I had some renovations done to it the past weeks. It's my gift to you, my love." As Jack finished speaking, he held his glass up high.

The guests stood and applauded. The small group gathered around Carolina and Jack, hugging them and again wishing them the best.

After saying all their goodbyes, Jack and Carolina were at last on their way home to their apartment. "Let's drive by the house so you can see it," Jack said. "Would you like to go in, or are you too tired? You're not your usual self, full of energy."

"I'd love to see it! What a great surprise. We only drove by a few times."

"I could tell by the way you looked at it, and I know how you love gardens, and this one had such excellent landscaping. I figured if you didn't like it, I'd fix it up and resell it."

"Always the wise businessman," she said with a smile.

"Here we are. Let's go in through the back. The entry is not quite ready yet. There was very little to do to update it, but I definitely wanted the kitchen as modern as possible as far as amenities. The cabinetry was duplicated to look old and in keeping with the Spanish style inside." Jack opened the back door, which led directly to the spacious kitchen. From there, Carolina could see all the way to the front door, the arched doorways creating a soft frame.

"Oh—this is exquisite. Jack, it's so beautiful. I can't believe this will be our home. I love the color of the walls; it looks like creamy butter." She was touching everything: the tiled counters in pale yellow and tans, the backsplash tile in the same pale yellow. "Our dinette will fit perfectly here," she said as she stood in the space under a Tiffany chandelier. "This Mexican tile on the floor is wonderful."

"Well, so far you love the kitchen. Let's go see the rest of the house. The plumbing has all been replaced and the electrical wiring was checked and redone where it was needed this past week. I did have the master bathroom completely gutted out and refurbished. The other bathroom had to be cleaned up a bit, the usual updates I do on all houses. On Monday new carpeting will be installed in the bedrooms and then it should be ready. The other surprise is that I've had speakers wired so we can hear our favorite music in the den, the master bedroom, and the patio. We can also choose a room exclusively."

"I'm in love with this house, Jack. Look at the view to the gardens from the dining room and the living room. Oh, there are French doors leading out from this paneled den. I guess this will be your office?" Jack nodded. Then he said, "Well, here we are. This is the master bedroom, and as you can see, it's the largest and has doors that open out to the garden. Here's a sample of the carpet that will be placed. How do you like it?"

"Oh, yes, very much. You do know my taste, don't you? The colors are all the soft ones I prefer. Blues, greens, yellows, and this bathroom—it's beautiful! Jack, I never expected anything like this. Oh, thank you so much," she said as she put her arms around him and squeezed him tight. They kissed lovingly, passionately. Her voice was husky as she whispered, "Too bad we don't have a bed in here yet."

"My little rascal wife, you can't wait to get your hands on me, can you?"

She took his hand as he led her to the hall where it turned a corner.

"What a perfect placement for a nursery."

"A nursery? Well, yes, we can use it for that when the time comes."

"It's going to be sooner than you thought—it should be in just over seven or eight months, I imagine."

"Caro, what are you saying?" They had stepped into the bedroom in the corner of the house, facing each other, their arms entwined as he asked the question with a lilt in his voice. "Is that why you've been so tired the past couple of weeks? You've been a little pale in the mornings. I thought you were working too much and too late. Come here, Caro," he said as he pulled her tight against himself. "Are you . . . ?"

"Yes, Jack. I haven't been to the doctor, but I've had all sorts of unusual feelings and discomfort and wonderful sensations. It's only been a few weeks, but I've never been late before. I . . . ."

He held her close, and in a low voice almost whispered, "That is marvelous news! We're going to start our own family." He held her head in his hands and kissed her on the lips. They held each other quietly as the sun went down around them. "I have to get you home now. I want to make love to my pregnant wife."

"There's so much to talk about, Caro," he said on the way home.

"Our schedule should be easing up. We had last minute requests we didn't want to get behind on. If I cut back, we have to hire another seamstress or two. I hope Maria and Edna know someone so we can hire quickly."

The phone rang as they were getting ready for bed. Jack answered, spoke a few pleasantries to Lisa, and handed the phone to Caro.

Lisa's voice was stilted. "I wanted to let you know

I won't be able to accept your invitation to see the shop tomorrow. I haven't seen my other cousins in quite a while. They thought you and Jack would be going out of town so they planned a get-together for Sunday. It's best that I spend the day with them. I hope that won't interfere with your plans."

"No, not at all. You sound a bit distant, Lisa. Is anything wrong?"

Again there was a lull at the other end. In a cool voice, Lisa asked, "Is Jack near you where he can hear you?"

"No, he stepped into the shower. Why?"

"I was going to wait and tell you later, but I may as well tell you now. I don't understand how you kept all the secrets from us, from your family. First, you left your husband, apparently with good reason, but you left your home—he called us at one point, saying how much he wanted to make things right with you, but you wouldn't even listen to him."

"But . . ."

"I have to say everything now. We've never had a divorce in the family. Then you moved in with this older man you knew for a very short time while you were still legally married to Joseph. You told us about the wedding you planned, but you never once mentioned he is Jewish. I'll have to tell them—I don't know how our parents will take it. Maybe it's not important to you, but you know it is to our family."

Carolina was silent, stunned, as she listened to her sister berate her for her decisions about her own life. A tear rolled down one of her cheeks as she listened in anger and humiliation.

"Are you there?" Lisa asked.

"Yes, I'm listening. Go on. Don't stop now, Lisa," she replied in a voice as controlled as she could manage.

"You've been distant from the family since you married and moved away. I've tried staying close to you and talking to you as often as possible. Yet, you keep such big secrets from me. You say you're happy, and I trust you are. But your family is shut out of your life. I have to hear from practically a total stranger what is going on in your life. Your business partner is involved with a married man. Another woman in your shop is being hunted down for abandoning her children. These are the people you're close to now, Caro."

Carolina's face grew paler as she listened to her sister's diatribe. She listened and nodded as she heard the truths being recited to her. Jack walked out, a towel wrapped around his waist. He stopped drying his hair in midair as he saw the look on Carolina's face. He listened in disbelief as he heard his wife speak.

"Today is my wedding day, Lisa." Her voice was calm and low. "A beautiful, happy day for me and my husband. I won't explain anything to you—I don't want to and I don't have to. This is my life now, here with Jack, and with my business partner and true friend. Our lives are none of your business. I don't care what you say to our parents. I'll call them myself later and tell them. Goodbye."

She placed the receiver down gently and looked up at Jack. He sat on the bed beside her and held her to him.

"I'm not going to cry, not today. It's been a happy day for us. You're all the family I have and need now," Carolina said.

Jack held her, not daring to say all the things going

through his mind. He understood that Lisa and her parents would object to this union. He and his family had been through so much because of their faith. His ancestors had changed the family name to avoid persecution, but it still followed them and showed its ugly head on occasion, like today, his wedding day. He wanted to protect his wife and the child they were expecting, wrap an invisible armor about them, never allow anyone to say one word against them. He felt his own tears roll down his cheeks. He knew that Caro mustn't see his pain.

The next morning Carolina was up early and prepared breakfast and coffee. They both laughed as she pushed away her coffee cup. "Somehow, it's lost its usual attraction."

"Let's not wait until tomorrow, hon. Let's go look at furniture this afternoon. I'll call my contact person at the store," Jack said.

"What a great idea. I'm sure we'll find everything we need." She hesitated before saying, "I have to call Greta to tell her we won't be meeting at the shop as we had planned." She didn't want to say anything to spoil their first whole day of married life.

Jack noticed the determined smile on her beautiful face. He kissed her cheek and said, "That's my girl."

A few minutes later the phone rang. It was Greta.

"Hi! I was going to call you when I thought would be a good time. We won't be meeting at the shop after all. I'll tell you about it tomorrow."

"Oh, well, okay." Greta hesitated without asking for any details. She wondered if it had anything to do with the heated discussion she had had with Lisa and the other members of the family. As far as she knew,

Carolina had not been aware of what had happened. "I hope everything is okay."

"It is. I'll tell you tomorrow. Jack and I are going to shop for furniture for our home. We stopped to see it on our way last night. It's so beautiful, more than I ever dreamed I'd have. I can't wait to show it to you."

"Schatzie, I keep saying I'm so happy for you and Jack. I can't wait to see it. What a great wedding surprise that was! He kept the secret very well."

The next morning Greta had just arrived when Carolina walked in.

"I'm betting you don't want coffee this morning? How about a cup of hot tea? That might be just right for you."

"Yes, I'll try that. There's so much to talk about. Where shall we start?"

"I think you should go first. You left me in suspense when the visit with Lisa was cancelled. You also have a serious look on your face, not just that of a newlywed. The good things first: did you get your furniture?"

"Oh, yes," Caro said. "We didn't take anywhere near as long as I thought we would. Jack has his connections, of course, through the company. We got the prices wholesale. Jack is so pleased with himself, as you can imagine."

"I knew he would go that route. But tell me—what happened with Lisa?"

Carolina's face turned somber and she clenched her fist to her mouth for a moment. "I have to be strong when I tell you what happened. I swore to myself I wouldn't cry or get upset talking about it. It was the last thing I expected to happen. She scolded me like a child because I hadn't said anything about Jack being

Jewish, and this second marriage in general. I guess it's important to my family."

"Schatzie, that has to be hard on you. I must admit—I knew something had happened. Lisa was upset at your reception and she wanted to say something to you then. I stopped her. I hope you don't mind my interference." Greta reached over to place her hand on Carolina's arm. Caro placed her own hand on Greta's.

"No, Greta. You're my friend. You defended me. Well, after she told me all her complaints about how I am living my life, I told her to stay out of my business. I was so angry. I still am. Jack knows all about it. He came out of the shower just as we were finishing the conversation and he saw how upset I was. I refused to let anything ruin our beautiful day. Oh! I had just told him at the house about the coming baby. He's so excited about it. We're setting up the corner bedroom next to ours for the baby's room."

"When are you going to the doctor to make sure? And if you are, we have to see how we're going to work out our schedule so you don't work such long hours."

"I'll call for an appointment this morning. It won't be right for me to overdo anything, but I want to be able to help with the design and creating the costumes."

"Of course. That's another reason I need to tell you something I've kept from you. It's been my decision to continue using Connie—I take her the material in the evening, then I pick up the items when they're ready."

"I suspected that. I respect your decision, and her work is excellent. Are the police looking for her? Lisa mentioned that. I suspect Jack's mother gave her that tidbit of information."

"From what Connie's told me, she's made some arrangement with her ex-husband so that it's not a police issue. She must have gotten in contact with him since she found out someone had come here looking for her. Her ex-husband has come to terms with the fact she won't be getting back with him and the boys."

Carolina winced at hearing this. She looked away, trying to hide her distaste for the whole situation with Connie. She had thought long and hard about the facts she knew and had at least come to the conclusion there are many different kinds of mothers on earth. Some mothers abandon their children. Some mothers ignore a child for reasons only they can justify.

Greta saw that Carolina was lost in thought. She got up to pour herself another cup of coffee and poured hot water for Carolina to brew her tea. She made a mental note to bring in a real teapot so they could steam tea.

"There's the little surprise you're expecting. Are you going to tell your family?"

"Not for now," Carolina said after mulling over the question. "I may tell them as the time draws near. I never dreamed I'd get this distant from my family. The one I miss the most is my dad—and Lisa. I'm not surprised she's so strict and unforgiving. I didn't think she'd be that way with me, though. My other sisters have been on their own for so long I've been used to some distance between us, though we get along pretty well."

"Don't worry yourself about it, Caro. You have all these good things happening in your life now. She may come around and you'll be friends with her again. Maybe when the baby is born she'll come out and meet her niece or nephew and realize how wrong she is. At least I think she's wrong. I usually don't like to give my opinion about anyone else's life."

"I know—that's what's so good about you, Greta. You accept everyone the way they are and you never judge. You don't even ask questions. I used to wonder how you could be so easygoing. Now I see you save yourself a lot of headaches and heartaches that way."

As she was returning to El Paso Monday night, Lisa dreaded bringing up the subject of Carolina's lifestyle. What will I tell them? she wondered. Carolina's far away and most likely will not return home any time soon, so what difference will it make to her? I really don't want to hurt Grandmother and our aunts and Mom and Dad! I have no idea how they will react.

"How was the wedding? Tell us, hijita." Her mother could not contain her desire to know all about the wedding as soon as Lisa arrived at her parents' house.

"Well, of course she was lovely as you can imagine— they had a small, simple ceremony. His family, our aunts, Angelica, a couple of friends. The wedding and reception were elegant, just like Caro."

"It sounds like it certainly was different from her first wedding," Aunt Mariana stated. "I'd love to see the pictures." She had tears in her eyes as she said this in Spanish. She took out a hankie and wiped her eyes. Lisa put an arm around her aunt's shoulders, murmuring comforting words in their mother tongue. It was no secret that Carolina had always been her aunts' favorite.

Lisa resolved not to mention anything regarding the

details of Carolina's life at the moment. She couldn't bear to hurt her loved ones. She wondered how Carolina could have made the choices she made, how she could stay away from her family as long as she had, and how she could turn away from their faith. She shook her head at the thought of the hurt and turmoil that would assault the people who cared the most about Carolina.

"Well, she's happy, isn't she? The last time I talked to her she told me how well everything was going for her and her new boyfriend, who is now her husband. I understand he cares very much for her. She sounded as if her life was what she wanted, at last. It was the day she and Jack went over to Margarita's house." Mariana's tone was as lighthearted as ever. "She told me again how grateful she was that I had spent so much time teaching her to sew. That's been her passion all her life."

"Yes, we have to remember that. It's her life. She's decided to stay in Los Angeles, and now she's married to someone who seems to be a wonderful man. I've always trusted your sister's judgment, Lisa," Don Miguel commented.

Mariana extended her hand toward Lisa and gripped her niece's arm so she could have her say. "In olden days she would have had to stick by her first husband and put up with whatever came her way. Those days are long gone, at least here in the United States. You girls have choices now. Circumstances are changing, and for the better. Your sister is right to get married again. Why should she have to stay alone for the rest of her life? From what I've heard, she has made a wise choice."

Fourteen

Jack sat back and surveyed what his wife, with the help of an expert gardener, Manuel, had accomplished with the backyard so far. Huge, old oak trees served as the backdrop for the flowerbeds she had designed all along the perimeter of the house. Carolina had extended the beds in an S-shape, where she was adding flowers and shrubs as well as other sitting areas with small outdoor lights. Two more covered patios had been added to the spacious garden.

Piped music, playing softly, could be heard around the garden and in the distant patios. Carolina smiled as she heard Frank Sinatra singing one of their favorites, "Strangers in the Night." Jack usually chose the music, fully aware of Carolina's preferences so they both enjoyed whatever was playing in the background.

"This reminds me of Grandmother's garden. Even in the desert of El Paso, her garden flourishes. That's where all big family events are celebrated. That's where we would have had our wedding reception," Carolina said.

"I can take you to visit your home any time you say, Caro. I'd love to meet your family. I feel that I know them from what you've told me. They sound wonderful."

Carolina was pensive a while before she answered, "They are. They all are. My aunts are warm and loving and kind to everybody they meet. My sisters are good wives and mothers, completely devoted to their families. Grandmother Ana loves to have parties, any excuse will do. All the women love to cook. My dad's cousin and some other men formed a band, so they play at most casual neighborhood functions. Sometimes, for no reason at all, they'll get together and play, and everyone will come around to hear them. Before you know it, a big party will be going on."

Jack reached over to take Caro's hand in his, a loving gaze in his eyes.

"I wish I had been there with you. It sounds so peaceful, and enjoyable." He wanted to tell her they could have that type of life as well. He felt the yearning in her and reached over to kiss her, wanting to be everything for her so she would not long for that other life she knew.

"I think we can go visit after the baby is born, Jack. We'll have to take her to meet all her cousins, aunts, great-aunts, grand-parents, all of them," she said with a merry lilt to her voice.

"You just said 'she'—I wonder if that's a premonition."

"Oh, that's right. I said that before, to Greta. It just slipped out."

"Maybe you're right. I'd love to have a little girl, just like you."

"Or a boy, like you."

Fifteen

The nursery was almost ready. The main components were in. The white crib and dresser were ready to be decorated. Infant clothes were washed and folded and lovingly patted as Carolina waited during what she hoped was the last week before the birth. Greta was helping her set up some of the finishing touches.

"Have you let anyone in your family know yet?"

"No. Lisa has never called me again. I haven't called her, either. After that awful phone call I had with her, there has been no communication at all. I may have to break down and call her."

"What about your aunts here in LA? You've talked to them. Do they know?"

"I couldn't tell them and not tell my folks back home. I keep making excuses for not going by, so my phone calls have kept them content for now. Oh, Greta, this has all gotten messier than I'd thought it would be. I've called during the day when I know only my parents are home. Even for the Christmas holidays, I managed to time the conversations so I wouldn't have to ask for Lisa, and Jack and I kept the secret of the coming baby."

"If you think about it, it's usually family members who hurt each other. I'll tell you about my problems with my mother, sisters, and daughter another time. Today we're getting this room ready for a very lucky baby. He or she is going to have a wonderful mommy and daddy. Once you have the baby, I think things will change for everyone. Jack's parents won't be so distant. Your family will accept his being Jewish and see only his goodness."

"When we called at Christmas, Jack spoke with my dad for the first time. They hit it off well over the phone. Jack again invited them to come for a visit. It's my mom who won't travel. I know why she refuses to come to Los Angeles, but of course she won't—and can't—tell anyone. That man—you know who I mean—lives here, though what are the odds they would run into each other?"

A week later Jack was holding the baby as his parents walked into the beautifully appointed room in the private clinic. Aaron and Melissa could barely contain their excitement and eagerness to meet their tiny, new sister. The proud daddy held her up so they could get a good look at the bundle in his arms.

"Mom, Dad, meet your new granddaughter. Melissa, Aaron, this is your baby sister. We've named her Karen Michelle. We'll call her Michelle for now and see what she grows into."

Jack pulled back on the pink receiving blanket as Michelle stretched a little and pursed her lips as if to nurse. "See how tiny and perfect she is. I think she looks like her mommy, but Caro insists she has my eyes and chin."

The elder Mortens sat on either side of Melissa, who was holding the baby, their faces happy, smiles from ear to ear, both reaching over to touch the newborn lightly, delicately. "I do believe she has Carolina's wonderful hair color," Arnold remarked.

A few days later, with the baby settled in at home, Greta was getting ready to leave after a quick visit with Carolina. "I could do some work here at home if you need me to," Carolina said. "Nanny is working out rather well. And you were right—Rose and Arnold have been angels, helping with dinner and being so loving and caring to me and Michelle. Their old ways are long gone and forgotten. Jack and I are so happy with the way they've come around."

"I'm glad to say I told you so. Bye, Schatzie and Baby Michelle." Greta blew a kiss at the baby and dashed out the door.

Caro prepared supper for Jack and herself, fed Michelle, and then lay down for a quick nap. Jack walked into the darkened room, assuming Caro was asleep. He tiptoed over to peek at the baby. He heard a muffled cry from Caro.

"What's the matter, Caro? Is everything all right?"

"I'm so glad you're home," she said with a sob.

"My goodness, Caro, what's wrong?"

Her sobs slowed down as she sat up and leaned in against Jack. He put his arms round her, patting her like a child, soothing her with kisses on her head and wet cheeks. "Just relax and tell me what has happened.

We'll take care of it together."

"Oh, Jack, I've been so miserable all day. I can't keep it from you any longer."

He waited patiently, feeling her soft body against his. They had not been intimate since before Michelle's birth and he felt the longings stir within him.

In the light of dusk he saw her huge brown eyes. Childbirth had given her a new glow, had further softened the contour of her fine features. He bent down to kiss her lips.

"Jack, I miss my family so much. They still don't know about the baby. Lisa was so ugly to me that time she called right after our wedding. I haven't told anyone in my family about Michelle. But I miss them terribly."

"There, there, my love. Hush now. I'll take care of this mess as soon as possible. I'll call them and tell them."

He began dialing the phone and sat next to her on the bed, holding her hand.

"Hello? Miguel? Yes, this is Jack. Yes, sir, we are just fine, thank you. How are you and all the family? Good! We'd like to give you some wonderful news, Miguel. We just had a baby girl. Yes, you heard right. Carolina had a beautiful baby girl. We've named her Karen Michelle. We call her Michelle. They're both fine, thank you. Yes, here's Carolina."

He held the phone out to Carolina. She stared at it and reached for it, holding it to her chest briefly. Then she smiled and said a timid "Hello?"

As she heard her father's voice, the tears rolled down her cheeks, and for a while she was unable to speak. Jack took the phone and explained, "She wants to talk to you, but you know how new moms are, she's pretty emotional right now. Oh, she's fine. She just has to get the crying out of her system."

"I'm here, Dad. Yes, she was born last week. She didn't weigh very much, just over six pounds, but she's perfect and healthy and she just eats and sleeps and gets her diaper changed. Yes, I'll wait."

"He's telling the others," she said to Jack as she moved the phone away. "He's very happy, and I hear the voices in the background asking when and how and why hadn't I told them. What shall I say, Jack? I don't want to hurt anyone and I don't want to get Lisa in trouble. I don't think she's home. I don't hear her voice. My aunts are there."

"*Sí, Papá, aquí estoy.* No, nothing's wrong. Jack is wonderful. He's the best husband and father, after you or on the same level as you. I hadn't said anything because—because I had a few problems early in the pregnancy and I didn't want to disappoint anyone if things didn't work out. That's all. And I've been working at my shop. You know I'm part owner now. And then we have the house, there's always so much to do here. The garden, too. You can imagine how much time I spend on my flowers, at least before I had the baby," she said with a light laugh.

She held onto Jack's hand, squeezing it with delight as she heard her family's voices.

"Yes, I'll see how soon we can manage a visit. I'm hoping we could stay a couple of weeks, if he can get away that long."

Jack quickly looked at his agenda and said, "We can go around the beginning of next month, if you're up to it by then."

"Did you hear that, Papá? Yes, absolutely, we'll stay with you and Mamá."

Jack took the phone. "We'll be in touch with you before then, Miguel. I look forward to meeting all of Carolina's wonderful family I've heard so much about. *Hasta luego*, Miguel!"

The family was abuzz in preparation for a big reunion at Grandmother's house. Aunt Amelia and Aunt Mariana started cooking and freezing as soon as they got the good news. The band was given ample notice so they could begin practicing. Grandmother got a crew to freshen up the garden. Tables and chairs were cleaned and repainted as needed. All the homes got an extra-good summer spruce up.

"Everything has to be perfect. We have almost two weeks to have it all in order," Grandmother announced as plans were finalized for what would be served and even the tunes the band would play. "Miguel, the band members have to be on their best behavior. Your cousin Francisco mustn't touch a drop of liquor the entire week before the party. Amelia, you're in charge of the kitchen. Delegate. You're the expert," Doña Ana commanded.

"Sí, Mamá. I'll have my nieces help prepare everything for me so all I have to do is put the ingredients together. We'll start at once."

"Mariana, make sure all the linens are washed and perfectly pressed. We'll use blues and lavenders, Carolina's favorite colors. We have that new set of china I know she'll like. Heavy paper plates for the children, naturally. I can't wait to meet another great-grandchild! Oh, and not one mention of that other man from anyone, understand?"

"This is a very important trip for you, Schatzie. Connie will be here every day to help out."

"Speaking of Connie—she took me aside yesterday and told me she understands my sentiments toward her. She knows what she's done is an unpopular thing with most women. She said she couldn't find the words, but that in her case, it was the only thing she could do, leave her boys. I didn't say anything, just nodded. I'll never understand her."

"In a way my situation is similar. My daughter is far away with my mother. We have little physical contact. I didn't want it that way—that's the way it's turned out."

"Oh, Greta, I'm sorry. I spoke without thinking. But in your case your daughter knows she can contact you anytime! I won't bring up that subject again. I'll call you when we get back."

"Have a wonderful time, Schatzie."

The baby slept through the short direct flight. Jack held the infant seat in his lap as Carolina's gaze was focused out the window. He could see she was lost in thought, though she would reach over to hold the baby's hand or show Jack a tight-lipped grin now and then. The airplane landed.

Sixteen

Miguel was waiting for them at the gate, twirling his base-ball cap round and round in his hands. He was leaning forward, eager to get a glimpse of the daughter he had not seen since her last visit with Joseph a couple of years earlier. He looked eagerly to meet the man who had so changed Carolina's life. He was determined to get off to a positive start.

He waved as he saw her. She was walking slowly, holding onto her husband's arm. Her husband was carrying the baby in the infant seat.

She waved back timidly. Miguel could not hold back his tears. When she got to Miguel, he crushed her in his arms, and then quickly let go of her. With both hands he took hold of Jack's outstretched one. He placed one arm around Jack in a warm embrace and bent down to look at Michelle.

"Papá, how good to see you! Dad, this is my husband, Jack, and my baby, Karen Michelle."

"Jack, it is an honor to welcome you to El Paso and to my family. Everyone is eager to meet the two new members of our family."

Jack returned Miguel's hug with his one free arm.

"Did anyone else come with you?" Carolina looked around.

"Mi hijita, we decided I would be here alone to receive you. There's so many of us. We didn't want to overwhelm Jack so soon," he said with a laugh. Jack immediately sensed Miguel's genuine warmth.

While in the front seat with Carolina's father on the drive to her childhood home, Jack gave in to the pleasant sensations of finally meeting and being with Carolina's family, looking forward to the parties Carolina told him the family would have, and being in her hometown. Though the heat was unbearable at the moment, he knew he'd adapt soon. It had always been easy for him to adjust to any climate, and this dry, intense heat was something he could prevail over and enjoy.

The well-kept neighborhood they drove into showed stately, older homes. "These heavy pillars are interesting," Jack said as he observed the architecture of some of the homes. "Wider at the base, not quite square, and they taper in slightly at the top. I see many homes on this block have the same concrete porch. It must be nice to sit out here on a hot summer evening."

"You see," Miguel said, pointing to his neighbor's porch, "some have enclosed it with screening. I'm considering doing that. I'd like to add circulating fans on the ceiling to help cool the place down. The shade from the trees helps." Chinese elm trees much taller than the house provided the needed shade. "I'll take you around the house to show you all the details after you're settled in."

"I'd like that very much, Miguel."

There was a sea of smiling faces, young and old, milling all around them as they entered Carolina's childhood home. Jack was soon in the midst of hugging and cheek-kissing, and oohs and aahs over the baby.

"A small group to start with," Miguel said. "I know you're familiar with the names. You'll get to know each one little by little. This is Esther, Carolina's mother."

Esther extended her arms in a welcoming embrace, which Jack warmly returned. Her slightly accented voice was soft as she said, "Welcome to the family, Jack. Now, I want to hold my newest granddaughter."

She took the baby from Carolina after hugging her daughter, held the baby close, kissed her forehead, and spoke ever so softly in Spanish to the infant, who opened her eyes wide. "She has beautiful dark blue eyes, but she looks like you, Carolina. She looks so much the way you did as an infant." Esther could not conceal the tears that welled in her eyes.

Jack noticed Carolina's observation of her mother's reaction to the baby. Esther walked over and sat herself in an easy chair where she held Michelle on her lap, facing her. She opened the lightweight blanket, caressed the baby's arms and legs, and gently ran her finger along the baby's face and hair. She wiped her tears as they ran down her face. Carolina looked away from her mother. She turned her attention to other family close to her.

Jack was impressed by Carolina's mother's trim figure and beauty, an older version of his beloved wife, with dark hair and eyes. Her unlined skin belied her age, which he figured to be in the late fifties. He was astonished by an aloofness he noted in Esther toward

Carolina. Her tone was warm enough and her actions seemed genuine, but he was puzzled by what his unfailing sixth sense told him. He made a mental note to analyze it all later. Now, he was immensely enjoying meeting these warm, wonderful people. He found it easy to converse with Carolina's sisters, Marta and Anita. He discreetly looked for Lisa, but so far she did not seem to be present.

Carolina soon had her older sisters on either side of her, the three chatting animatedly. Jack admired the older sisters' thick dark hair, the curls pulled away from their faces.

He could hear snatches of Spanish now and then. At one point he answered flawlessly in their mother language, to cheers from the small group. Miguel questioned him on his ability to speak Spanish so well.

"I've always loved the sound of it. I made it a point to study it and I take advantage of the chance to practice at work with some of the men who work for me."

Women's voices came from the back of the house. "Oh, it's my Tías, they're here!" Carolina dashed toward the kitchen. "Tía Amelia, Tía Mariana! My dearest aunts!" They formed a trio as they hugged, the two older women caressing Carolina, stroking her hair, proclaiming their love for their niece in Spanish. Carolina and her two aunts soon became a quartet as Grandmother Ana walked in and Carolina rushed to hug her.

"Mi Abuelita querida!"

"How I've missed you, mi hijita. We want to meet your baby and your husband," Grandmother Ana's voice, strong as ever, filled the kitchen.

Carolina called to Jack, who was soon by her side.

"Jack, these are my favorite women in the world: my grandmother, Mamá Ana, and my aunts, Amelia and Mariana."

"Ladies, Carolina has told me so much about the three of you, I feel like I know you. It is a great pleasure to meet you at last."

"*Hijo*," Doña Ana said in her regal voice, "*ya eres parte de ésta familia.* You are my granddaughter's husband and the father of my great-granddaughter and you are forever in our lives. It is a pleasure to welcome you to our family."

"*Muchas gracias*, Doña Ana. That means everything to me, to be part of this beautiful family. I am honored." Jack leaned over to kiss the older woman's proffered cheek. Carolina's aunts followed suit. Carolina was beaming as she saw how readily and lovingly Jack had been accepted. For the moment she forgot the other problem gnawing at her. What would they say when they learned of his Judaism?

The afternoon floated along wonderfully, Carolina relishing the attention and love she so fondly remembered. She caught sight of Lisa's cool glance, and not even that soured the day she was enjoying. She had not seen Lisa arrive. She was not surprised at her sister's cool demeanor.

Her husband joined the men outside in the back as they sat around the shade of the old trees, the cold beers providing a welcome slake of the unending thirst in the hundred-degree heat. Jack felt at home and wanted to have the moment last forever. Jack sought out Miguel and Esther to thank them for their hospitality.

"Esther, and Miguel, I want to thank you both for today, for letting me become a part of this family so easily and joyously. My love for Carolina has included her family from the moment I got to know her."

"Jack, this is your home now," Miguel said in a low, deep voice, with Esther nodding and smiling happily beside her husband.

Later that night, Carolina reached over for Jack, whispering to him that she wanted him to make love to her for the first time after Michelle's birth. She clung to him, loving his closeness, not daring to tell him this was the very room and bed where she had heard the terrible truth about herself, so many years ago. Maybe lying here with Jack, like this, feeling him deep inside her, the memory would fade and the room would have new meaning for her, she hoped.

Jack immensely enjoyed the stroll through the neighborhood where he could see more of the turn-of-the-century and 1920s architecture on their way to Aunt Mariana's for lunch the next day. They pushed a borrowed stroller, hand in hand.

Mariana and Amelia were careful not to monopolize Jack. They also timed the courses so one of them was always present at the table. They did not want Jack to get snatched into another group as Anita and Marta's young children and teenagers showed their enthusiasm in meeting Jack and hearing about the Mortens' life in Los Angeles. The teenagers in particular asked about the current peace demonstrations and hippie movement. Jack was brief in stating they were lucky in that they and those they knew well were barely touched by such events.

"It's been easy so far to avoid any confrontations and stay out of areas where there's anything major going on. There are still many people who don't or won't get involved in anything like that." After they ate a quick meal, the youngsters left to join their friends, leaving the adults to their own afternoon gathering.

Halfway through the delicious meal of tacos and enchiladas, with only adults present, Lisa abruptly asked, "Have you thought of having the baby baptized while you're here? That would be so practical!" with a light lilt to her voice.

Carolina and Lisa had spoken only a few words to each other. Although Lisa had held her niece only once, as one of her sisters had passed her along to someone else, she had looked lovingly at the baby.

Jack cleared his throat. "We haven't really thought about that, Lisa. This trip was planned spontaneously. What do you say, Carolina?"

"Oh, I guess you don't baptize in your faith, do you, Jack?" Lisa's voice was cool as she slowly made her statement, making sure she had everyone's attention.

Grandmother looked at Jack for what seemed a long time, her eyes unwavering from his face. She seemed to be studying his features. Her expression was noncommittal. Finally she spoke, sweetly and clearly. "Your last name is Morten. Was it changed from something else?"

"Yes, it was. It was Morgenstern two generations ago. My grandfather changed it to avoid persecution. His father had some problems defending his Judaism. Yes, we are Jewish," Jack said, his voice firm and unapologetic. Carolina was smiling proudly at him.

Across the table, Miguel and Doña Ana cast what could only be called puzzling glances at each other. Lisa and Jack were looking back and forth at Miguel and Ana and caught the furtive glances. For what seemed a long time, neither Miguel nor Ana spoke. Miguel and Grandmother Ana seemed to be debating whether they should state whatever secret they held.

Lisa could not keep quiet any longer. "Why are you two looking at each other like that? What is going on? I asked a simple question. Jack announced he is Jewish, and now the two of you look so—well, strange."

"Let's finish our meal, and then I'll tell you," Miguel said softly.

"No, Dad. What in the world are you and Grandmother hiding?"

"Hija, you'll wait until we're finished eating. We might tell you then. That's final." Grandmother had spoken.

The remainder of the meal was eaten in silence, no one daring to ask any more questions. Amelia and Mariana were rather piqued. They had worked hard, as always, preparing a wonderful repast, and now all everyone could do was hurry and finish. The suspense was palpable.

"Let's not wash the dishes yet. We'll just clear the table so we can find out what could possibly be going on," Lisa impatiently commented.

As soon as it was cleared, they gathered again around the table, seated in the same places they had all been in before. All faces turned first toward Grandmother, then toward Miguel, at opposite ends of the table. The two were tightlipped. They looked at each other, then around the room. Carolina followed their line of vision, wondering what mystery they would announce.

Grandmother cleared her throat. "Miguel, you tell them." Her voice was firm, yet sweeter than anyone had expected.

After a while and several deep breaths, Miguel began. "We found this out some time ago, when Doña Ana had been settled here for some time and she received papers on the sale of her lands and property. She received some other documents which she showed me and which we felt we should keep secret, at least for the time being. They had been hidden away."

Everyone was staring quietly at him, in awe. Amelia, Mariana, and Esther did not dare look at Grandmother. What secret could she have kept hidden all these years? they wondered.

"To make it easier for Grandmother Ana, after I found out, I told her my family has the same secret, hidden as long a time as hers. I found out when I was a young man, before I married, and I was afraid Esther would not accept me. All my life, my religion, the Catholic faith I grew up in and have loved so much, meant everything to me. It still does. It was the same for Doña Ana and her family."

No one moved as Don Miguel spoke in a soft, quiet voice. He paused to let his words settle in everyone's minds. He thought, I have anticipated this day for years—the day I would tell the truth about all of us.

He continued after a brief pause. "This is what we are, what we have been for generations, Catholic. But— many, many years ago, before we were Catholic—we were Jewish. My family went to New Mexico from Spain, and then came here long before I was born. But when they left Spain during the Inquisition, they were Jews. They had to hide the fact to survive. They hid the truth and became Catholic. Well, Grandmother's family did the same. It was in the documents that were found in the secret lining of a box that came with her property. The same story—people who were Jews who converted to Catholicism to survive. In secret, they still held on to some ways of worship to honor their Jewish faith. Most of those traditions are lost now." His voice was almost a whisper as he spoke the last words.

When Miguel finished, everyone was stone silent. They looked at the table or at their hands or at the walls, but not at each other. Jack, too, sat still, almost holding his breath as he heard Miguel's story. His thoughts were on the suffering and persecution that had followed those of his faith. He did not dare glance at Carolina—not yet.

A sniffling sound broke the silence. Slowly, those gathered around the table sought out the sound and found Lisa, tears streaming down her face. Lisa made no effort to stop the tears or cover her face. Grandmother stared at her, handed her the ever-present handkerchief, and pressed it into Lisa's hand. Lisa let it lie there in her hands, limp on the table.

Lisa was shaking her head back and forth now. She did not trust herself to speak.

"How could this be true?" she finally said in a hoarse voice. "How could no one have mentioned this before? It's not fair. I am a Catholic, that's what I am and what my family is. Nothing will ever change that. Ever."

"Hija, I think you should go into one of the bedrooms and rest a while. You're very upset now. Please, go now." Grand-mother's voice was so gentle. Lisa looked at her grandmother, still shaking her head in disbelief. Lisa left the table.

"I knew you all would have to know the truth sometime. I guess this was the best time. Well, Jack, we've gone full circle, haven't we?" Don Miguel's face was serene, finally having told his family the secret that had haunted him and his mother-in-law for countless years.

Jack wanted to get up and hug the man, embrace him and tell him how wonderful he was. He himself had tears in his eyes as well, but he didn't want to weep openly and get sent out of the room by Doña Ana. He wanted to stay and be part of the family and enjoy their presence. He looked at Carolina with more love, if possible, than he had before. She caught his look and smiled back, seeing the absolute love in his eyes.

"We never did settle the question. Are you going to baptize the baby?" Aunt Amelia asked, thinking of the baptismal party she would start planning.

"We're here for about two weeks, Tía. I don't know if that's enough time to make arrangements."

"We can talk to Father David. He'll work things out." Don Miguel knew his friend the priest would manage somehow.

"One of my sisters and her husband would be the logical choice for godparents. I'd like that, if it's okay with you, hon," Carolina said.

"Whatever you decide is fine with me. If you can get it done while we're here, let's do it."

The grand party Saturday night was better than anyone anticipated. The musicians were all sober and in top form. They performed better than ever. The huge array of food was excellent. The warm evening was cooled by lovely breezes not too strong to stir up the desert dust. Neighbors and friends were invited along with all of the immediate family. Some were Carolina's schoolmates and were happy to see her and meet her new husband. Jack commented it was the best party he had ever been to. The family gathered again for the baptism on the following Sunday. The godparents, Anita and Fred, held a reception at their home with Aunt Amelia's wonderful assistance.

"Here we are celebrating my granddaughter's baptism, in an ancient tradition, and there are men getting ready to land on the moon! I praise the God of Abraham for all our blessings," Miguel said as he held up his glass of beer, and the others cheered on. Jack and Miguel exchanged looks of mutual respect and love. Anita held the baby and smiled at everyone.

The next morning Carolina told Jack she would like to spend the day with her aunts and grandmother, just the four of them. Esther had asked that Michelle be left in her charge.

Jack had seated himself to eat a solitary breakfast when Esther came in to warm Michelle's bottle. "I'm here to help with the baby, Esther."

"No, Jack. You sit and relax and enjoy a few moments of quiet. I can imagine you're tired of all the noise from our family."

Jack could not believe his luck. He had hoped

to get time alone with Esther. He had not forgotten his impression of an odd bond between Esther and Carolina from the first day. He poured himself a cup of coffee and stood leaning against the counter, his quick mind going at its usual lightning speed.

"It's been great for me to meet all of you. I'd wanted to see Caro's childhood home, where she spent her first years. How was she as a child, Esther?" He looked directly into her eyes.

She was silent a while as she sipped her coffee and looked out toward the backyard. Her thoughts seemed far away. She sighed and held the cup in her hands, almost caressing it, as she began to speak. Her voice was similar to Carolina's—it had the same soft, gentle quality.

"My girls were so sweet and special when they were little. Miguel and I would get them all dressed up to take them out. He was always so proud of them. Carolina was his favorite. My sisters also made her their pet, but no one ever minded. As the youngest it was natural. She was always a good child, an easy child, never any problem at all."

Jack had kept a relaxed attitude as she spoke, but he made it a point to watch her facial expression and her eyes as she spoke. He could not put his finger on it. What was missing? She's warm enough, seems loving enough, but there is something not right, he told himself. He felt uncomfortable all at once, as if he were betraying Carolina. Perhaps his wife was not aware of this subtle lack of—something.

Esther said, "Tell me about your parents and your children. Are they so very different from us? To me, all people are God's creatures. He loves all of us, but somehow we can't love one another. I've never understood how someone can be cruel to another person because of their religion or color."

Miguel walked in then, washed his hands at the sink, and sat down to join them. "How are you this beautiful morning, Jack? And how is my lovely wife?" he asked Esther as he kissed her cheek and squeezed her hand.

"Jack was about to tell me about his parents and his other children."

"I'd like to hear about your children and your parents. Family is most important," said Miguel with a warm smile as he joined his wife and son-in-law.

Jack would always look back on this day as the start of his and Miguel's relationship, beyond that of in-laws, as Jack spoke fondly of his parents and children, recounting anecdotes from his youth as an only son, and how close he, his parents, and his teenaged children had become, especially after the children's mother left.

Seventeen

1976

Festive decorations filled the patio and garden areas that had been prepared for Michelle's seventh birthday party. A small group from school would attend as well as her grandparents Rose and Arnold, and her brother, Aaron. Melissa, her sister, was away on a college trip planned months ahead. Greta was away on her semiannual trip to Germany to visit her daughter and family; a happy reunion had occurred shortly after Michelle's birth.

The years had flown by. Michelle had unknowingly created a miracle in her immediate surroundings. Her paternal grandparents had become so smitten with her that all unfounded misgivings they may have had about her mother had disappeared. As Michelle grew, Rose and Arnold's love for the child blossomed. Michelle was blessed with an easy disposition. She had her father's dark blue eyes but otherwise resembled Carolina, with delicate features, an oval face, and honey-brown hair with auburn highlights in soft curls.

"Michelle is the joy of my life," Jack often said to whomever happened to be within hearing distance.

Informal and formal photographs of his daughter were
discreetly placed throughout his office. Her sweet
voice on the phone charmed him when he would take a
minute or so from his busy schedule to call her.

Jack and Miguel often spoke by phone for a long,
comfortable chat. Carolina marveled at the relationship
her father and husband forged, but she was not surprised.
Miguel could talk to anyone about anything. Eventually,
Lisa warmed to her youngest sister again, but it was not
the same as before the breach.

Jack, true to form, had fallen in love with the dry
desert city of El Paso. Miguel would tell him whatever
was pending in the way of family festivities, and
Jack would work in a visit for himself, Carolina, and
Michelle, sometimes leaving Carolina and Michelle in
El Paso for an extra week or longer with the family. Jack
was especially happy to see how loving Esther was to
Michelle.

He once caught Carolina looking from a vantage
point at her sisters gathered around Esther. The pain
on Carolina's face was obvious to him and it crushed
him. He could not bring himself to ask her about it.
She did not suspect he had any knowledge of the
situation, which is how he thought of it.

The morning after the birthday party, Carolina
stepped out of the shower, eager to get dressed and be
on her way to work. She was working on special projects
for the dinner theater, which she wanted to finish before
the family left for their planned visit to El Paso. With
Greta gone to Germany, she had to oversee most of the
work. The unusual draperies she had designed for the
backdrop of the play that was about to open were due
that day.

Jack had not risen out of bed for his shower, so she reached over to wake him. Instead she stood frozen, her hand on his shoulder, aghast at the sight of her beloved Jack. His eyes were open, his mouth was twisted to one side, and he was breathing, but he did not respond to her. The color drained from her face as she looked around, stunned, wondering what to do. She called out to Claudia, her house help and nanny.

Claudia saw the grief-stricken look on Carolina's face and dropped the plastic water glass she held in her hand. The two women stood numb for a few seconds, looking at Jack's slumped figure on the bed. Claudia went to the telephone next to Jack's bed and, thumbing through the phone book, found the police department's number and dialed.

Claudia took a deep breath as she regained her composure after talking to the police department. "The ambulance should be here any minute, Señora," she said to Carolina.

"Please go into Michelle's room and make sure she does not leave her room. I don't want her to see her daddy like this," Carolina said as she was holding Jack's hand with one hand, stroking his face with the other.

Before Claudia had time to see to Michelle, the doorbell rang and Claudia ran to answer. The paramedics stepped into the room where Jack lay and began checking and preparing him to be placed on the stretcher. Carolina grabbed her purse and began following the crew. There were already tubes attached to his arms and an oxygen mask on his face. Claudia stepped out of Michelle's room, motioning to Carolina that Michelle was sound asleep.

Though Caro was pale, there was a firm set to her jaw. She squeezed the younger woman's hands. "Take care of Michelle," she uttered, as Claudia nodded somberly.

Carolina answered the necessary questions as clearly as she could.

"What time did you find your husband like this?"

"It had to be right around six fifteen."

"When was the last time you saw him awake and alert?"

"It was last night. When I got up, I went straight into the shower, around six."

"Did you notice anything when you got up and before you went into the shower?"

She hesitated slightly before answering, wishing she could turn the clock back. But her mind had been on her work, her plans for the day, all the projects she had been so diligently working on the last few days. "I—I didn't look at him. Not until I went to wake him, which I don't usually have to do."

Finally they arrived at the hospital. Time had no meaning for her. It seemed an eternity since she had found her husband unconscious, if that was what it was. All the commotion and machines and people rushing around and others asking her to go first to one place and then quickly to another—it was all so foreign to her. She wanted Jack to be all right, to wake up and take her home, and be the Jack she knew. A specialist finally took her aside and told her Jack had suffered a massive stroke.

She nodded with a wan smile forced out of habit, and she sat in the chair after the man had left, looking down at her hands, wondering what to do. Don—I have to call Don, she thought. She found her little phone book and went to the pay phone across from where she was sitting. The phone must have rung twenty times before someone answered.

"Eva, hello, it's Carolina. May I speak with Don, please? Yes, Eva, it's urgent."

When Don came to the phone, which took a while, he told Carolina he had been in the shower. She shrugged. Of course, it's early and everyone is showering, she thought. She wasn't sure how she told Don what had happened. She found herself nodding into the phone, realizing he had already hung up, and she went back to the chair. When Don arrived, he ran over to her and took both her hands.

"My God—Carolina. I'll talk to the doctors and see how soon we can get Jack back home. He'll be fine, you'll see."

Don disappeared down the hall and it was a long time before he came back, slumped down next to Carolina, took her hand, and just sat there, still and quiet, avoiding looking directly at her. A doctor motioned the couple to a private office down the hall, out of direct traffic.

"I'm afraid the news is bad. Mr. Morten suffered a massive stroke, a brain hemorrhage due to elevated blood pressure. We have him sedated now and are doing everything we can to control the bleed. It will be days before we can say if he'll survive. I tell my patients and their family the truth. We also can't tell what condition Mr. Morten will be in if he survives. He'll be transferred to a private room as soon as he is able to leave the critical care area and you, Mrs. Morten, and Mr. Hanson can stay in the adjoining alcove, as you see fit. I do hope we are able to save him."

Carolina looked up at the doctor's face; the rugged, craggy lines on his pale face told her he must spend most of his time indoors. She wondered if he had a family, a wife, and if so, what she was like.

Don spoke, his voice low and softer than she had ever heard.

"I—we appreciate all you are doing. Please, do everything that can be done, and keep us informed." He reached up to shake the physician's hand and noticed his own was trembling. The doctor nodded at them and left the room.

Again, the two were silent, staring straight ahead. Carolina, at least, was not aware of how much time passed before Don cleared his throat and stood up, saying he had to notify everyone at Jack's office. "Do you want me to call his parents, or will you do that? Carolina, anything you want me to do, I'll take care of it. You tell me what you want me to do." He sat down, slumped in the chair, and put his head down in his hands.

Carolina placed her hand on his shoulder, and in a barely audible voice stated, "I'll have to notify everyone, his parents, his children, my family, and somehow get Michelle settled somewhere because I'm going to be here as long as I'm allowed." She stood up. "Can you please take me wherever I can make the calls? Will you go to his parents? They should hear the news in person, I think."

Don stepped out and returned almost at once.

"They said you can stay in here and make whatever

calls you need. I told them to charge everything to the office. I'm going in to work to notify his crew. I'll be back with whatever you need from home. You just tell me what you need, Carolina."

"Thank you, Don. I'll have to let you know. I'm not sure what I'll need and when. As soon as I've called my family, I'll be by Jack's side, either in this office, or somewhere nearby. That's where you will find me."

Eighteen

Greta had picked what she hoped were perfect gifts to take with her to Munich. She would leave a week before Michelle's seventh birthday, sorry to miss the big event, but that was the best flight connection she was able to get, and she was eager to see her daughter who, by now, had settled down and away from her rebellious years. Greta called her mother the day before the flight.

"Mutti, according to Lotte, Monika is fine now that she's no longer dating Rolf. Monika herself told me she realizes he was the wrong man for her and is happier now with Dieter." Greta breathed a sigh of relief as she spoke.

"We have Monika's birthday party to plan," Helga, Greta's mother said. "We'll decide when you get here. I can't wait to see you, mein Gretchen."

"Me, too, Mutti. I'll get to stay an extra week this time. Carolina has everything under control at the shop."

On Greta's arrival, Monika was at the airport and the first to run to her mother to welcome her home.

"Oh, Mom, it's so good to see you," Monika said in English. "I want us to speak only English while you're here so I can practice."

"My dearest Monika," Greta said, embracing her daughter tightly, "I'll speak anything you want. I'm looking forward to this time with you. My dear sisters and mother, give me a big hug, all of you." They all took turns embracing Greta.

She called the shop in Los Angeles, confident everything was going smoothly as she had left it. Yes, everyone said, nothing new to report. Carolina was at the dinner theater checking on the costumes, doing whatever fittings had to be adjusted, doing minor alterations on the set.

"What I would like for my birthday," Monika said in as mature a voice as she could garner, admitting to herself how young she sounded when she thought of her days of running around with the wrong crowd, "is for all of us to dress in our traditional costumes and spend the afternoon at Hofbrauhaus. Dieter's family will join us."

"Our brothers will be here from Hamburg, but their wives can't make it. We'll have to reserve the room as soon as possible. I'll take care of that," Lotte said, smiling at Karin. For once, Lotte got in ahead of her more forceful sister.

The entire Neuberg family and Dieter and his parents, along with his sister, attended Mass the morning of Monika's birthday, as part of Monika's wish. After Mass, a light, quick breakfast at Helga's was followed by everyone dressing in their finest. The men put on their lederhosen, with the leather shorts tied at the knees and crisp white shirts under the leather suspenders. They also had their hats with goat's hair tassels. The women had neatly kept their dirndl in closets to wear on such occasions. Greta still had hers from years past and she sighed with relief when everything fit perfectly: the blouse with puffed sleeves, the crimped skirt and apron, even the corset and waistcoat. The women decided to wear identical chokers for the party.

"I can't believe the day has finally come, Mutti," Monika said in German, hugging her mother as they were about to leave the house. "The last few years are a blur as I realize the wrong path I took a few times. Thank God I was able to grow up and see how foolish some teenagers can be. I'm happy you never saw me at my worst."

"I knew what you were going through, as you must be aware by now. One of your aunts was always in touch with me and we kept our hopes and prayers up for you. We knew you would see the light."

"Some of my friends from that time were much worse, Mutti. They did such strong drugs and some were not as fortunate. I heard one of the girls had to be hospitalized almost a year. I only experimented lightly, so looking back, I was always aware of the stupidity some of us go through." She was silent as she finished getting dressed. "Oh, I've wanted to tell you something special. Dieter wants to propose marriage at the party. I haven't told him yet if I will accept. I think we should date another year before we settle down. What do you think, Mom?"

"As long as you have any doubt about getting married, you shouldn't. You are at a point in your life where you can enjoy your youth. Do you want to travel? You can come visit me and even go to school there for a year or so and see how you feel about Dieter. Or you can even have him come to Los Angeles with you. Would you like to consider that?"

"Oh, Mom, what a great idea! I'll talk to him about that."

"It was thoughtful of your father to bring his gift to you early. It's an exquisite watch. Will he join us at the party? You know he is always welcome."

"He and I talked about it and he said he will drop by for the prosit but won't stay much after that. It's fine with me. He and I have as good a relationship as possible, and I even see his other children sometimes."

"I'm so glad, Monika. It's best for everyone. Now let's get going to your party! The others are outside waiting for us, I can hear them calling."

Several of Monika and Dieter's friends were included, and the party turned out as grand as Monika had wished for and envisioned since she had known her mother would be with her to celebrate her twenty-first birthday, a huge turning point in her life. And, she thought, she might accept Dieter's proposal. She had convinced him to wait for a time when the two would be alone to propose. At any rate, she felt she was on top of the world that day.

Later in the week, Greta was out with her sisters when she heard Carolina had called. Monika had spoken with Carolina, who called to say everything was fine and to wish her a belated happy birthday, stating she had not been able to get through on the special day.

Almost a full week passed before Carolina called

Greta again. She could not wait any longer to tell her friend about Jack's illness.

"I'm taking the next flight back to Los Angeles, Schatzie."

"I'm so sorry to spoil your vacation."

"My family and I have enjoyed each other's company tremendously. Now I must return home to my friend who needs me. My family will understand."

Helga and Monika both comforted Greta as she told them the news.

"My friend's husband is in bad shape. I have to get back and see if there is anything I can do, at least be there for her."

"Mom, I understand. I know you and would be surprised if you did not return right away. I'm glad you were here the weeks you were able to be here with me and all of us."

"Call us and let us know how Jack is. Give our love to your friend Carolina," Monika told her mother at the airport. "I love you, Mutti."

"I love you, my dear Monika. Thank you for understanding me as well as you do. I hope you and Dieter will decide on going to school in LA. You would stay with me, of course. It's something great to think about."

Nineteen

Carolina's relationship with Jack was so secure she never once felt uncomfortable in living out her faith and, in fact, as she quietly delved into his Judaism, she found herself drawn to the beauty of being married to one of God's Chosen.

The day Jack suffered the stroke, the day life forever changed for Carolina, she turned, as always, to God for strength and peace. In the immediate hours after the horrific event, Carolina felt lost in a chasm of despair. Don had to leave to go to the office to secure whatever it was Jack and he did. That was all she knew and all she wanted to know. Jack's office was in good hands so that the workers could continue their necessary work. Everyone's livelihood was at stake. So was the Couture Shoppe.

Carolina found a tiny, nondenominational chapel on the first floor of the hospital. She stepped into the dimly-lit, quiet room, and after a minute or so heard piped-in music, barely audible. It sounded to her like angels humming. She knelt, head in her hands, and wept silently, though there was no one else in the room. As she prayed, she felt an infusion of strength and peace, yet this peace she felt was new, stronger and deeper within her. The humming continued; it was the most beautiful sound she had ever heard. She felt a hand on her shoulder and turned around, startled, but there was no one there. Yet she was surrounded by an inexplicable warmth and goodness in the midst of her sorrow. She reluctantly left the chapel after some time.

"Here's some fresh coffee for you, Mrs. Morten. I thought you might want some," a nurse with a kind smile told her as she returned to the unit. "I know times like these are tough on the family. Let me know if there is anything I can do or get for you."

"I shouldn't have stayed away so long, in case you needed me. But I found the chapel and went in to pray. The music in there is exquisite. It brought me out of my sorrow for several moments. Thank you for your thoughtfulness." Carolina took the cup and sipped, smiling at the nurse.

As the nurse stepped back to the station, she had a puzzled look on her face and asked, "Aren't electricians working on the first floor wing, by the chapel? I read a notice about that this morning."

"Yes, why?" her colleague asked, as she reviewed a chart.

"Well, Mrs. Morten says she heard music in the chapel, but that whole side of the floor is without electricity, just lights that run on battery so visitors can use the chapel. The office staff is working on another floor because of that."

"She must have imagined the music," the other

nurse replied, not looking up from the chart.

When Don returned and found Carolina sitting in the same office she had been in when he left, he saw a firm resolve in her face. Her eyes were not troubled. Her face looked serene.

"Carolina, any news?"

"No, everything is the same. They're running the necessary tests," she said in a steady and calm voice.

He looked at her in wonder. "I wanted to tell Jack's parents in person, so I went over and broke the news to them as gently as I could. You can imagine how distraught they are. They'll be here soon. I've sent a chauffeur. When I spoke with Melissa and Aaron they asked how you were doing, Carolina."

"I have to be strong. I have Michelle to think of and you and I have businesses to run that many people depend on. We have to be strong."

"My God, Carolina, you amaze me. I noticed right away when I came in that you seem changed. I was afraid this might break you. But I see you stronger than I ever imagined. Don't try to take on more than you can bear."

"Thank you. I'm aware of how much you and I will lean on each other in the coming days—or longer."

"Have you had anything to eat?"

"No. I haven't felt hungry. The nurses brought me coffee; that's enough for me now."

"You can't let yourself go too long without food. I think we should go get something light in the cafeteria. Let's at least go see what might be available."

When they reached the dining area, it was closed. Don suggested they get something across the street.

"I don't want to leave the hospital."

"Well, I'll go get something for us. Wait here."

"All right. I want to be where I can be found if they have anything to tell me, though."

"I'm sure they would page you or find some other way to locate you."

Don came back accompanied by Jack's parents, who would have run to Carolina if they had been able to. She stood and clung to the two of them, Arnold's tall figure towering over the two women.

"How did this happen, Carolina? He's always been so healthy, never even been to a doctor as far as we can remember. What happened?" Rose asked in a weak voice.

"Come, sit down, Rose," Arnold said. "Carolina will tell us whatever she thinks is necessary. We don't want you to think we blame you, my dear. Rose is understandably upset and has been asking these same questions of me since we got the news."

The three of them sat at a garden table in the patio where a few other people were also sitting around in various stages of concern. In one corner a family was huddled, crying.

"The only thing I could think of to tell the doctors was that he had complained of a slight headache the last few weeks, but nothing to cause him or me concern."

"I heard you were quite upset when you first got here with Jack."

"Yes, I was, I—. It's all a blur, but I do know that after I went to the chapel and prayed I felt a peace and strength I did not have before. I can't explain it any other way."

"What about Michelle? She's with Claudia at the house, isn't she?"

"She is. I called my sister Lisa and she's on her way here from El Paso to stay with her or take her back with her. It may be best that they go back where there are several family members to help out. Michelle loves to go there to visit. I prefer that she not see Jack as he is now."

Rose began to weep and both Arnold and Carolina reached over to comfort her.

"I called Greta in Germany. I couldn't bring myself to tell her what happened. Her daughter answered and told me they're planning her twenty-first birthday celebration next week. I had intended telling Greta, but couldn't at the last moment. This is such a special time for her with her family."

"We understand, my dear. What about the shop? Who's taking care of the business?"

"There's a woman, Connie, who helps us quite often. I called her and she said immediately she would be available all this time, as long as it takes. I had to tell her not to mention anything to Greta if she should call, though I doubt Greta will call again so soon. When she arrived she said as long as everything was all right we wouldn't hear from her. Connie will do a great job. She's been very responsible when we've needed her. Good thing the costumes that were so urgent had just been completed."

"Don is taking care of Jack's business, of course. That man is worth his weight in gold," Arnold Morten remarked quietly.

"Let's go inside now and see if maybe we'll get news.

I must warn you, Jack does not look like his old self," Carolina said.

Melissa and Aaron arrived late that evening and were informed by a physician about everything that had occurred. Both were devastated and they clung to each other. They were allowed to tiptoe in briefly to give their father a kiss. Melissa could not take seeing him in the condition he was, hooked up to all sorts of foreign machinery. Carolina found Melissa sitting on the floor in the hallway, sobbing quietly, her head buried in her arms. Caro sat beside her and cradled Melissa to her, letting her express her grief. She cried with her stepdaughter. Finally, Melissa spoke.

"You've been so wonderful to Dad. I want to thank you, Caro. I always wanted to tell you that but felt some guilt, betraying my mom. But Mom was never like you. I can see that now that I'm an adult and on my own. I don't know why Mom wasn't as loving and cherishing as you have been. I guess that's a private matter between my parents. The way you and Dad are together is the way I'd like to be when I meet the right one for me." Again, she started crying, quietly this time, leaning in to Carolina, who sat patiently by her stepdaughter's side.

"We have been very fortunate," Caro said. "I didn't know I'd ever meet someone I could love as much as I love your dad. I was married before. You know that, don't you?"

"I vaguely remember hearing something about that when you two first met, but I didn't pay much attention to that."

"Well, it's a story I've mostly forgotten by now.

It was rather unpleasant at the time, but I had to go through that to find the right man for me. I'm sure you will, too, if you haven't already. Aren't you seriously dating someone now?"

Melissa nodded somberly.

By the third day, as part of her routine, Carolina wrote key words that the doctors mentioned, such as "blood pressure stable" and "lab results within normal limits," and she recorded specific lab values that apparently meant Jack's physical condition was stable in a little notebook. She gave Don the information as soon as he came by and counted on him to help her figure it out. Most of it seemed like a foreign language to her. She asked the doctors a few questions, but she knew not to hold them up. She could see at a glance the delicate condition her beloved Jack was in. There were times she was not sure her newfound strength would hold. Jack's father asked her to call him daily, and she usually did several times throughout the day. Carolina found that having Jack's parents to talk to about his condition also helped her keep her courage, and stating aloud what she understood was happening to Jack cemented it all in for her. Jack's stroke may have been preventable, but there was no sense blaming him or herself at this point.

It all had been too much for Rose, and Arnold was concerned for her deteriorating mental health as well. Aaron and Melissa spent most of the second day with Carolina until she shooed the young adults out and back to their normal lives. They tiptoed in and spent a few precious minutes with their ailing father.

"It won't do anyone any good for you to hang around here with me. I'll keep you posted by phone and let you know the minute anything happens. Don or I will call," she told them.

Carolina stoically accepted the news of Jack's minimal improvement. She could see for herself that the Jack she knew and loved was somewhere deep inside this other person, and no one could say when and if there might be a change. She prayed faithfully every day, asking God for Jack's health to return, and, she added, if it did not please God to perform this miracle, then she asked for strength for her and the rest of his family to accept whatever happened.

She went home one afternoon to kiss Michelle goodbye as she was leaving with her Aunt Lisa to stay in El Paso. Mother and daughter had been in touch by telephone from the hospital, with Carolina explaining as well as she could that Daddy was sick and could not come home. She said that she would be home as soon as she could get away.

It was the first time Carolina had ever been away from her daughter for any extended length of time. When the Mortens visited in El Paso, Michelle would usually spend an evening or two with one of Carolina's sisters and the younger cousins. But that had been different.

Several days had passed since the fateful day, and Carolina hadn't been home since. She found that the house was unchanged. Her garden was thriving, as always, tended so well by Manuel, the gardener. The house was spotless, nothing out of place. It is almost eerie, Carolina thought; my house is surviving very well without Jack and me.

Michelle ran to her. "Mommy, I'm so glad you're home. I've missed you. How is Daddy?" She sounded so grown-up. Carolina stared at her child, smiled, and held her close, holding back the tears she felt welling up. I mustn't cry now, she sternly told herself.

"Well, aren't you the little lady? Are you ready for your trip?"

"Mommy, I can't wait to leave, but I had to say goodbye to you. I'd like to say bye to Daddy. Can I call him?"

"Right now, darling, he's having all kinds of tests done to him to see what's making him so sick. We have to pray very hard so he'll get better soon. You and I—we have to be strong for him. When he's better I promise we'll call you wherever you are."

Lisa had arrived a couple of days before and had been to the hospital, with Don driving her there. The shock of seeing Jack helpless had been rough on Lisa. She had grown to appreciate her brother-in-law on his visits to her parents and had seen the excellent relationship Jack and her father enjoyed. Jack's kindness to her despite her now admittedly horrible attitude toward Jack and Carolina's marriage had humbled Lisa. She was truly disheartened at seeing this vibrant, loving man so debilitated.

"We're all very glad you're allowing Michelle extra time with us this summer, Caro," Lisa said, hiding her own grief, aware the adults had to be stronger than ever around Michelle. "Her cousins have all sorts of plans: outings, picnics, parties, you name it. She'll have a great time, won't you, Michelle?"

"I sure will, but I'll miss Mommy and Daddy. Will you come over soon, Mommy?" The child looked tearful.

"Honey, I'll try very hard to go as soon as possible. Even if Daddy isn't well yet, I'll come over to visit with you and maybe bring you back."

Mother and daughter hugged and clung to each other. Carolina wondered if she would be able to go through with her plan. Maybe Michelle should stay here, with Claudia, and Carolina could come home every night, she thought. She almost suggested this, but she looked at Lisa and knew she could not change the plans so suddenly and abruptly. She made a promise to herself to go visit as soon as possible.

The taxi arrived for them and Carolina was glad she could not change her mind and spoil everything for Lisa and Michelle, who by now was happily scooting into the cab's back seat, Lisa right beside her. They waved cheerfully out the open window, shouting their goodbyes, Carolina at the open door, waving until the cab was out of sight.

Carolina immediately went to her bedroom, closed the door, and lay weeping on the bed, hugging Jack's pillow to her. In the dark she looked around the room that had been so much their own haven, a cozy and comfortable space completely theirs. She could see their bodies on the bed, making love every night and often during the day as well. They were so happy in this room. Jack would read the newspaper as she sat and sketched for whatever projects she had going. He would stand quietly behind her and kiss her neck or cheek. Or they would lie in bed, snuggling, and watch television. When

Michelle would join them, the three of them would lie in the bed, talking, laughing, reading a book to Michelle. They were so happy, the three of them. Why? Carolina asked. Why? Of all the men in the world, why did this happen to my Jack, my own dear love?

She dozed off and, startling awake, looked at the clock. It had only been an hour. She had to hurry back to the hospital. She mustn't stay away from the hospital where her Jack was lying, connected to all sorts of tubes and machines that were keeping him alive and giving him a chance to return to his old self, the beautiful and kind, loving Jack everyone knew.

When she decided to call Greta again, it was over a week after it—she didn't know what to call what had happened, so she thought the word *it* would do— happened, and Jack was opening his eyes now and then and trying to move his good arm. She had not dared to hope for more. There were moments when she thought it had always been like this, with him lying there, and she, down the hall, alone in the big empty hospital room.

Greta was devastated when Carolina broke down and told her the news.

"My family will understand, Schatzie. I'm taking the first plane back to LA," Greta said. She informed her family, and Monika was the first to insist Greta must return to California and her friends as soon as possible.

As soon as Greta arrived at the hospital, she was updated on all that had happened. "But how, Schatzie?" she asked after the doctor had left. "How did such a thing happen to a man who seemed so healthy and never showed signs of anything being wrong? I don't know what comfort I can offer you." Greta cried like a child; Carolina tried to comfort her friend but ended up weeping as well.

Jack started to show tiny bits of improvement. Most of the time he was alert enough to nod or shake his head, and when Carolina got close to him, he would whisper her name or monosyllables. It was too painful for Rose to see her only son so dependent on others for all his activities, and this trial had aged her visibly. She kept in touch by daily phone calls or an occasional visit. Aaron and Melissa came in on weekends.

Carolina's family also telephoned regularly. Greta came in almost every evening, insisting on taking Carolina to walk around the perimeter of the hospital, with Carolina resisting but secretly eager to get out in the fresh air.

The day came when at last Jack was to be transferred to a private clinic to continue his convalescence. The doctors were quick to tell Carolina that Jack's progress was better than anyone had expected, but they would not give any false hope of great improvement. Her intuition told her he was never to completely return to his healthy, wonderful state. Somehow she knew those days would remain a beautiful memory.

Jack managed a wave with his good arm, and his smile was almost straight as he was wheeled off the unit.

Twenty

It's too early for anyone to be calling, Carolina mumbled under her breath as she reached for the phone. After confirming Michelle was all right, Lisa told Carolina the grim news about their father's accident.

"Dad was coming home from the store. We were told by the police that a truck, a cement mixer, turned the corner and lost control, skidding into Dad as he stepped onto the street. At least they have a witness who told them the whole story. The truck careened into him, pinning his legs against the curb. He's been in surgery for several hours. The doctor told us they doubt his leg can be saved. I came home to get clothes for Mom. She says she won't leave until she knows he's all right."

"Oh, my God. I'll get the first flight out, Lisa."

"Call me as soon as you know how your father is doing, Schatzie," Greta said when she received the grim news. "Will Jack be told what happened?"

"No. I've called the clinic and I've told Jack I'm going to visit Michelle. I don't dare tell him what's happened to Dad. I don't want anything to upset Jack. Everyone at the clinic knows not to mention a word."

Carolina took a cab from the El Paso airport directly to the hospital. She found her father's room and saw some of her family standing in the hallway, others in a waiting room nearby. They spoke in whispers as they hugged, all shaking their heads in disbelief, the teenagers in tears.

Lisa tightly grasped Carolina's hands with hers. Esther was at Miguel's bedside, holding his hand. He seemed to be asleep but occasionally would utter a low moan. Esther's pale face had a look of grief, which she tried to cover with a wan smile and half-hearted wave to her daughter.

Carolina placed an arm around her mother's thin shoulder. She was shocked to see how aged and frail her mother appeared. Esther looked into Carolina's eyes. Both women forced a smile at each other.

"I'm going to be brave like you, Caro. You've been taking care of Jack all this time and you've done very well. I'm proud of you, hija. Now it's my turn to take care of my husband."

"We're all here to help you, Mom." Carolina felt guilty for feeling content to get Esther's attention and consideration. "I know what you're going through is tough for you, Mamá. Seeing him like this is especially painful for you." Carolina brushed her mother's cheek in a light kiss.

Carolina called Jack the next day and let him speak with Michelle. She finally confessed to Jack that her father was ill, but told him it was nothing serious, a touch of pneumonia. She told him she would stay on to visit and spend time with Michelle. She knew she may never be able to tell Jack that her father's leg had been amputated below the knee.

A representative of the cement company appeared at the hospital. The man spoke with Esther and Marta's husband, stating they acknowledged the accident was due to their faulty equipment. For the present, the hospital bill would be covered in full. The man stated the company would settle for an equitable amount and suggested that when Miguel was in better condition he perhaps would care to negotiate with the company himself. The representative also assured the family they were free to consult an attorney despite their generous offer.

As Miguel recovered, he brushed aside the idea of fighting to get a higher amount. "Their offer sounds pretty good to me. I'm not after money, as long as I recover enough from this accident so I can pay all the bills."

After weeks had passed and Miguel was well on the road to recovery, Carolina felt it was time to get back home. She had never been away from Jack this long before.

"Hija, I know you want to spare me sad news about Jack, but I can take it. Tell me the truth."

"Oh, Dad, I'm always optimistic and want to believe someday he will be his old self again. But I also have to be realistic and face facts. He has improved, and he's walking on his own, slowly and with canes. His speech is the hardest for him. It takes him much longer to say what he wants. I do need to get back to him."

"The doctors told me I can have a—what did they call it—a prosthesis, yes, that's it. It will be fitted to my leg and I'll be able to walk like I did before. I'll be going to a rehab center every day for a while."

Just a week later, the family gathered around Don Miguel, cheering him on as he took his first steps with the help of the therapist. Everyone, including the doctors, agreed Miguel made great progress despite his injury, due to his tenacity and faith. Carolina decided she had to return to Los Angeles, this time with Michelle.

A year quickly passed and Carolina and Michelle were home in Los Angeles, their routine of visiting Jack at the clinic comfortably arranged during the school year. His progress was slow, but after a year his speech was comprehensible. Most evenings the family had their meal together at the clinic.

One morning, as Carolina approached the clinic, the sight of the ambulance pulling away made her heart skip a beat. Jack's nurse ran toward her, waving Caro down.

"We called you, Mrs. Morten, but you had already left the house. That's Mr. Jack," she said, pointing to the ambulance. "He's had a setback. He's on his way to the hospital."

Carolina followed and pulled into the emergency entrance. Again, the sounds and sights assaulted her: the tubes in Jack's arm, the mask of oxygen, the stretchers. She remembered the routine. She steeled herself—the doctors nodded at her as they rolled him away, shouting their orders. She knew which hallway to take. She stopped by the tiny chapel.

She bowed her head in prayer, her tears flowing. "I'm strong, I have God's peace," she said aloud. "Jack is not well. Help me cope, dear Lord."

She left the chapel to make the necessary phone

calls.

"He was just taken in, Don. He's had another massive stroke. You better get his parents. I'm calling his children." She also placed another call, to her family in El Paso. And she called Greta, who arrived at the hospital almost at the same time as Don.

The doctors were frank and offered no hope. Jack was hooked up to machines keeping him alive as his family said their goodbyes. His children Aaron and Melissa walked in, holding each other's hands, and separated to stand on each side of him.

"We love you, Daddy," they said together.

Melissa spoke. "You're the best dad anyone would want. Everything you ever did for me is forever in my heart." She kissed him as she held his hand. She felt a slight squeeze of a finger from his hand.

"Aaron, he can hear us."

"Dad, it's me, Aaron. I—I love you, Dad." He choked on his tears and was unable to continue. The two walked out together.

Arnold led Rose to her son's bedside, holding her arm to steady her.

"Son, we know you can hear us. Melissa said you squeezed her finger. Aaron will be fine, you know that," Arnold said. He spoke slowly, waiting for his beloved son to understand what he was saying. He choked back tears. "Mom and I are here, son. We know you've had a rough time. We'll take good care of Carolina and Michelle, we promise you. I love you, son."

Rose bent down to kiss her son's forehead. She was crying and unable to speak, and held Jack's hand with both of hers. She bent to his ear and said, "Love." Arnold led her away. Carolina saw Rose's stooped figure walking toward her and she broke down in tears. She turned her face to the wall.

"It's our turn, Mommy." Michelle tugged at her mother.

Michelle's soft little hand tucked into her mother's. Carolina braced herself to be brave for her daughter. They stood a few moments, Michelle taking in the sight of her father, and she placed her hand in his.

"Daddy's hand is cold. I need to cover him." She climbed up on the bed to reach for the sheet and fell into the crook of her father's arm. Her head rested naturally on his shoulder, as it had so many times, as recently as the past week when he had still been at the clinic. She caressed his face and pushed herself up to kiss his cheek. She felt his arm move to hold her.

"Daddy's moving, Mommy."

Carolina had seen Jack instinctively tighten his hold on his daughter. She smiled at him through her tears. Her face leaned in toward his, and her teardrops fell and merged into his tears, running down his cheeks. He lay still again.

Michelle was taken out by a nurse. Carolina was alone with her husband. He opened his lips slightly. Carolina bent down to hear.

"Cah—roh—lee—nah, mi—amor, I love you."

His eyes were closed. She could see the flicker of his eyelids as he slowly spoke the words he struggled so hard to enunciate. She stroked his forehead. She kissed his lips ever so gently.

"I love you, Jack, mi amor."

He seemed to be sleeping comfortably as she stepped away. The family was called in moments later to be told Jack had died.

Twenty-One

The Morten family sat on two long sofas along one wall in the paneled, dimly lit attorney's office as the attorney walked in. After a brief introduction, he produced a sheaf of papers from which he read Jack's last will and testament. Carolina was astonished when her portion was read. She would have financial control over his company with 51 percent ownership, with a board of directors appointed to oversee general decisions. Don would continue to run the physical plant and office and manage the various projects, with 10 percent ownership deeded to him. Aaron and Melissa each received 10 percent, and the remainder was to be held in trust for Michelle. Jack's parents received a sizeable amount of money that would cover them for the rest of their lives. Greta McLean was to receive one hundred thousand dollars in tribute for her long friendship with Jack.

A codicil noted that in the event Carolina was to remarry, her company assets were to be held in trust, separate from all monetary funds from whomever she wed.

Carolina was stunned when she learned the actual amount of money now in her sole possession. Millions. She thought bitterly that she would trade them for Jack's life without hesitation.

Lisa had been waiting in the hall for Carolina and Michelle.

"How did it go, Caro?"

"My daddy left all of us a lot of money, Aunt Lisa.'"

Carolina, Lisa, and Michelle drove home in silence.

Sitting on one of the patios, Carolina served lemonade to the trio.

"Money has never been the focus of my life, of our lives. Jack managed our finances and we lived comfortably, as you can see, but never in an ostentatious manner. I'm going to set a portion aside for my family in El Paso to be used as you all see fit."

Lisa shook her head. "Dad will get his settlement for his accident in most likely a few weeks. It's quite a bit, Caro. I know he won't accept any money from you. Set up charitable foundations, if you'd like that. I'm sure you'll find good use for it. Dad already said he will do that."

"Mommy, let's all go back to El Paso where we can be together with Grandpa Miguel and Grandma Esther," Michelle said.

Weeks passed, each one much like the one before for Carolina. Lisa had stayed on to spend time with the sister she loved the most and to make up for the hurt she had caused. Taking over the care of Michelle was the most pleasant aspect of Lisa's visit. Claudia, the nanny, came in mainly to keep up the housework.

One day Greta called to say she was coming

over with sketches to show Caro; she figured it was something to get Carolina's mind off her grief.

"Look at the sketches we just received—I've got them on the kitchen table," Greta reported shortly after she arrived.

Carolina did not show any interest as she half-heartedly ruffled the papers.

"Lisa, take Michelle with you back to El Paso. I'm taking Caro to Munich—that is my proposal. Listen to me, Caro," Greta said as she placed her hands firmly on her friend's shoulders. "You've been moping around your house, not even coming in to the shop. You're thinner than ever. Go with me and meet the family you've heard so much about."

"That's a great idea, sis," Lisa said. "Take time away from all your surroundings. Michelle will be fine at home with me and all the family. You know how she loves her cousins."

"Oh, yes, Mommy, please. I want to go with Aunt Lisa. Say yes, Mommy. We want you to be happy again."

Carolina's eyes brightened as she dabbed a single tear. She was aware of how she was bringing her daughter's spirits down along with her own. The smiling faces were full of anticipation as a smile slowly changed her own face. Michelle was hopping up and down, a huge grin on her face.

"Where's your passport?" the practical Greta asked.

"I'm sure it's put away in my desk."

"I'll make arrangements—we'll leave as soon as I can get the tickets. Schatzie, you'll soon be your old self again. Mother's cooking will cheer you up quickly enough, you'll see." Greta's warm laugh echoed in the kitchen. "I'm going to let them know they're having more company."

During the following days, Lisa and Michelle prepared to return to El Paso.

"I know it will be hard for you to be apart from Michelle, but Greta's idea to take you away from your sorrow is the best I've heard. You've been focused on Jack's illness, then Dad's accident, the business you run—this will be a good break for you, sis. Michelle will be in excellent hands. Once school starts I'll take her with me, if that's okay with you," Lisa told Carolina.

"Of course, Lisa. I know you want the best for her, as I do. Being with all our family is the best for her. She'll be busy with school. She'll have her cousins she loves so dearly. It will be hard for me to let her go, but I do see I have to break my routine. Greta and her family will be the cure I need. I'll call at least every week. You can reach me at Greta's mother's house—Greta already confirmed that should be fine. Just remember the time difference."

It was early morning as the airplane approached Munich. Carolina had awakened and freshened up, and now gazed in awe at the sight below. For as far as she could see there were different shades of deep emerald. As they got closer, the greens turned into forests, and soon she could see the individual trees clearly from high up. When they stepped out of the plane, three women were waving at them. Carolina was immediately aware of the sounds of German. As she approached, the women quickly switched to English.

"Welcome, welcome! We are so happy you are here,

at last," one of Greta's sisters said.

Greta introduced Carolina to her sisters, Karin and Lotte, who hugged the arriving visitors. "We've heard so much about you we feel like we know you, Carolina," Karin said.

"Thank you all for having me on such short notice."

"Here's Mother. Carolina, this is Helga, my mother."

A tall woman with dark blond hair in a chic bun stood in front of Carolina, a smile on her face. "Gruss Gott! Carolina, we are all very sorry about your loss, dear. We hope your visit with us will help you even a little."

Carolina looked into the striking older woman's brown eyes, sensing an immediate connection with her. "Thank you for your wonderful welcome, all of you," she said as she hugged Helga and again embraced the younger women.

"Gruss Gott, Frau Neuberg," Carolina said. She had been practicing—her accent was excellent.

"Please, dear, call me Helga."

Carolina commented to all of them how lovely their city looked from above.

"Ah, yes, we have a most beautiful historic city. Bavaria, especially in the summer, is unsurpassed," Karin said.

"This is your home for as long as you wish. This was my parents' home," Helga said. She spoke in virtually flawless English with a slight British accent, occasionally giving in to the German pronunciation of some words, as did Greta and her sisters. Helga took Carolina to her room. "The room overlooks my garden. I am aware that you love anything to do with flowers, shrubs, and trees. We have that in common, you and I."

Carolina felt at home at once and commented, "All of you remind me so much of my family in El Paso." Her spirits were soaring, and she felt the depression she had endured lift as if a vapor were rising before her face.

Monika and Dieter, Greta's daughter and her daughter's fiancé, arrived in time for supper. Greta had brought Carolina up to date on the pending marriage— it seemed that Jack's illness had impacted Monika and Dieter's plans to attend school in Los Angeles, and they had recently become engaged after all. "They decided to stay in Munich, get married, and later come stay with me in LA," Greta reported.

After the meal the group settled in the garden, beneath white umbrellas covering the round tables set under an enormous chestnut tree. Carolina recognized some of the flowers and shrubbery and made a mental note to ask Helga what the others were. She could already see herself helping Helga work in this marvelous canvas of nature. She took in the forest smell of the garden, a new aroma for her, with deep pleasure.

For a few moments there was a lively discussion in German with Karin the natural leader, from what Carolina could figure out.

"We definitely have to start with Altstadt. There's nothing better than sitting outside, having a good meal," Karin said in English. The group nodded in agreement with Karin.

Early the next day they drove from Grunwald, the neighborhood the Neuberg family called home. Carolina took in the sights from the front seat. She looked around in amazement, like a child. She didn't know where to look first. Lotte pointed out they were on Ludwigstrasse, on their way to the center of Munich's Old Town, Altstadt.

Caro was in awe as she saw centuries-old buildings, their massive stone bulk in pastel colors. Karin, a teacher, was quick to point out the Gothic architecture, the dominant style. As the group walked toward the main attraction for tourists, Marienplatz, Carolina felt a rebirth. She allowed herself to be carried along by the euphoric sensations.

I will never be the same again, she thought. I love being here. I want to stay here forever.

Karin eagerly conveyed her knowledge of her beloved city. "The architecture here is a mixture of Baroque, Gothic, rococo, and even neoclassical. You will see many Catholic churches here, some of the most striking in the world. The largest Gothic church, Frauenkirche, is down this street."

They walked slowly, allowing Caro to take her time with all there was to see. They entered a church, called Asamkirche, and found the interior ornate marble in varied shades of pink and the fresco paintings breathtaking.

"This artwork is incredibly beautiful. Can we get postcards to send to my family?" Carolina whispered, as she took some holy water, blessed herself, and knelt down and said some prayers, as did the others.

"This is a Catholic city, different in history from the rest of Germany. You can feel the warmth all around. The name itself means 'The Monk,' Munchen," Karin said.

They crossed the pedestrian street to a restaurant,

Augustiner, where they occupied an outdoor table under a blue and white umbrella.

"I never dreamed it would be like this, Greta. Thank you all, Helga, Lotte, and Karin, for letting me be a part of your family, and you, Greta, for bringing me here to your city," Carolina said. They all lifted their drinks in a toast to their guest.

"You are welcome to stay with me as long as you like, Carolina. My home is your home," Helga replied.

Carolina reached over to hug Helga. She noticed a man staring intently at her from a table inside the dining establishment. He politely looked down at his plate and discreetly turned away from her. She soon forgot about him and, as the happy group finished their meal, they talked about where they would continue on their excursion.

The next couple of days were a whirlwind of sightseeing, with Carolina exclaiming over every detail. Karin and Lotte's husbands joined the group for supper one evening, again at an outdoor restaurant. They had finished their meal when Johann, Karin's husband, stood up to greet a friend. Carolina was surprised to see it was the man she had seen at the restaurant, the one she caught looking at her, just days before. Johann brought him over and said, "Karin, remember my friend Henk van der Kerk from the office? He's here having supper."

"Well, have him join us if he's alone," Helga remarked. The others voiced their agreement.

"Henk, this is my wife's sister, Lotte, her husband, Peter, and her other sister who lives in California, Greta. My mother-in-law, Frau Neuberg. And this is Greta's friend, Carolina Morten, who is here visiting from America. It's her first trip here so we have much to show her."

Henk shook hands with the others, then bowed politely before Carolina and extended his hand to hers, waiting for her to respond. Carolina smiled sweetly and felt his large hazel eyes taking her in. She slowly placed her hand in his.

"I am so happy to meet you. What a beautiful name, Carolina. May I call you that?" His accent was charming as he pronounced her name in Spanish.

His old-fashioned, European manners are so pleasant, Carolina thought. She wondered if he would mention seeing her at Augustiner days earlier. Henk pulled up a chair between Carolina and Karin, and positioned himself so that he could look at Carolina as he faced the group.

"May I ask where you are from, Carolina?" His disarming smile gave him an air of boyish naïveté.

"I'm originally from Texas; my family is Mexican-American. We are American," she stressed.

"Will you allow me to tell you—you are quite beautiful. Forgive me for staring at you."

"Thank you, Henk." Carolina looked away briefly. She hoped no one noticed her exhilaration as he spoke to her. His smile was open, frank. She felt comfortable talking to him, as if she had known him a long time.

"I understand you work with Johann." Her voice was soft, and, she admitted to herself, she was flirting with him. His gaze on her face gave her a feeling of warmth she had missed. She almost felt guilty as her thoughts were not on Jack for the first time in months.

"Yes, I'm an accountant and director in the same company."

"Your accent is different from the others."

"I'm Dutch, from Rotterdam, but I've lived here and worked with this company for three years. I love it here and will stay as long as I can."

"Is your family with you?"

"My daughters live in Holland with their mother. I've been divorced about four years. I go visit the girls every few months and, of course, they come to visit me."

Monika and Dieter arrived at that moment and joined the group. Seating was rearranged and Carolina made it a point to move a couple of chairs down from Henk. I certainly don't want to seem forward, she thought. The old modesty instinctively kicked in. She would have to lean forward to catch sight of him.

The merriment of those assembled resounded along the boulevard, along with the pleasant chatter of other guests at other tables. The evening was seasonably warm, the slightest breeze occasionally stirring the napkins or ladies' skirts. The meal had been excellent and now everyone was enjoying their beer or wine and the camaraderie. It was late when they hugged their goodbyes.

"Henk, you must come and have dinner at my house. I'll prepare one of my family's favorites, *schweinebraten*," Frau Neuberg said with a smile.

"I will be honored, Frau Neuberg. I am free and at your disposal."

"Well, day after tomorrow I will expect you at six in the evening. Here is the address," she said, handing him her card.

Twenty-Two

Henk van der Kerk's cheerful disposition had seen him through the break-up of both of his marriages. He should never have run off and married at the tender age of nineteen, he admitted. He met Louise, his second wife, during his last year at the university. They had two daughters, Miranda and Marike. The opportunity for Henk to be the director of accounting of the large electronics firm in Munich was perfect timing after his second marriage failed.

After the initial onslaught of guilt and ensuing gloom, he was soon his old cheerful self, whistling as he walked along, greeting neighbors, always a kind word for anyone who crossed his path.

At work, his lighthearted personality quickly gained him a following. He ran the office smoothly and everyone wanted to please this kind, likeable Dutch man with the boyish good looks. At one point he tried growing a moustache to appear older, but he soon tired of grooming it and gave it up.

One day, he had gone to the tourist area for lunch

and noticed Carolina as she walked with a group of
ladies into a church. He was immediately intrigued by
the lovely woman with the olive skin and dark auburn
hair. As luck would have it, he recognized Karin, the
wife of one of the men in his office, in the group. He
could not believe his good fortune as they entered the
restaurant where he was seated, having just finished
his meal! He tried to be as respectful as he could while
he listened to the small entourage from a nearby
vantage point at the restaurant. His heart sank as he
heard she was a tourist, thinking he would not have
the opportunity to meet her—he wanted at least that, to
meet her—and possibly even talk to her.

At the office the next day he approached Johann,
Karin's husband, and told him about the woman he'd
seen with the group. He discreetly mentioned his
interest and Johann suggested, "I'll see how we can get
you two introduced."

A day later, Johann, nicknamed Hans, knocked on
Henk's office door. "We are to have supper tonight at the
Hofbrau, around seven, I would say," Hans reported.
"I have to warn you, though. The lady you saw, the
tourist, recently lost her husband. Greta, my sister-in-
law, brought her over here to get away from everything
that has saddened her so much. She may not be ready
for any type of relationship."

Henk reflected a moment. "Oh, I am sorry to hear
that. Well, don't worry, it may not lead to anything,
but at least we will have a chance to meet. I'll be most
discreet, you know me. I will be a perfect gentleman."

"Yes, I do know that of you. Otherwise I would not
go along with any plan to meet this woman."

"I'll be there. And, thank you, Hans."

When they met that evening, Henk had not been prepared for the wave of emotions that hit him. It was not just her beauty that struck him. It was her softness, the color of her skin and hair, the fragrance emanating from her, and then her name, the way it rolled off everyone's tongue. His breath was sucked out of him. He detected her modesty as she gazed away from him, but he felt her presence as if she were reaching her hand to him, touching his face with the hand she had placed in his. He could have floated away down the street, or reached up to the stars and plucked one down for her.

They would see each other again. Helga had invited him to dinner at the house where Carolina was staying. He said goodnight and again held her hand for a few moments, saying he looked forward to seeing her again. She had smiled at him and looked directly into his eyes.

She had not mentioned one word about Henk to anyone all day, but she had thought about him throughout the day. She felt herself shudder excitedly as she looked through her clothes, wishing she had many more to choose from. Well, she would get busy and take out Greta's sewing machine. Or maybe she would buy some. She settled on lightweight denim slacks and a multicolored cotton blouse, keeping a matching denim jacket nearby for the cool evening.

Henk arrived promptly at seven. Music was playing and everyone was seated in the living room, joking, laughing, and chatting amiably as Carolina entered the room. Everyone said "Gruss Gott." Henk stood up and took her hand, wishing her a good evening. She thanked him and asked how his day had been.

After dinner, as they were all seated outdoors at the round tables, Henk and Carolina again found themselves conversing comfortably. Within hearing distance of the company, Henk invited Carolina to lunch.

"If you can get away from your wonderful hostesses, Carolina, I'd love to get to know you before you have to return to California."

Carolina nodded shyly at Henk. I feel young again, and I very much want to get to know this sweet young man, she thought.

"The weekend is coming. We were planning a picnic out in the countryside to show Carolina the mountains. Would you like to join us, Henk?" Greta said. She had noticed Henk's interest in her friend and wondered how Caro would react to this boyish-looking man. She needs to move on, Greta thought, feeling a pang of sadness as she thought of Jack.

Plans were quickly made for a family picnic in keeping with the Neuberg tradition. Carolina felt comfortable meeting this man in the safety of the Neuberg family. She again thought of how strong an impact the city was having on her, almost as if she had been here before. As everything was new to her, she wondered what the huge attraction could be that was pulling at her. Yet deep within, she felt it was more, something more than just the beauty of the city and surroundings.

Saturday morning they piled into two cars and drove toward Wasserburg, where they entered the historic Renaissance town. They walked through a narrow street, almost an alley by modern standards, where she touched the centuries-old walls as they passed a building being refurbished. The rough-hewn bricks spoke of all the people who had passed by through the town's several hundred years of existence. Carolina was in silent awe. She hoped to spend more time getting to know the small villages and towns such as this one.

Without a doubt, I am going to live here, she thought. I want to be a part of life here. I want to experience everything Munich has to offer. Her mind whirled as she worked out the logistics of how she would manage. Surely her daughter would eventually come to stay with her. She would find an American school in this cosmopolitan country. She would buy a house or apartment for the two of them.

"There are many businessmen renovating these wonderful centuries-old buildings. You'll see some have already been transformed into cafes and boutiques," Hans' voice broke her thoughts. "Many have also been rebuilt as apartments with the external details preserved."

She did not reject Henk's invitation to sit at the picnic table with him. She was keenly aware of his interest in her and admitted to herself she was flattered, though he seemed considerably younger than she. To her surprise, she discovered he was merely two years younger.

Henk came by every evening, bringing a bottle of wine, and one evening he brought a roast beef—his contribution for all the meals he was sharing with the family. During the day Carolina would go on excursions, usually with Karin, who was the self-appointed instructor, and other times all the women went along. They spent an entire day at Nymphenburg Castle, walking through the formal French gardens. The huge golden carriages impressed her, as did the enormous paintings, and she had several photographs taken, sure her family at home would appreciate them. The Baroque architecture of the palace fascinated her.

Henk took a day off from work, and to celebrate his freedom he suggested a trip to the outdoor zoo, the Tierpark Hellabrunn. The women joined him, and again the merry group made the most of the outing. Carolina insisted on treating for lunch. Afterwards, she and Henk strolled through the gardens. Happy to be alone with Carolina, Henk asked, "Will you go out with me, just the two of us?"

"I'd like that, Henk. Yes, I'm sure we would have a good time."

"I've wanted to ask you to go out all along. It's been good for us to get to know each other. I think you're a wonderful woman, Carolina. I know what you recently experienced." He was silent. She understood his silence.

"It has been so peaceful for me here despite all the activities. I assumed you knew what happened—that I lost my dear husband earlier this year. Everyone has been so kind. Being here in Munich with these new friends has been so good for me. I had no idea my life would change so much. Thank you for understanding."

Henk silently sat on a bench. The warmth of the sun and the scenery made the moment surreal for him. He admitted to himself he was falling in love with this woman. She was sitting next to him, telling him how she had suffered and how happy she was now. If I wake up and it's not true, I will be most disappointed, he thought.

But right now, listening to her, having her close to him and seeing their relationship begin as a delightful friendship was incredibly romantic.

"My daughter is doing well after the loss of her father. She's staying with my family in El Paso. Michelle's very happy with all her relatives. I call her almost every day. She's nine years old now. You can imagine how our lives have been since our loss."

"My daughters are ten and eleven and have also adjusted to my absence. Children adapt to life."

They talked amiably as they walked back. He reached for her hand, holding it lightly in his. It seemed so natural to both of them.

"Schatzie, you don't mean that! You want to stay *here*?" Greta said "here" as if it were the ends of the world.

"Yes, Greta," Caro said in a voice lower than usual. She was prepared to fight for her newfound freedom and peace. "I decided after the first day we arrived, and no, it doesn't have to do with the fact Henk and I met and have become friends. Helga and I talked it over one afternoon. She understands me and completely supports my decision. We've become quite close, Helga and I. It won't be a permanent move, but I'm not going back with you this time. I'll stay and possibly rent an apartment or a house later on. I've seen handicrafts and other art around here that have given me ideas of opening my own boutique, a place to sell them in LA. I'm not sure yet. But I am eventually going to have a home here."

"But what about your daughter and the business? Our business? You're a big part of the success of the Couture Shoppe. And your house, and Jack's company? I really don't understand your sudden change in attitude. Have you told your family?"

"I was afraid you wouldn't understand my feelings. I guess I don't expect everyone to understand. No, I haven't told them yet, though I asked Lisa if she could continue to take care of Michelle. That would be different, of course, if she said no. But in that case, I'd just bring Michelle over here."

"I really think you need to give yourself time for such a huge move. You've just lost your husband and you're going through a traumatic time. Stay for a few more weeks and then decide. Wait until the winter comes along. You're not used to the cold and snow. Carolina, I've never told anyone what to do, and as your friend I don't intend to start now—but, really, Schatzie, you have to give yourself time to see if you can stay here."

"Things have changed for me, Greta. It's hard for me to explain, and I don't think I can explain. I feel a new life for me, beginning here in this city. I have never been on my own or made any really major decisions on my own. I love Munich. I feel that I belong here. It's home for me down deep inside. I can't explain it. You'll have to trust me."

"Caro, I know how beautiful it is here. I grew up in Munich and know its attraction. I guess you're right, though. That is how I felt about Los Angeles when I arrived there so many years ago. It felt like home. California will always be home for me. Oh, my dear friend—I hope you're not reacting to your loss."

"Greta, if I don't like it I can always go back. I'm a

plane ride away. Think of it as if I'm on a long vacation. And you're the Couture Shoppe, you always have been. You have Connie to help you run it. I'll have to go back when the time I'm allowed runs out," Carolina said, referring to her visa to visit West Germany. "We'll see then how things are going."

"Does anyone else know?"

"Only Helga. I don't want to say anything, least of all to Henk, until I see how that goes. We're going out tomorrow night for the first time alone, just the two of us."

"He is really a great guy, isn't he? I've never met such a likeable man before. I hope he's not the reason for your plans to stay. Well, I don't intend to meddle in your life—that's not my way of being." Greta muttered something under her breath in German.

"I've been afraid you and everyone else will think that. But I can assure you and tell you from my heart I reached my decision well before I got to know him. Probably the first few days I was here. I felt an exhilaration being here—I don't know how to explain it. I feel different. Actually, I feel complete for the first time in my life. Even with Jack I did not have the freedom in my mind I have right now."

Carolina was silent for a few moments before she continued, in a soft but firm voice. "Greta, in these last three weeks I have grown in ways I did not know was possible. I'm not the same person who left Los Angeles. I know that losing Jack made me realize how alone we all are. Each one of us must make our own way in life. Jack will always be the love of my life. Nothing and no one will change that."

Carolina continued when she saw Greta's pensive

stance. "You and I have survived rough times and we've come through with a great business." She was silent a moment as she thought of what she wanted to tell Greta, who was listening intently. "You're more like a sister to me, someone I trust completely. Don't think I'm running away from the life I left in LA. You've made a completely new life in America and you cannot explain to your family here why your home is over there now. I have to stay here, at least for a while, and I have to give myself the chance to continue growing as I feel I am right now."

After a few more moments of silence, Greta spoke less urgently. "You're right. You have to do what is right for you. It's just so sudden and unexpected. I hope your family won't blame me for taking you away," she said as she shrugged, and a tight smile slowly appeared on her lips.

"I'm my own person now. I don't need permission to do what I feel is right for me."

"Well, the trip over here certainly has been different from what I had expected, Schatzie. I'll leave on time next week as planned. Paul has called me several times and is missing me as much as I miss him. If you choose not to talk about your decision I'll make sure no one else finds out. My mother will not say a word."

"Yes, for now that's how it must be. I won't offend her by looking for somewhere else to live, not yet, anyway. Let's go. I have to go shopping and get some decent clothes. Evenings here are cooler than I expected."

Most days Carolina spent hours tending to the garden with Helga, the two women conversing about everything that came to mind. Their friendship grew, as they had both sensed it would from the beginning.

Carolina spent an hour trying to decide what to wear from the outfits she had purchased for her first solo date with Henk. She tried different hairdos. I don't want to appear as eager and excited as I feel, she thought happily. She was satisfied with her makeup and eventually settled on light gray slacks and a lightweight navy sweater. A pale gray pearl necklace complemented the outfit and a navy blazer completed the ensemble. She was surprised how well everything fit, considering it was not custom made. When she was ready she was almost giddy. She was going out with someone who had been a stranger a few short weeks ago in a foreign land, and she could hardly wait to be alone with him at last.

Greta answered the door and welcomed Henk amidst the customary Gruss Gott. "I'm glad I get to say goodbye to you, Henk. I'm leaving tomorrow. In fact, I'm going up to bed now so I can be well-rested for my trip." They both said their goodbyes and Henk wished Greta a safe trip home. He wondered why Carolina was not leaving at the same time.

Carolina stood up and went into his outstretched hands. They kissed on the cheeks three times in Dutch fashion. Greta laughed softly as she pointed out that Henk and Carolina had apparently coordinated their clothing for the evening. Henk was clad in a light gray mock turtleneck sweater and navy slacks. His sandy blond hair, neatly combed back, stressed his boyish attractiveness. Henk and Carolina walked out the door hand in hand.

Twenty-Three

Henk pondered his fabulous luck. He happened to be at the right place the day he caught sight of the woman with whom he was now in love. He was sure it was love as he shaved the morning after their first date alone. He went over every detail of their night out, remembering how everyone laughed at their matching clothes. Carolina had been quiet, more so than usual, and he rightly assumed she was being cautious and possibly uncomfortable with a new man in her life. She had told him so at the restaurant.

"We hardly know each other," he had volunteered, "even though we have been together almost every day the past couple of weeks. I know you've based your trust in me on the friendship and work relation I have with your friend's brother-in-law. Carolina, you've been through a hard time, losing your husband, coming to a foreign country, and then you and I meet and we seem to get along so well. Of course you have to be careful. I also know very little about your life in America."

She noticed his accent was more pronounced and

that he seemed a bit emotional. So unlike Jack, she thought as she caught herself comparing the two men. She had promised herself not to do that and had almost succeeded. Now what? she asked herself. Do I continuously compare him to a man much older and totally different, at least in outward appearances? Someone who meant the world to me? And who always will?

"Oh, I know you can't help but compare me to your husband. Excuse me, I must bring up the subject. And I think he was most fortunate to have your love. I also know I must be different in many ways, or else it would be too painful for you."

He's reading my mind, she thought, and laughed softly.

"Carolina, you enchant me. I don't want to seem forward and frighten you away from me. Please accept my compliments to you, as they are meant from the heart."

Carolina looked at the man sitting across from her and admitted to herself she found him appealing and she enjoyed his interest in her. Yes, it is time to move on, she said to herself, firmly, as she smiled sweetly at him.

Henk invited Carolina to spend a week in the mountains of southern Bavaria. They could book separate rooms, he discreetly suggested.

She was excited as she packed her bag and realized she would have to buy warmer clothing for the mountains. The thought of spending days—and nights—with Henk was tantalizing. She found him attractive and easy to be with. The thought of being intimate with Henk gave her a twinge of guilt, but she shook it off as she thought about going on with her life.

"Henk has become someone I can spend time with, someone to talk to, and a most pleasant companion. I am not sure I am ready for more, but I am willing to give ourselves a chance. Life is so different here, and with you," Caro remarked to Helga as she was preparing for the trip with Henk. "I know my family means well, but they treat me like the youngest daughter that I am, as if I am still fifteen. It helps that I can speak openly with you, Helga."

"You are your own person. You don't owe anyone an explanation or excuse for what you choose to do. Of course you have to be careful. You're in a foreign country, and you will be alone with a man you met recently. But my family knows him as an excellent, trustworthy person with a most pleasant personality. It's been good fortune for you both to meet. Take the chance! If it works out, fine! If not, at least you tried."

What a difference, Carolina thought, from the way my family is reacting to my staying here and to what they would say to the whole idea.

After telling everyone how much she inexplicably loved it there, Carolina could not have imagined her mother's reaction to the news of her staying on a few more months in Munich. Esther could not have told anyone the memory that was stirred in her, of the evening Robert told her some of his family history. They had been sitting on Esther and Miguel's back porch, having lemonade and holding hands as he told her his paternal grandmother was from southern Germany.

Bavaria, he had said.

"I can hear her voice, singing a lullaby to me in German," Robert had reminisced. "She would hold me and tell me how she longed to see 'her' Alps again, how she loved the woods around her family home."

Esther fought back tears, as she knew she could never tell her daughter the reason for her love for Munich and Bavaria. It must be in her blood, she thought. She knew she would have to call Robert to tell him the news. It had been a long time since she had heard his voice, but she felt this was important and worth the call from the phone booth. Carolina is in Munich and has decided to stay there for some time. Esther understood her daughter, but the only other person who would understand anything about such an unusual turn in her life was Robert. Yes, she had to call him. She wondered what he would say to this turn of events in Carolina's life.

Henk and Carolina set out with high expectations. The drive south was more than Carolina had imagined. The roads went through forests she had only seen in movies. She ran her fingers through the moist earth and touched the mossy trees, hundreds of years old, as they stopped to walk around. She wondered why she felt such strong emotions as she caressed the trees and shrubs and took in the incredibly enticing aroma of the forest. Yes, she always loved this type of nature, but to be so moved by what she was experiencing seemed odd to her. She would not have missed out on this for anything, she told herself, smiling joyously.

Henk drove as slowly as possible without creating a traffic problem, pulling over as Carolina asked. He, too, was greatly enjoying the rolling hills and verdant pastures, the idyllic landscapes against the huge German Alps. They made it to their destination, the conjoined town of Garmisch-Partenkirchen. Henk informed Carolina the area was the site of the 1936 Winter Olympics. He read in his guide book that the two villages had been merged into one at that time despite the rivers Loisach and Partnach that separate them.

"This town is so quaint. Oh, I'm so glad you chose this as our stop. I feel as if we dropped into a fairytale. The paintings on the buildings are so unusual and lovely," Carolina said about the different scenes and landscapes painted on white walls depicting anything from trees and flowers to ornate patterns.

"This is the hotel where we're staying," Henk announced.

They walked into the grand entry hall of the huge four-story hotel. He had booked two adjoining rooms. As they stood at the registration desk, she placed her hand on his and in a sweet, low voice said, "You can get just one room, Henk."

They went into a cozy room with two double beds, and a separate sitting area. The view of the snow-capped mountains from the large window was breathtaking. Carolina stood admiring the view. Henk stood behind her, placing his arms gently around her. She leaned back against his chest, her head nestled into the crook of his neck. She turned around and gave in to his soft, warm kiss.

In the room later that evening after a wonderful supper, both of them ready for bed, Carolina and Henk snuggled on the small settee. He kissed her gently, waiting for her response. She touched his face with her hand and smiled. A tear rolled down her cheek as she pulled away from him.

"I'm sorry, Henk," was all she could muster, a wave of nostalgia for Jack overpowering her. She forced herself not to break down.

"I understand, Carolina. You don't have to say anything more. We're both tired and need a good night's rest."

"I . . . need time alone right now. It's the first—"

"You don't have to say anything, Carolina. I understand perfectly. You have all the time you need to—make a fresh start. Goodnight, my dear friend."

After sleeping for most of the first night of their trip, Carolina stirred, keeping the images of the dream before her, willing herself to recall every detail. It was the same as several mornings before—a man, his face a blur but the hair and general characteristics clearly not Jack's, was bending over her, kissing her tenderly until she gave in to passion and allowed him to make love to her. The dream had made her feel the warmth she had missed all these months without Jack. Their love life had been so full. They had made love almost every night of their blissful marriage, their bodies in perfect alliance with each other. To dream of another man in this fashion was unexpected yet welcome at this point in her life, at age thirty-four. She had missed the physical contact with the man she loved, but had accepted it as part of his final days. Now this—a new man being physically intimate with her—was a foreign sensation. Could she go through with it? Was she enough in love with Henk to give in to him and her own desires?

She heard Henk in the shower, singing a popular tune. He came into the room, a towel around his waist. She slowly pulled the covers off herself. She had removed her pajamas.

He leaned down over her, caressed her auburn hair flowing on the pillow, and kissed her lips lightly. She gently pulled him down to her breast and gave in to his kiss, allowing the kiss to grow into a passionate loving hint of what was to come. Their bodies became one; a tender, new emotion was born as she took in the sight of his body on hers and in hers, and she knew she would come to love this man.

He held her lovingly, gently tracing her face with his fingertips. They made love again, in heated passion, giving in to their need for each other. He whispered in Dutch to her, teasing her as she tried in vain to pronounce the words he said.

They spent the day walking around the Alpine village, looking in awe at the Zugspitze, the highest peak in the area. The stunning churches, one a medieval building, the other in Baroque architecture, were inviting. Carolina knelt in prayer by herself at an altar. Henk rightly assumed she was praying for the soul of her departed husband and, he hoped, also for the beginning of their relationship.

Twenty-Four

"What's wrong, Miguel?" Esther asked.

"Ay, querida, I don't know where to begin. Sit down. You too, Lisa. Both of you need to just listen to me. It's quite a shock." He shut his eyes for a few seconds, and, shaking his head, slowly began his tale.

"One of my friends, Pedro, told me a few days ago. He has seen Fred, Anita's Fred, coming and going from a house down by his in-laws' place, in Ysleta. I went with him this morning to see for myself. I didn't want you to say anything to ruin my plan, that's why I never said anything until now."

Both women were staring at him, each one clutching one of his hands.

"It seems, my dear Esther and Lisa, that our Alfredo has another woman and family. I saw it with my own eyes. I was there early, the time Pedro tells me he sees Fred coming out, and sure enough there he was—the door opened and he stepped out. A woman, about ten years younger than Anita, patted his cheeks and kissed him goodbye. Then, a little girl, about two, ran to him, yelling, 'Daddy, Daddy'—he picked her up and tossed her in the air, like he did with his children when they were little. He kissed them both and ran to his car down the block."

Miguel pulled his hands away from his wife and daughter and put them to his eyes, unable to control the tears running down his cheeks.

"What do we do, Miguel?" Esther's voice was weak and tremulous, and then she, too, broke down in quiet sobs.

Miguel wiped his face with a kitchen towel and sat there shaking his head, wondering how he would handle this unexpected situation.

"We have to tell Anita." Lisa's voice was firm. She had wiped her tears. "We'll have to get her over here and break it to her. She may not want to leave Fred. He's been such a good husband, or so it seemed, until now. There's no way we can keep this secret."

"Lisa, you're right, of course. Call her and see if she can come over by herself. We will tell her together."

"How will Anita take her family falling apart?" Esther asked no one in particular.

"That's just one of our daughters, Esther. The rest are doing fine."

"That's what you think, Papá. You may as well know, now that we're talking about our family problems. Carolina is traveling in Bavaria alone with a man she met just a few weeks ago. That's why she's staying in Munich."

"What are you talking about, hija?"

"I haven't told you yet because it didn't seem like the time to tell you. You both know she won't be returning to Los Angeles. But the other part, the one about the man, I finally got that out of her. She admitted she had not wanted to say anything about him—this new man."

"Esther, did you know any of this?"

"Some of it, but not the whole story. I didn't know about the man who's traveling with her. I do not agree with Lisa that she's doing anything wrong. She's had a bad time with Jack's illness and then his death. She needs time to get over everything, and she found a place she loves." Esther looked away, afraid to say anything that would reveal her own feelings and thoughts about the hidden mystery to Carolina's love for Bavaria.

"You're right, she has been through so much. Carolina has matured away from us and her ideas are not our old ones. I'm more upset about Anita and Alfredo. What will happen to them, to their family?" He shook his head to clear away the picture in his mind of his son-in-law and the other woman.

Lisa picked up the phone on the kitchen wall to call her sister. Anita answered.

"Hi, are you busy?" Lisa asked. She tried to sound lighthearted. "Come over for a few minutes."

After Lisa hung up the phone, Don Miguel said, "The other thing I have to discuss with the two of you before anyone else interrupts—I'm going to meet with the attorney about the money. There will be a check for me—it should be more money than I ever dreamed I'd have. I'm going to put it into trust funds for my family. But now, of course, I have to rethink any of it going to Alfredo. He won't get a penny, I can tell you that." He was silent a few seconds. "I believe I will get more than a million dollars, possibly close to two million."

The two women stared at Don Miguel. No one spoke for a long time.

Esther said, "Miguel, what are you going to do with all that money?"

"The attorney told me I could possibly ask for more, but I refused. That really seems like a fair amount, and thank God I have all the material possessions I could ever want. I will discuss with the attorney about setting up trust funds for college for my grandkids, and then you and I can remodel like we've talked about, Esther. Lisa, you're a sensible girl—woman. I leave it up to you to give me suggestions about investing so that your mother and you don't have to think about what to do when my time comes."

Lisa nodded solemnly. With all the other projects she had going and the moral problems she was faced with, she had almost forgotten about the pending financial settlement for her father's accident.

Lisa said, "For one thing, Caro has her own wealth—I understand Jack left her quite a large sum. She has more than she will ever need or spend. She told me before she left for Munich she wanted to give you and Mom enough to live on. I reminded her then of this settlement of yours. I'll find a competent advisor to guide us, Dad. You'll be part of every decision, not me. Let's try to keep this between the three of us for now, in light of what you've discovered about Fred."

Anita walked in the front door. She found her family sitting glumly in the kitchen. She helped herself to a glass of tea and sat down, a wan smile on her face.

"You certainly don't look like you have good news.

What is it? What's happened?" Anita asked quietly.

"Anita," her father began slowly, calmly, willing himself, the distinguished patriarch of the family, not to break down, "it's not easy to tell you what I've just confirmed today. I don't know if you suspect Fred of being unfaithful to you."

"I wish I could say I have never had my doubts. When we were first married I know he had problems settling down, though he was the one who insisted we marry when we did, as you all remember. But why are you asking me now? What do you know?"

"Well," Miguel spoke slowly, "I saw with my own eyes this morning that Fred—Alfredo—has another woman and family. I say this bluntly because I have no other way to break it to you, Anita, my dear daughter. I hate to see you go through anything painful, but what I'm telling you is the truth."

Anita was quiet for a few moments and looked down at her hands in her lap. Without looking up, she said softly, in a weak voice. "Maybe I knew. Maybe I didn't want to think about it and thought it would all go away. He's always been good to me, you know that." She moved her hand to include the three sitting before her. "He loves our children. He's an excellent father." She was now in tears. "He's all I have, now that our kids are grown and almost on their own. If he knows that we know, he'll have to leave. I don't know if I can handle it. I'm going now. Please don't tell anyone. Not yet."

They looked at each other in silence.

Anita continued in a bitter tone, "I know you and everyone around us see the Sanchez family as the paragon of the 'perfect' family, but the truth is, we're not. I wish we were, but we're not." Even in her moment of humiliation, which obviously this was, Anita held her head high and used as proper language as possible. A voracious reader, though she had not attained higher than a twelfth-grade education, she took pride in her vocabulary and read all of Lisa's school workbooks. She smiled bitterly at her family.

Esther hung her head, knowing full well her own contribution of imperfection to the family. If I could turn the clock back I would, she thought, clenching her fists to keep from crying out her own ugly truth. But then I would not have our wonderful Carolina, she remembered.

"Si, hija, you're right," Esther said, using her tears for her daughter and for herself. "None of us can be perfect. Take your time in deciding what to do, though it will be hard for us to treat Fred as we did before."

Anita hugged her parents and sister and got up to leave, wiping the tears running down her face. Esther yearned to hold her daughter, to protect her from what lay ahead. Anita walked out quickly through the back door.

The week was almost up. Carolina and Henk would return to a routine, but of what? He hadn't the courage to ask when she would return to America. He was sure their relationship was good and true, but what about when she left? Deep in his heart he knew he would follow her anywhere. He was determined he would meet that challenge when it arrived.

Carolina's desire to be fully immersed in Bavaria

was insatiable. Luckily for Henk, her appetite for him was proving to be most mutually satisfactory.

Carolina was surprised to hear how ordinary Lisa sounded on the phone on their weekly telephone conversation. She had expected an inquisition and even a scolding. But Lisa did not bring up the subject of the new man in Carolina's life.

"Oh, it was the most interesting trip I've ever taken. Imagine a fairy tale with castles, forests, quaint villages, houses decorated with paintings on them. But tell me, what is going on? Mom said you have a lot to tell me."

After she told Carolina what they had learned about Fred, Lisa added, "It may not seem like the worst thing, but for Anita it is."

Carolina was surprised and shocked to hear the news.

"Does Fred know that his secret is out?"

"No, he doesn't. He comes and goes as usual. What's worse is Dad will be getting his settlement for the accident and he had planned to have a family meeting to announce it. He intends for all of us to keep it from Fred. He says Fred will not get one penny of Anita's share. It's causing Dad a lot of stress."

"I hope none of you will be hard on Anita. She really needs all the support the family can give her and not be told what she could have or should have done. At times like this I could hop on the next plane and be there with you. I'm not sure when I will be back, but most likely in a couple of months. That's my plan for now."

Carolina told Helga Lisa's news. Helga shook her head in empathy.

"Schatzie, can you keep a secret? No one knows—certainly not my family." Helga said. Carolina nodded silently. "It happened when I had been married about ten years. I had the four older ones and was expecting my last girl. I found a letter in my husband's pocket. Oh, my—it went on and on about how 'wonderful' he was and how lucky she was to spend time with him. It was two pages that just about killed me to read. I confronted him that night and at first he denied the whole thing. I had the letter and showed it to him. He wouldn't talk for a long time. Finally he broke down and begged me to forgive him and to stay with him. I stayed. I went on with all the daily things of married life. Our girl was born. I rarely spoke to him unless I had to. He told me over and over how sorry he was, and as far as I know he never saw the woman again. For me it was never the same again. I hid it from everyone. The only one I told was my friend Elisabeth, who had been through something similar. And now, you know."

"Thank you for trusting me in sharing such a painful memory." Carolina confided her own story about Joseph to Helga, who said, "I don't know which is worse—another woman or another man!"

Twenty-Five

～～～～

"Don, I think it will work out profitably. The buildings along the block of the Couture Shoppe have a nostalgic 1940s feel to them. There are a couple of stores across the street already doing well that are drawing in the elite. They're selling top-quality antiques and rare art objects. The street itself is low traffic at any given time. We'll take our side of the street, clean up the buildings, keep them in the forties style. We'll place benches, neat little trees, shrubs and flower beds, another couple of shops along that line, at least a restaurant, a café or two to bring in traffic. The vacant lot next to our shop will get painted to resemble a forties-era soda fountain, with a park area, and again comfortable benches with covers and an outdoor eating area. At the corner is a lot that can be made into free parking for the merchants and their clientele. The shop in the space next to ours will be the bakery and curio shop—two different entrances, but clearly the aromas will bring in people. I'm shipping you several crates of what I've found so far and suggested pricing. I'll be coming in to finalize the whole idea so that by spring everything will start to function. Don't offer more than you absolutely have to for the buildings that we'll buy."

Don was silent a while. Carolina could hear him tapping his teeth with a pen, as was his habit. It could be rather annoying, but right now it indicated he was giving her ideas serious thought.

"You just might have something, Caro. What was it you said about music? You'd have forties music piped along the street? That sounds great! Benny Goodman, Sinatra, Glenn Miller, the great swing music many people love. I'll look into acquiring the building next door and get the word out to the other tenants and get their ideas on it back to you."

"I should be there by the end of the month. There's no reason the Couture Shoppe can't be a huge draw, as we get all those high society ladies in there already. The new shops will entice them in and get them in the door, at least. See what the other tenants would like to offer along that line. We can provide any renovations they may need, at a reasonable price, of course."

"Caro! Did you absorb ideas from Jack, or what? It all makes sense and frankly, I do think you have a great idea. I'll get started on everything right away and get back to you. Are you at the same phone number?"

"Most of the time I can get messages at Helga's. I spend quite a bit of time scouting the area for treasures. I know many people in LA are sophisticated, and some won't be impressed by my gift items. But I know some in the higher income brackets will want to have the latest finds from Europe. Mark my words."

"I have to agree with you."

"Let me know as soon as you get the shipment and

tell me what you think. Get Eva's opinion. I'll be eager to know. Thanks, Don."

Carolina's heart was pounding as she hung up the phone. On the last weekend trip around villages she had found an artisan, a craftsman who carved and painted quaint curio items, replicas of well-known statues representing artists and composers, using delicate workmanship she had never seen before. In one village she met a woman who sold handmade linens, dainty items she believed could become treasures. On a hunch, she had bought several and taken them back to Helga and Greta's sisters. The women were familiar with the representations of the carved figures. The linens, of course, were traditional items already in most of their homes. Some carvings were Christmas figures, angels, elves, and curious little gnomes that were delicately proportioned. Others, such as nutcrackers, were larger and somewhat cruder in their presentation, but nevertheless interesting. She had also found paintings, scenes of the area that looked like pictures in a fairy tale. She encountered various artisans who would be willing to consign their goods. She had signed contracts with several and paid them a fair price. She would see what her return would be and negotiate for more. Her hope was there would be a market in LA and possibly other outlets.

Helga was impressed with Carolina's inventiveness and knack for locating art objects, and one day she said, "I know of some artists who would love to get recognition and extra dollars for their work. Would you let me take you to them?"

"Of course, Helga. I trust your judgment. We can

get a few items and see how well they sell. I'll keep track of who the craftsmen are. I'm looking for as much variety as possible. You tell me when you can go, and we'll get moving. I'll take care of all the expenses for the trip. I also need to find a small warehouse somewhere, nothing too large or expensive for the time being, until we see how everything moves. I'll have to figure out prices, possibly with others' input. I'll see what tourists are paying and work out a good price all around."

"I haven't wanted to bring up the subject since I respect your privacy, but does Henk know how much money you have? I imagine he has a vague idea since your husband had a business that you inherited."

"I haven't said one word, nor have I given any indication of what I have access to. I'm really not comfortable with it, as you may have guessed. I'm grateful, of course, but the thought of huge amounts of money has never been of importance to me, or to my family. Certainly we want to live full lives, get an education, see that our children fulfill their goals, but focusing on money is not what drives me."

"I thought as much; you are down-to-earth, you have more interest in being creative, enjoying nature, and having good relationships with those around you. That is one trait I admire about you, Carolina. I believe Greta is much like that. My parents left me with a sizeable inheritance that thankfully was intact after the war."

They sat down to have a cup of coffee. Helga continued her story. "My husband was a banker, and so was my father. They worked together. That is how I met my husband, Erhardt. When they saw what was happening here in the 1930s they wisely transferred funds to secret bank accounts. I never found out where. There was also some hidden away here in this house along with Mother's jewels. After the war Erhardt got my father's money and transferred it to me, the rightful owner. I opened a perfume shop in the tourist area and only recently sold it. I've always been a hard worker. Greta remembers me being home and cooking, but I was always involved in some business or other. Helping you will be most pleasant for me. I especially like spending time with you."

They were both silent for a while as they enjoyed their morning coffee. Carolina could tell Helga had something else on her mind and waited for Helga to speak.

"I've wanted to discreetly bring up the subject of the Holocaust, as I know through Greta that Jack is— was—Jewish. Both Erhardt and I despised the actions that brought about the suffering of Jewish people. But we were both helpless, as were so many others, to declare our true feelings. Anyone was subject to being shot if the truth came out, and our own families were also threatened with being killed. We did the best we could, under the circumstances."

"I know, Helga. Greta and I talked a little about it. She and Jack made their peace well before I came along. I'm glad you told me. And now, let's discuss our travel plans."

"I can be available any time. You let me know when you want to leave on, what did you call them, expeditions? I haven't heard that word before. It sounds more serious than the pleasure I'm sure the trips will be."

"I look forward to the expeditions, as I'm thinking of them already. I'll keep notes on which artist sells what. I'll keep meticulous notes. You and I will have a wonderful time together."

Carolina told Henk her plan. They were snuggled in bed in a bed-and-breakfast chalet on another of their weekend trips, with a view of pine trees and mountains from the open window. She had been silent for several minutes.

"Henk, I've been waiting to tell you something."

He looked at her with dread, fearing she was going to tell him she was leaving. She recognized the look on his face and laughed softly.

"No, I'm not leaving. Well, for a while I am. I'll be going to Los Angeles and to check on my family—my daughter in El Paso—and set up this business idea I have. Henk . . . I'm going to be coming back, probably in a couple of months, and I'll be settling here, in Munich. I haven't wanted to say anything as I didn't want to pressure you into any type of commitment with me. Whatever happens between you and me has to happen freely."

He leaned over her, not touching her, with that boyish grin that made him so lovable to Carolina.

"You have given me something I had no idea existed. I thought I knew what love is. I believed I was in love with my former wives. But the—what is the English word for it?—the fullness I feel with you is more than I ever dreamed I would have."

"Fulfillment?"

"Yes, that must be the word! We are happy together,

aren't we? I know you had a wonderful love with your husband and I cannot compete with that. I don't intend to. I am just what I am, and I offer myself to you in every way. If you wish, eventually we can get married. Here, in Europe, it is not necessary."

"I am very comfortable and at peace with you. I had such a wonderful husband and truthfully, I do not believe I will want to marry again. It will be a shock to my family that I will stay with you and not have a legal marriage."

A month of business and pleasure passed quickly. Carolina was more in love with Bavaria every day. There were times she could not find words to express the unusual joy she experienced coming upon quaint scenery as they turned on a mountain road and entered villages she'd only imagined existed. She would be breathless for moments, taking in the extraordinary Alpine beauty. Henk and Carolina parted with promises of phone calls and spoke of how quickly they would be together again. Helga was saddened to see her friend leave, yet happy at the thought Carolina would return to establish her own home in Munich.

She flew directly to El Paso to see her daughter and to get a feel for Michelle moving to Europe with her. The reunion was emotional, as she had expected, with mother and daughter clinging to each other. She caught up on the news on her father's huge financial settlement for his accident. Certainly it was more than anyone had expected he would receive. At the final meeting he was offered close to two million dollars.

A tight circle gathered. No other members would be allowed at present. Not even Anita was to know the extent of the settlement. It was unfortunate that no one believed she would not tell her husband of the money her father was to receive and share with the family.

"I hate to say we don't trust Alfredo, but we don't," Miguel's voice was emphatic. No one had ever heard him speak in such harsh tones. "He is not worthy of being a member of this family. Still, we have to wait for Anita to make her decision. She has not yet confronted the man."

"I can understand how difficult it must be for her. Remember, none of the rest of you has experienced such conduct in your own lives. You've been fortunate or maybe just have been fooled," Carolina said, and then thought bitterly about her own mother's betrayal and winced as she spoke the words. She was afraid that truth would be obvious on her countenance, so she kept her eyes diverted from her family.

"I know it will be difficult, if not impossible, for you all to understand why I am going to stay in Munich," Carolina continued. "And yes, I have made up my mind. I'll be getting a house when I go back, and at the moment I am looking into taking Michelle with me. There are excellent American schools, or, for that matter, private European schools where she would do well, I'm sure. I might take her for a few months to see how things go for her."

"Well, you are an adult. You don't need our permission to do whatever you choose in your life. Carolina, I'm proud of you. You're confident in yourself, and though I wish you would stay here, I respect your decision. Also, for your peace of mind, this is Michelle's home as long as you and she wish." Her father's solemn voice gave her the approval she still wanted despite her newfound independence.

"Thank you, Dad. I hoped you'd feel that way. The rest of you may not, but that is not going to influence me. I'm also going to Los Angeles to open a business along the block where the Couture Shoppe is. I haven't told Greta yet. This will be my own project. Of course, I'm using funds I have from Jack's company. I'll purchase a building, a couple of vacant lots, and remodel to create a cozy block, no automobile traffic, in a 1940s theme. Mine will be a European bakery, and I'll also import handcrafted items I'm finding around Munich. I have faith my ideas will work."

Lisa beamed at her. "Wow! That does sound interesting. Is it what you sent us as gifts? They certainly are unusual and delightful. I've gotten comments from my friends wanting to buy some. I've been meaning to tell you, but this other family situation has taken up all our attention."

"Yes, that's just some of the items I've found. I want to get these curios over here before the world discovers them and they lose their novelty and appeal. Greta's son-in-law is studying to be a baker. I have to see about getting him a visa and permit to work. Don is looking into that aspect. We've kept it from Greta, mostly as a surprise to her, and also because we're waiting to see that he can get a work visa."

Carolina set time aside to speak privately with Anita a day after her arrival, just the two of them. Anita's eyes welled with tears as they sat in Anita's kitchen having breakfast.

"I've heard all about the ideas you have for your

own business and I am so proud of you, my youngest sister, going out on your own, living in Europe, making your own decisions. Because of what's happened with Fred, I've decided to go to school and possibly go into teaching, like Lisa. I've enrolled and have already started classes. I didn't say anything because I wanted to be sure I could handle it. I've been so stuck in my home, tending to Fred's every whim, that I forgot myself. Well, not any more. My classes are coming along well. You know I love to read, so it's been easier than I expected."

Carolina reached over and hugged Anita. The two could not hold back tears. "I am so proud of you. You have overcome something negative in your life. I want to shout to the world that you don't need Fred to get approval, you can do it on your own, sis. When will you tell him to leave?"

"I know everyone wants me to do it soon. I am preparing myself to face up to it in the next few days. Seeing you and talking to you has given me the courage I need. You survived losing the husband you loved so much and who loved you completely. You have given me the inspiration I needed. Now that I am doing well in school, as old as I am, I can handle what comes along in life. I'll tell him soon, you'll see."

"We're here for you. You won't be alone."

Twenty-Six

As the cab dropped Carolina off, she stood outside, not sure what would happen as she entered her home. The cab driver left the luggage at the front door as she requested and drove off. She had purposely not told Don when she was arriving. She wanted to be alone. It had been terrible for her to leave Michelle, though it would be for a few weeks only, until school was out. That would give her the time she needed to get some of her projects settled.

As she stepped inside, memories flooded over her. Immediately she felt tears stinging her eyes. Everywhere she looked she sensed Jack's presence. She walked throughout the house, touching some pieces, pausing now and then, reliving memories.

After having checked every room, removing sheets covering the furniture, she sat on her bed and sobbed. I can't be here and look at everything Jack and I treasured, she told herself. This is our home—his home. It's too painful. I'll remodel. I have to. The bedroom will be first.

She called Don the following day.

"When did you get in? Why didn't you call?"

"I wanted to be home alone. Along with all the other plans I have, I now want to totally remodel most of my house."

"Of course. I understand. It must be very difficult for you to be there without Jack. It's hard for me to be here at the office without Jack, so I can only imagine what it's like for you. Did you bring Michelle with you?"

"No, she's in school, and I think it would be traumatic for her to be here, also. It's best to protect her from the painful memories. I'll come by this morning if you have time in your schedule."

"I should be free by ten. I have news for you on what you asked me to look into. I've made offers and they've been accepted. The other tenants along the block have been very receptive."

"That sounds great. I'll see how soon I can get there after ten. I have to meet with Greta. She doesn't know I'm here either."

Carolina drove slowly along the block that she planned to redevelop, her mind racing ahead with visions of the shops she was planning. It may seem like a quaint idea for LA, she thought, but if I like the curios and my family does as well, there is no reason others shouldn't. The quirkiness of the idea would be the hook that would bring people in. The empty lot next to the Couture Shoppe will be the first thing to get done, she decided.

She walked in through the back, as usual, and stood at the table where Greta was having coffee and reading the newspaper. Greta gasped as she glanced up and saw her friend standing before her.

"Oh, mein Gott, Schatzie—it's you! You sneaky woman! You had me wondering when you were getting back. I should have known you'd do something like this." Greta came around the table and the two women hugged. "You look terrific. You look even happier than when I last saw you."

"You look wonderful, too. It's good to be back, even if it's only for a few weeks. There is so much to talk about, Greta. You'll never guess what ideas I have for this block. Sit down so I can tell you. If you have time, of course."

"Yes, yes—I have all the time in the world. Get your coffee and sit and tell me. First, how is everyone at home, in El Paso and in Munich?"

"Everyone is fine, both places. Health wise, everyone is fine—there's things going on with my dad and the others that I'll tell you about later. All my family and yours send you their love. I have packages and letters for you in this bag." She placed the tote bag on the table.

Greta sat open-mouthed as she listened to Carolina's ideas for the block, nodding now and then, shaking her head in amazement at other times, but always with a positive grunt, as she did not want to interrupt her friend and partner. Greta loved the idea of paintings on the walls on the lot next to the shop, similar to Garmisch-Partenkirchen. She had many questions while Caro spoke, but she let her get to the end.

"I've saved this part for the last—the bakery will be European style, with mouth-watering authentic pastries like the ones we ate in the coffee shops in Munich. I have a German baker lined up—Don is getting clearance for a visa for Dieter. Monika and Dieter will be here, at least for a while as they try life in America," Carolina reported. She saw the look of pure delight on Greta's face.

"Oh, that is too wonderful for words. I hope they like it here. It's hard to say, you know. Some people can't adapt." Her voice was soft as she was considering all the possibilities and work ahead for all of them. "They can live with me until they find a place they like. Oh, it will be so good to have Monika here with me. I can't believe it, Schatzie."

Carolina briefly told Greta what was happening with her folks and Anita. Greta just shook her head. They switched back to Carolina's business plans.

"Don has the last two shops at the other end committed. They're going to remain in the same business, just get the buildings cleaned up, painted, and some decorations to fit in the theme. The others across the street are negotiating with Don."

Since Carolina had returned to her home she'd had a sense of uneasiness, as if someone were watching her. Maybe it's my imagination, she thought. She called Don to tell him her concerns.

"I've seen a car in the area each evening when I get home." She gave him the description.

"I'll have it looked into, Caro. Is every door and window locked? You really shouldn't be home alone. Let me get you a guard. It will be the best for you."

Carolina heaved a sigh of relief as she said yes. "I've been reluctant to go this far, but I do believe I'll feel better. Where will they stay? I really don't want anyone in the house."

"I'll take care of everything—there will be someone out there in a car. It will be set up so someone will cover when one of the guards needs a break."

"Good. I guess it's for the best. I'll only be here for two or three weeks; then I'm going to El Paso. While the house is being renovated do whatever you think will be necessary."

She had not turned on a light, so she could look out the window. There was the car, down the block. She could see it perfectly well. She could see the outline of a man facing her house sitting in the driver's seat. She felt a chill, though oddly, not fear.

Don called Carolina in El Paso to let her know how the progress on her house was going.

"By the way, Caro, I do have some news on the man who's been hanging around. He stopped at the house while I was there and asked if the house was for sale. I'd had a trace put on the car so I knew his name. I saw him right after we started work on the house. He gave me his information and it jived—it's Russell. A man named Robert Russell—says he's interested in buying the house if it goes on the market. Seemed like an innocent sort of older man." There was no response for several seconds.

Carolina tried to make her voice as nonchalant as possible, despite the pounding of her heart. "Tell me about him."

"He had gone in the house while the men were working. I happened to walk in and saw him in the living area looking around. He was very polite, quite a nice man, actually. Didn't seem like the type to scare anyone, but I did find it odd that he'd been hanging around."

"What did he do?"

"Well, he was just looking around. I don't see what difference it makes since the house isn't on the market."

"Do you have his number? I'd like to have it, just in case."

"Sure, here goes." Don gave her Robert's address and phone number. "Oh, he also asked where the owners are."

"I believe it's someone Jack knew," Carolina said. "Yes, he'd mentioned that name. He may just be interested in the house."

She hung up the phone and went immediately to one of the empty bedrooms, shut the door, and locked it. Her heart had not stopped pounding and her hands were trembling. She looked at the address and phone number she had written down and saw how shaky her writing was.

Oh, my God. Why is he—that man, my . . . father—hanging around my house and asking questions? she wondered. Over and over she repeated the words to herself in low whispers. How she longed to be able to tell someone, to talk about it and bring it out in the open. He was the man she'd seen in the car and the one from whom she'd felt no fear. Of course not, she thought. There was no fear to be felt from someone she knew loved her without really knowing her.

A timid knock at the door shook her out of her

thoughts. She opened it to find Michelle standing there, a huge smile on her face.

"Mommy, come see me. Grandpa's teaching me how to hold the bat and swing slowly so I can hit the ball. I've already hit it about ten times. Come see, Mommy!" She took Carolina's hand and pulled her out of the room.

They were in the same place she had stood so many times when her father had taught her the same tactics. She saw the look of adoration on her daughter's face as he pitched the ball. He always had patience for a child. She went over and kissed his cheek. Whatever thought she had of contacting the other man was erased from her mind.

Twenty-Seven

"I'm not surprised, Don. This is perfect and even better than I'd hoped for." She walked around quickly to each room, calling out to Don, telling him how well everything had turned out. The newly enlarged entry hall was now a more spacious welcoming room. The living room was unrecognizable from the former setting. The kitchen was updated with the latest in cabinetry, flooring, and color.

The mural in her bedroom was exquisite. It was identical to the picture of Garmisch-Partenkirchen she had provided. She could almost see herself standing in front of the buildings. The geraniums in the containers looked real. The muralist had captured the paintings on the houses.

"I'm glad you like it. I can see why you're so fond of this place you're going back to. You've changed. You seem stronger. Jack would be pleased to see how you've gone on with your life." Don continued, "I've saved the best for last. The one man who was holding out has agreed to sell, so you'll have your parking area next to the Couture Shoppe. That frees up the space on the other side, the one you want to turn into a cozy sitting area, if you still want to do that."

"Yes, I do. I have pictures of places around Munich that have such spaces next to businesses and they're so inviting. Shoppers can sit and relax and drink their coffee. The open space will be between the bakery and the Couture Shoppe. What do you think of the European Shop for the name of my curio store?"

"It sounds fine. How about European Curio Shoppe with the same spelling of 'shoppe' like your other store?"

Carolina nodded, smiling as she heard the name.

"We'll get started on your business venture as soon as possible," Don called out as he left Carolina's house.

She mustered courage to go into Jack's office for the first time since his initial stroke. His office was the one room untouched for remodeling. She removed the tarp covering the desk and touched the pens he used only at home and the other fixtures on the massive mahogany desk. She opened one of the deep drawers and took one of his journals that held notations he made of business meetings, as well as ideas he had for upcoming contracts. She reached back and found another smaller journal and wondered why she had never seen it before. The journal opened to the middle. She smiled as she ran her fingers along his handwriting. She saw there were notes on the many times they had traveled to El Paso. Some notations were cryptic, initials and brief messages, but she could figure them out as they were referrals to her family. Her mind whirled as she read his notes. She felt a chill and wondered why she had never seen him writing in this particular journal.

Lisa is okay now w/ me, has accepted me.

Miguel took me to his cousin's home. Comments followed on that particular visit.

She started at the first page of the book, their first trip home with Michelle as a newborn.

Alone with Esther as planned! Can't figure out her attitude toward C???? Noticed it the first day. Saw a distant look in Esther's eyes when she spoke of C as a child.

The C was underlined. She remembered the day as if it were yesterday. Carolina had gone to visit her aunts and grandmother. When she returned she found everyone else had left, leaving Jack and Esther alone, though her Dad had returned briefly. What had they talked about? She continued reading his notation.

Something secret—see it in her face. Resentment? Why? Holding something back. See the difference when she looks at her other daughters. C has never said anything. Is C aware?

Carolina sat open-mouthed, the color draining from her face. There was no doubt about Jack's knowledge of something wrong between her and her mother. Jack's astuteness and analytical nature had never failed him, she could see that clearly. She turned the pages, looking for more. Every visit they had made had prompted notations. She stared at one page toward the end and said aloud, "I can't believe this. No, it's not possible."

Jack had written R. R. and a phone number. She recognized the number as the one she had recently gotten from Don. It was Robert Russell's phone number in Los Angeles. How had Jack gotten it? And why? From the date, she could see it was written during the year before his first stroke. She went on reading vague notations, some were about conversations with Miguel.

Then she saw it—his notation about one month before he fell ill.

Connection to R. R.? Got report. R. has family in EP, same name as C. Do I tell her???

Her hands were trembling as she reached further back into the drawer. She retrieved a sheet of paper rolled up with a rubber band tightly wound around it. This was not at all like Jack. All his correspondence was neatly stacked or in files. She cut the band and tried to smooth the paper open. It kept curling up. She placed it face down and smoothed it. Her mouth was dry. She sipped the lemonade and began to read the typed report. The date on it was one day before Jack's notation in his diary.

The investigation of the gentleman seen outside The Couture Shoppe and outside your residence on more than one occasion is complete. He is Robert Russell, Junior, age at the present time: 65, residing at - - - in Los Angeles. Previous address in El Paso, Texas at - - - . Mother's maiden name: Carolina Hernandez, married Robert Russell, Senior, in El Paso, 1910, both now deceased. Property deeded to R. Russell Jr: grocery store at - - -, said property now titled to son of said R. Russell.

The document listed his occupation. It further stated that Mr. Russell had no criminal record of any sort, not even traffic tickets. Apparently Mr. Robert Russell was an upstanding member of the community. It was signed by a private detective with an address outside of Los Angeles.

Jack and his family are fond of investigating people, she thought bitterly. She picked up the phone and called Greta at the shop. Luckily, Greta answered and was surprised to hear Carolina's voice.

"Do you have time to come over after work? I have something really important to discuss with you in person."

Greta heard the anguish in Carolina's voice. "Of course. I'll be there as soon as I get free." She could not imagine what could be wrong, but there was definitely something going on.

Carolina greeted her friend at the door a couple of hours later, hugging her tightly.

"My, what a change this is," Greta said as she looked around. "It's lovely, Caro."

"Thank you. I'll pour you a drink. Would you like a beer?"

"Yes, thanks. I'll wait and see all the changes later. I can tell you need to talk."

"Oh, Greta, you can't imagine what I've found. It's a journal Jack was keeping. I am so confused and angry and hurt at the same time. I really don't know what to think."

"Don't tell me he had a secret life you didn't know about!"

"No, it's nothing like that. Here, sit down and I'll tell you what I found. He knew, Greta—Jack knew all about my secret. All these years he knew and never let me know. I believe he wanted to protect me. He wasn't sure that I was aware of the secret."

"This sounds intriguing. How did you find out?"

"I found a journal while cleaning out his desk. I finally decided to go through his papers and get on with the pain of putting his things away. I have to back up and tell you—right before I left for El Paso this past winter, I saw a man in a car watching the house. I was afraid at first, thinking someone wanted to break in. I told Don, who set up surveillance and found out about the man. It's him—my real father. He's been watching me, apparently for years. That's what Jack discovered—he was watching me at the shop and here at the house. I guess Robert just wanted to see me and know about my life."

Carolina began weeping softly. Greta got up to get her a tissue and handed it to her.

"Jack had an investigator check him out. Jack figured everything out. Everything. He was good at doing things like that, you know." Caro smiled as she said that. Greta nodded.

"The report says Robert lived in El Paso. In fact, Jack knew my grandmother's name: Carolina—how original," she said wryly. "It's all in here," she said, holding the report. "A fool would figure out the truth. Why would this man be following me around? The grocery store his mother ran was just blocks from my parents' home. It tells how he was in El Paso the year before my birth. I don't know how the investigator went that far back, but it's easy to imagine. His mother's store must have kept records."

"Well, it's not that bad. It isn't anything you did or could have helped. I don't think you should grieve over this now. Jack is gone. It would have been interesting if you had been able to talk to him about it. Would you have wanted to? You know Jack would have continued to love you, no matter what. What will you do with the papers?"

"I'm not sure," she said, wiping her face and

sounding more relaxed. "I wanted to talk to you about this since you're the only one who knows. I can't let my family find out about it. It would destroy my father. Miguel, it would destroy Miguel." She sobbed after she said his name. Greta got up and put her hands on Carolina's shoulders.

"I wish I had the right words to say to you. I understand how hard it is for you," Greta said. She had tears in her eyes.

"Oh, I didn't mean to make you cry, Greta." Carolina got up and tried to laugh off the emotion. They hugged spontaneously, happy to be reunited.

"Are you coming to the shop tomorrow?"

"Yes, I'm trying to get everything settled for my new venture in the next few days. I'll be leaving soon. Henk and I will most likely move in together as soon as I get back. He's hinted about something big as a surprise for me and I'm afraid that's what it is—that he wants us to live together."

"What do you mean, you're afraid? Don't you want to?"

"Oh, yes, I suppose I do. He's wonderful to me. I'm a very happy woman when I'm with him. But I'm happy by myself, too. He still has no idea how much money I have at my disposal. I sometimes wish I didn't. The idea of wealth has never appealed to me. But that is not the most important thing to me. I'm afraid when he does find out he will react differently from what I expect. I really don't know what he will think."

"You were wise not to let him know. It's always a chance a woman takes when a man wants her for her money. I keep my financial information from Paul even though we're together almost all the time now. His wife is getting worse and he says she may not last much longer. He talks about marriage. I really don't think I want to marry, no matter what. I feel terrible waiting for his wife to get worse and die. It's not a way to live, at least not for me."

"You have a solid relationship with Paul."

"It's been a secret for so long, we're both used to living like this."

"Greta, I almost called him on the phone—Robert. When I found out from Don that he's been watching me all this time, I felt so bad for him. I remember he told my mother how he would always love me. He sounds like such a kind person. But I can't go against my father, my dear Miguel. It's best I just leave it like it is. I'm going to leave the country and probably will be back only for short periods of time. I'll be in El Paso a lot, and that might keep Robert away from me. I wonder if he's in contact with my mom."

"What an unusual love story theirs is," Greta commented. She saw Carolina wince as she spoke the words. "I'm sorry, Carolina. I know it's a hard topic for you, but you may as well face it. They must have loved each other very much."

"I know. I wish sometimes I had never found out. How different my life would have been. I wouldn't have married Joseph to get as far away as young as I was. But then, I wouldn't have come to LA and met my precious Jack and had my wonderful daughter, and met you!"

They both laughed and settled back, content in each other's company.

The weeks flew as work on the shops progressed quickly. A shipment of two large crates arrived the week before the European Curio Shoppe was set to have a soft grand opening. By soft, that meant the store would open without fanfare until business indicated everyone was ready for the rush of a grand opening. Carolina was pleased with the variety of items Helga and Henk sent. As Carolina had predicted, the women who had their unique clothing designed by Greta immediately flocked to the new store, and brisk business was soon evident. Carolina called Munich for two more shipments. One of Greta's customers asked if her cousin in Austria could send some of his paintings on consignment and Carolina said yes after seeing one in the customer's home.

The other shops soon followed suit. First the café next to where the bakery was to be located, and then the tobacco shop across the street. Carolina was most pleased with the clientele that was attracted to the boutiques.

Twenty-Eight

The sky was clear, but there was definitely a chill in the air. Carolina wrapped the coat around her as she waited for Henk to bring the car around. He had presented her with a bouquet of freesias and lavender crocuses. He had kissed her long and passionately as soon as he was able to hold her as she walked off the plane. His eyes sought hers, hoping to see the same longing he had for her. It was early March, just days before his birthday. Helga and her family were going to celebrate his special day, and it would be a welcoming party for Carolina as well.

"If you're not too tired from your trip we can go by and look at the house I found for us."

"Is that your surprise?"

"I have enough in savings for a house in a nice neighborhood. It's about the right size for us. It has two bedrooms. I think we don't need more than that. I know you'll love the gardens."

They drove to the house and yes, Carolina loved the gardens. "I do love it, Henk, and how touching of you to do this for us. There is something you must consider, though. I'll probably bring my daughter to live here, and there's always the chance others in my family will come to visit. My niece Elena just graduated from the university and she's talking about coming to stay in Europe a year or so. I'm not sure this house would be large enough. Has the sale gone through?"

"No, it hasn't. I knew you would want to decide, so I told the owners you would be here later this month. It took you longer to come back than you'd first said, so I've kept the owners waiting. I might buy it anyway for my daughters to stay in when they come to visit with me."

Later, at the Neuberg house, as Henk talked about the house he and Caro might soon move into, Helga caught Carolina's eye, silently asking her when Henk would find out about Carolina's wealth. They excused themselves and met in the kitchen.

"He doesn't know, does he?"

"Not yet. I wanted to tell him today, but he took me directly to the house. I couldn't tell him then. Oh, Helga, he's so happy buying this house for us. I can't spoil his happiness. I did tell him the house would need renovations, which I do intend to get done as soon as possible, if we get that house. I just think I'm getting into a situation where I'm not comfortable."

Twenty-Nine

Robert Russell's weathered face belied his heartache. He shook his head and ran his fingers through his white hair as he thought about her, as he had for the past twenty-five years. He took out the album where he kept her pictures. Some Esther had given him the year she turned fifteen, when he first learned of her existence. Other pictures he had carefully cut out of the newspaper after she moved to Los Angeles.

He had found her first wedding picture when he heard she had married. It was easy to get the Salinas paper in Los Angeles. Then she had married that prominent contractor and there had been a larger picture of the couple, which provided him with a closer look at her.

He admired Esther's courage in calling him with news about Carolina, as he had asked her to. He knew how hard it was for her to call, having to go to the phone booth down the block with her coins so there was no evidence of her calls. She told him she memorized the number to his shop, though she kept the handwritten one, in reverse order, in an old wallet in a drawer.

He could count the times he and Esther had spoken. Each word was indelibly imprinted in his mind. He would go over and over everything Esther said until it was memorized. There was very little about their time together or the few times they had spoken on the phone that he could not remember as if it had happened yesterday.

The guilt followed him everywhere. He loved his wife, Marjorie. She was a sweet, caring, unassuming woman who deserved the unconditional love she received from her children—and from him. He would never be able to explain how he happened to fall in love with Esther that summer. There was no reason on earth for them to have met, and for the two of them to fall in love with each other was incomprehensible. But they had—it had been a magical time. She was the prettiest woman he had ever seen. But that was not enough for him to fall in love to the point he would have left his family for her, even given up his life, so to speak. There was her character, her kindness, the soft way she spoke, and her accent. Even after all the years, she had a slight accent that charmed him. He would have taken her as far away as possible so no one would ever have found them. His fantasy gave him peace and pleasure, and then the guilt set in, as always.

Marjorie had never known, or if she had a hint of it, she hid it completely from him. There were times he caught her looking wistfully at him. The year Marjorie died a piece of him died also. He had loved her deeply and she had known he loved her.

He and Marjorie raised a granddaughter, Carol,

after his son and the girl's mother, Hannah, divorced. Hannah eventually recovered from her drug use, but the years left a rift between child and mother. Carol was named after Robert's mother, and she was the joy in her grandparents' lives. She was a nurse now in a big hospital, and though she lived on her own, she visited him often.

As the years passed after Marjorie's death and because of his son's prolonged absence in Carol's life, Robert and Carol grew closer than ever. He briefly confessed the facts of Carolina's existence and told Carol of his yearning to leave a recording of how Carolina came to be. It had been painfully difficult for Robert to admit to an imperfection in his love for Marjorie, and it was especially hard to admit it to his beloved granddaughter.

Shortly after Robert told Carol about his desire to make a recording about his time with Esther, Carol visited him with a gift. She announced, "Grandpa, I've brought you this tape recorder like you asked. I promise I won't be upset with you or treat you differently after you've recorded your story. You'll always be my best pal. Whatever happened in the past is done. I want very much to know about this woman. We even share a version of the same name."

"Honey, you have no idea what a relief it will be to get it all out. It's been haunting me all these years. Your darling grandma would have been so hurt and upset. That's why I've kept it so closely guarded. I don't want to keep the secret from you any longer. My son won't care. Your aunt in Colorado may want to hear about it someday. You can keep the secret, and if someday you want to share it with anyone, that will be your call."

"I'll turn it on for you. This is what you press," Carol showed him, "when you want to take a rest or to collect your thoughts. It's the newest model of recorder I could find. I'll be back in a few hours. Will that be enough time?"

"I hope so. I want to do it all in one swoop. Once I get started, though I know it will be painful for me at times, I don't want to stop."

"Grandpa, the doctor told you you're fine. I'd tell you if I knew there was anything serious going on with you."

"I know, sweetie, but at my age you never know what may happen. I want to do this before it's too late. I want her—my daughter—to someday know how much I loved her. I don't want her to be shocked when she hears the truth about herself . . . and me. Her family has always been close. It will be a terrible shock for her to know the truth about us. Do you think you could stay nearby her when she hears it so if she feels bad you can help her?"

"Yes, I will. That's a promise." She kissed his cheek and ran out the door before she broke down.

Days later, Carol took a few minutes away from her hospital unit. In an empty room she picked up the phone and dialed the number to the Morten Construction Company. She asked for information on contacting Carolina Morten, pronouncing Carolina correctly in Spanish.

The receptionist hesitated slightly. "Mrs. Morten has returned to Munich."

"Oh, I see," she hesitated, not prepared for such an un-expected response.

"Is this regarding orders pending at the European Shoppe or the Couture Shoppe?"

"The European Shoppe. I misplaced her number and need to place an order as soon as possible." Carol felt her heart skip a beat at her luck in getting a break. She was determined to find Carolina no matter what.

"Here it is." The woman gave Carol the number. "How do you like the art pieces you've gotten so far?"

"We all love them. Customers keep asking for more." Carol figured her answer was right. Carolina must have another business going. Her mind raced with the information she was getting. How would she ever get the recording to her so far away? She realized that she couldn't take the chance of sending it over and that she had to think of something. The first afternoon she was free she found the shop in Los Angeles and found the art pieces interesting, especially the paintings. At least I'll have a point of reference, she thought. She even purchased a replica of a grandfather clock, about a foot high.

Carolina answered the phone early on a Saturday morning while Henk was out puttering in her yard. The woman identified herself as Carol.

"Mrs. Carolina Morten?"

"Yes, this is she." Carolina assumed the caller was interested in ordering, as her business was doing well.

"I hope I'm not calling too early. I'm not sure of the time difference."

"It's eight in the morning. It's not too early."

"Well, I'm calling about the art pieces you are supplying to the European Curio Shoppe. I fell in love with some of the paintings and wondered how I may purchase some to sell in my own store. I'd like to meet with you when you come to LA, if that's possible." Carol had her fingers tightly crossed.

"Sure. I should be there early in November. I'd be happy to call you and see when we can set up a time to meet. What kind of shop do you have?"

Carol bit her lip. She wasn't sure she could carry out her fabrication.

"I'm looking at a shop north of LA. I'm not sure yet." She winced, as she was afraid to get in too deep with her story. "I'd like to talk to you directly when you have time and get your opinion on what may work for me."

"I'll be happy to do that. I can call you a few days after I arrive."

"Thank you for your patience with me. My name is Carol. Here's my number: 213-555-7370. I look forward to meeting you."

As she placed the number in her notebook where she kept information on her suppliers and buyers, it occurred to Carolina she had not gotten the woman's last name.

Thirty

"Now that Carolina is settled in her house, it's time to discuss my wedding. I want to invite Carolina and as many of her family who can come to Munich. It will be an almost traditional Bavarian wedding. Dieter and I have decided the parts we want left out."

Helga looked at Monika in awe. She was proud of how well the young woman was doing, almost finished with her studies, planning her wedding, and now going well into adulthood.

"I called my mom and she loves the ideas I proposed. She's looking at who she will leave in charge of her business and wants to be sure that her friend Paul will be able to make it also. It's really going to be grand, Mutti. Wait till you hear all my plans."

Monika always called Helga "Mutti," and Greta was accustomed to being called "Mom," even in German. "Dieter and I have decided we won't have the Polterabend, but we definitely want all our guests in traditional Bavarian clothing, so that means everyone from the US will need to get fitted in plenty of time."

Monika looked at her list and said, "We'll wait till I talk to Mom to go over the rest. But we've spoken with the priest in Wasserburg and reserved the inn for the end of July."

"That's excellent, Monika," Helga responded. "I can't wait to get everything going. You haven't asked, but I do agree doing away with some of the more difficult traditions is a good idea. Throwing old dishes and smashing them for Polterabend has always been a nuisance to me, though I have given in when anyone's insisted on it. Also, sawing a log as you leave the church can be a bit unusual for American guests, don't you think?"

"Mmm, yes, I do have to go along with you. Dieter and I still have much to decide on. For example, the band to lead us in procession to the church. We haven't decided on who it will be."

"Well, there's time, but you know you have to get these bands lined up in time so everything will go smoothly."

"I'd like to call Mom when Carolina comes over later today so they can get in their opinions. What do you think Carolina will say about her family wearing the dirndl?"

"I do believe she will like that. We do have to discuss it with her, though, regarding whoever makes it over from El Paso."

Carolina and Henk stopped by later that afternoon.

"Gruss Gott. You both look like you have something special to discuss. I can always tell, especially on you, Monika," Carolina said.

"Yes, Caro, I'm planning my wedding. I need to call

Mom now so she can hear all the details I have so far. How is your house coming along?"

Henk had stayed in the living room and was out of hearing. Nevertheless, the women spoke in hushed tones. "He's still a bit annoyed I purchased my own larger house in this neighborhood. As much as I wanted to please him, it does not feel right for me to move in with him and also to be in that smaller house. He will use it for his daughters when they come to visit. He's content with that for now."

"You have to do what's right for you. I may be young, but I can see that at this point in your life you want to make your own decisions and live where you want to live. If you really want to stay with Henk he will have to understand that. Don't you agree, Mutti?" Monika spoke up.

"Absolutely—there was never any doubt in my mind when you found your house, the bigger one with land and more privacy, Carolina. You need the space for all your projects, for the van you use on your trips, and for your sewing. When your family comes to stay with you there will now be plenty of room. You really don't owe anyone an apology."

"Yes, I know, and thank you both for being so understanding and supportive. I care for Henk, but it's not time yet for me to commit as he would like. I have no intention of meeting anyone else, anyway. We are excellent company for each other. Oh, there he comes."

Carolina smiled broadly at Henk, who put an arm around her. He had gotten over his pique at her purchasing her own house. He had been shocked to learn of her wealth when she finally told him. They had been at his apartment and she began speaking about her life in Los Angeles. After a minute or so she had stated matter-of-factly she was in control of several million dollars, though not all in cash, she had been quick to point out. Much of it was in Jack's company's holdings and property. He had stared open-mouthed at her as she spoke. He had a hard time taking in the facts, and even though he himself earned a comfortable income, it could not compare to hers. She was earning income even as she sat and spoke to him. Jack's company was doing quite well without the founder, thanks to his foresightedness and business acumen in choosing Don and the board of directors.

Henk smiled at Carolina, as he had since the day he discovered the truth, and went along with whatever she suggested, though she relied on him for decisions on their daily routine as long as it did not impact her new business venture or her family. She had told him she wanted their relationship based on mutual respect and trust, and so far it was working out well.

Guests started arriving in Munich the week before Monika's wedding. Arriving from El Paso were Lisa and Michelle, along with twenty-two-year-old Elena, Anita and Fred's daughter, who had recently graduated from the university and, in her own words, was ready to see the world. Carolina insisted on going alone to the airport to have time with her family, especially with her daughter, who was now ten.

"I hope you get the rest you need today before the start of all the activities," Carolina said to her niece and daughter. Again Michelle clung to her mother, the two walking with arms entwined around their waists, smiling and enjoying each other's presence.

Once at Carolina's house she showed them around the property. "This is the room I've set aside for you, Michelle. I hope you like it."

"Oh, Mom, it's great. I do love it, and I love being here with you. I know you want me to come stay with you, so this is a good chance for me to see if I like it enough to stay. I hope you understand. It's not easy for me to give up the home and friends I have in Texas."

"Of course, my darling, I understand. Take your time getting acquainted with the house, the neighborhood, and eventually with Greta's family. I won't pressure you in any way. Whatever you decide will be fine with me. I know it's hard for us to be apart."

"But I understand you so well, Mom. I know you need to be where you're happy and where you can do what you have to do. I'm not a little girl anymore and I am proud of all you've done since we lost Daddy. Look," she said, taking out Jack's picture in an unbreakable frame, "my daddy is always with me." She leaned into her mother, letting Carolina hold her as the young girl knew she needed to do. They hugged tightly, and then Michelle continued unpacking. "I'm going to run outside and get familiar with the house, Mom."

"You do that, honey. I'll be helping your aunt and cousin get settled in. Later this afternoon, after you've all rested a bit, we're going over to Helga's. You'll start meeting some of the family."

The afternoon was a whirl of everyone getting to meet everyone. Helga had cooked the days before so she could enjoy the company. Her house was filled with people, laughter, cooking aromas, and gaiety, just as she liked. Everyone was made to feel welcome.

Henk was invited, as were his daughters, Miranda and Marike. Carolina invited Henk and his daughters to dinner at her home several evenings before the wedding so his family and hers could get to know each other. Carolina and her company had all spent the day cooking a traditional American dish of pot roast, vegetables, potatoes, and salad. Michelle had baked a chocolate cake. Elena thoroughly enjoyed the cooking session.

"Aunt Carolina, thank you so much for letting me come stay with you and getting to meet Greta's family. I haven't given you the gift I brought you, we've all been so busy and I still need to finish unpacking." Her lilting laughter filled the kitchen.

Carolina remembered her niece as a young girl, certainly not this lovely, mature young woman with a delightful smile on her face, her black curls bouncing as she merrily joined in the housework.

"I'm so glad your parents allowed you to visit me. I know how strict your father usually is." Carolina immediately regretted bringing up the subject of Elena's father. Everyone was as angry with him as ever.

"I know it's been hard on all of us after what my dad did to Mom. You don't have to be afraid to talk about him. He's my father and I love him, but I hate what he did to our mother, who always did her best for all of us. I won't mention that again now that I've said what I had to say." Elena leaned into her aunt for the hug she knew she would get. Elena's dark eyes were full of joy despite the temporary somber mood. It did not take long for her to return to her usual upbeat, happy self.

"No, we'll not get into that subject, Elena. You're here to enjoy yourself and get to spend time with me in my home. I look forward to showing you around this beautiful city I now call home."

Conversation flowed smoothly as the group ate their dinner. Henk's daughters were fond of Carolina and enjoyed meeting the other guests. The out-of-town guests got fitted for their wedding attire the next day. The dirndls were tried on and colors decided upon.

"I love this deep, dark pink on the apron and corset, Mom. Will you wear a similar color so we're almost dressed alike?" Michelle was enthralled with the charm of the traditional Bavarian wedding dirndls.

"That's a great idea, Michelle. I'll take this almost identical color; it has a touch of bluish tint as I turn side to side, but it's definitely pink. We'll wear the same blouse. Look, here are two that are the same, one in your size and one for me. Won't we look wonderful together?" The two giggled like schoolgirls, happy at their luck in finding similar outfits.

The wedding day was wonderful. The wedding party arrived at the inn in Wasserburg to walk in procession to the church a block away. The women in their festive wedding dirndls, all in white blouses with puffed sleeves with crimping on the ends, accompanied by long skirts and brightly colored aprons, and the men in their black suede lederhosen made for a wonderful sight as they entered the church. The group from Texas was especially impressed with the men's outfits with embroidered flowers on suspenders and along the pants legs. The frock coats on some of the men had striking silver buttons.

The bride was radiant with white ribbons in her bouquet. Her dirndl was elegant with a dress of intricately embroidered white silk with organza. Her vest and apron were pale lavender with blue tint. Flowers adorned her hair, which she had let grow longer for the day. The men's lederhosen were elegant in black suede, the pants going to just below their knees. In following the tradition, the sides were embroidered.

After the Mass and marriage ceremony, the entire wedding party walked in procession back to the inn where the restaurant was decked out and reserved for Monika's special day. The orchestra, the typical oompah band, played usual Bavarian wedding music. Though everyone other than the Americans was speaking German, or most likely the local dialect, Carolina was not sure, all of Carolina's guests greatly enjoyed the wedding and joined in the merriment.

"This is an experience I'll never forget, Auntie," Elena said during a lull in the music. "I'm going to write everything down as soon as we get back to your house so I won't forget one moment of this. Also, I've taken so many pictures I'll have to get a loan to develop them all," she laughed.

Elena always seemed to be smiling and happy, no matter what the circumstances. Carolina's daughter was quieter and seemed more reserved and introspective, which did not surprise Carolina, as both she and Jack seemed to be that way. Elena was soft-spoken, yet merry and full of laughter. At one point Carolina noticed one of Greta's nephews, Frank, had not taken his eyes off Elena. Frank was engaged, though his fiancée had not been able to attend the wedding. He was seated across from Carolina, Michelle, and Elena. Lisa was seated alongside Henk's other daughter, Marike; the two had seemed to hit it off and were conversing almost constantly. Henk was across from Carolina and next to him were Marike and Frank, directly across from Elena. The latter two smiled at each other and he would often lean across the table to talk to Elena, asking questions about her home and her choice in career, and, in general, seemed interested in the young woman.

Carolina was dismayed with Frank's obvious interest in Elena, but she was not in any position to do anything about it at the moment. She hoped it was just a passing fancy. Frank himself was not the problem, rather she thought ahead of the complications of a long distance relationship for her niece and Helga's grandson, if it came to that. Considering the young man's engagement, it may not come to anything, Carolina thought.

The evening was as memorable as everyone hoped it would be. The bride and groom danced with as many guests as possible following their tradition. Helga's happiness at having her family together on this special occasion was evident. She basked in time spent with her sons and their wives and adult children. Carolina and her group felt the warmth and hospitality extended to them. Henk relished his opportunity to connect with Carolina's family and included his daughters in the newly formed circle of the combined families.

Thirty-One

Greta thanked God for her faith and the stoicism that saw her through any obstacle. Her daughter and son-in-law had now been living comfortably in an apartment near her home for almost a year. Dieter and Monika had adapted quickly to life in America. The bakery was a success, with Dieter creating delicious European pastries and breads. An assistant eased the load, giving him a couple of mornings off of the demanding schedule. Paul's wife had passed away, peacefully, and Paul, too, was more tranquil than ever. It seemed life could not get better.

"How did I happen to get an illness such as this? Why now?" Greta asked her doctor. She did not go into details as to how well the rest of her life was going. She would not bore him with the story of her life.

His answer was not satisfactory: "It just happened." But for the time, it would have to do.

Greta would not tell anyone. Not yet. Let everyone enjoy this first summer here with me, she thought. Paul had again proposed, but she had convinced him it was not at all necessary that they wed. They were happy the way they were. Not even Carolina must know, especially not Carolina, Greta decided. I don't want her to go through another dreadful illness again," Greta said to herself aloud.

The months had passed slowly since Greta's discovery of her illness after her daughter's fabulous wedding. Carolina would not be back in Los Angeles until the fall. The two women called each other at least every week and caught up on whatever was going on. Greta was glad Caro was far away. She knew she could never keep such news from her friend if they were together.

"It's an old house, as you remember, large rooms, and so much privacy with the big wall around it. The house itself is almost too big, but I have found I do need that much space, and Henk stays with me most nights. He was a little unhappy a few days, thinking I would find some reason to complain that he cannot afford what I can. But he's back to his old cheerful self again, always singing or whistling. He's such a pleasant man. You know, he's only two years younger than me," Carolina reported in their most recent phone call.

Greta listened to her friend. She knew the area of Carolina's house well. Close to Helga's in Grunwald. She closed her eyes as she remembered the house she'd visited only a few times during preparations for the wedding. It had been full of laughter with Carolina's family.

"I had a feeling Michelle would not want to stay in Munich, despite all the temptations I placed before her. Instead, Elena stayed with me. I'm enjoying her company so much."

"Is Frank still showing interest in her?"

"I'm afraid so. I know he calls her. It's really upsetting to me, knowing he's engaged, but my niece and he are both adults. I can only tell them what I think—no, what I know—is wrong, but I can't force them to listen to me."

"Well, he's my nephew and probably has some of my stubbornness. If he's interested in someone else he must let his fiancée know as soon as possible. Of course now I am nostalgic and want to come for a visit. I know I have to wait until we are not so busy in the shop," Greta lied as she thought of the treatments awaiting her, knowing she would be too ill to travel anywhere.

"Greta, please leave Connie in charge and come over. I'd love to have you stay with us for as long as you can. You know Connie can take charge. The bakery is in good hands. The art shop is running smoothly with Mae and Christine there. You don't have a good excuse."

Greta laughed as she heard her friend try so hard to convince her to make the trip. Greta knew Carolina was right. She could take time off to make the trip. But she could not—and would not—tell anyone the real reason for her not being able to leave the country.

"I know, Schatzie, let me see what I can do. Don't make any plans until I tell you, okay? There's Paul, you know. He wants to be with me every day now. There is no reason for us to be apart anymore. You'll be shocked to know we are considering moving in together."

The next few weeks Greta was feeling better, eating well, and showing no signs of her illness or the medicine she was taking. Maybe I can beat this awful cancer, she told herself. Being with Paul openly certainly boosted her mood. Their life together was blissful and harmonious.

If Paul noticed a change in Greta he did not say anything. He was free of the stress his wife's illness had caused him. Paul and Alice had no children, so there was no one else to occupy his thoughts. For the first time in years he could come and go without considering a visit to see Alice. The last few months she had not recognized him at all, but he still made the daily trek to the nursing home where he made certain she was comfortable.

By mid-summer, though, Greta was no longer able to hide her illness. Paul went with Greta to the doctor, confirming his worst fears. He was devastated but held up a brave front for Greta's sake. Paul at first had been in denial, refusing to believe Greta's weakened condition could be anything serious. Paul insisted on moving in with Greta.

"I will take care of you, Greta," Paul said in a firm voice.

Monika finally got the truth from her mother.

"Mom, why on earth haven't you said something? I want to help you with everything. I don't want you to lift a finger anymore." Monika had been almost angry that Greta had not divulged the reason for her losing weight and feeling run-down. Her daughter did not tell Greta how pale and drawn she looked. Monika knew she had to keep her mother's spirits up, as much as

possible, at least. She informed her mother she would
be at her side every day, even with Paul there also. Greta
had just nodded, grateful for the love surrounding her.

Monika cried into her pillow when she got home the
day she found out. She had held back until she could
bear it no longer. She did not break down in front of her
mother. She was crying bitterly when she told Dieter
the news early the same evening.

"I can't believe this is happening, Dieter. Now, when
Mom and I are finally together and you and I are living
here so close to her."

Dieter did his best to lessen his wife's anguish,
but was frankly at a loss for words. He felt Monika's
pain.

"At least we are here with Greta," he said. "Who
knows how much longer we will have her with us?" He
was realistic enough to understand there was only so
much medicine and the doctors could do, and it would
be a matter of time before Greta would not be around.
He was kind and gentle with both Monika and Greta,
stopping by to prepare hot tea and light biscuits for
the two to have on the evenings when Monika visited
with her mother. He served them on wooden trays with
German doilies Monika had brought with her. They had
intended to keep some of the old country traditions,
and this was one of them.

Paul was at Greta's side when Monika was not
present. He would leave Greta and Monika together as
much as possible, knowing how much they needed to
be together.

Greta lay back on the large, overstuffed easy chair,
her feet up on the matching ottoman with Monika in the

chair next to her, the one that had been William's. Mother and daughter were together every day and would sit and talk about anything that came up, with Monika often asking her mother to tell her about her life in Los Angeles during the first years she was there. Monika never tired of hearing the stories her mother would tell her, keeping them safe in her heart, to be memorized so she would someday tell her own children of their grandmother's life in America. She started keeping a journal to jot down notes on all her mother told her, about William, their trips to the beach that Greta loved so much, and the funny stories Greta remembered, like the time William fell in a lake while bicycling and the time Greta and William broke their porch swing.

"I've called Mutti, my grandma Helga. She says we have to take you home. She wants to see you, Mom. My aunts and uncles say the same thing. I had to tell them," Lisa reported when she saw her mother growing weaker.

Paul went with Greta to tell the doctor they were leaving for Munich. "It's the best road for Greta to take," Paul said in as cheerful a tone as he could muster. Greta nodded, a wan smile on her face. "We'll leave in two days. She'll be at her mother's house," Paul reported.

The doctor embraced Greta warmly as the trio stood. "I wish you the best, my friend. I'm glad I got to know you, though not under these circumstances."

"Me, too," she said, and waved around the office to his staff as they left.

The picnic late in July was the last time the group living in Germany had a happy time together. They had all been there, and later they would reminisce on that last warm, sunny, fun-filled day. They had trekked out to the forest in caravan, taking three cars, as there was not enough room in two. Carolina, Henk, and Elena were in one; Karin, her teenagers, Stefan and Karl, and their father Hans were in the second; and Helga was with Lotte and Peter, along with Frank and his two younger sisters in the third.

Karin called them over to Helga's the following Saturday.

"It's urgent," she said on the phone. "Get here as soon as you can."

She hung up before any questions could be asked. It was late that Saturday morning, and when Carolina's trio arrived, the others were already there. Their glum expressions spoke volumes.

Carolina ran to Helga, grasped her hands, and looked into her eyes, which were teary. Helga looked well otherwise, so Carolina's bewildered expression went around the room.

"What is wrong?" she asked softly, her eyes wide, moving over to Henk and Elena.

Karin held out her hands as if to calm and quiet everyone.

"It's the hardest thing I've ever had to say," she said in English so the American guests could understand and she would not have to repeat. Henk put his arm around Carolina and brought Elena close in to them.

"Mother got a call this morning, just a while ago. She called me as soon as she hung up so you can see we're all still – was ist das wort? – oh, yes, reeling from the news."

Karin and Lotte moved in closer to their mother as Karin spoke, their arms tight around Helga. Helga put her hands up to her face.

Karin continued, "Greta is sick, quite sick. She's got cancer, and it seems like she does not have much time left. Monika called to tell us. Finally she got brave to call us and tell us the terrible news. Mother talked a long time with Monika. Greta would not talk on the phone. Finally Mother convinced them all to bring our sister home—to Munich—as soon as possible. Paul and Monika will bring her. Dieter cannot make the trip and leave the bakery on such short notice."

Carolina slumped down, held up by Henk and Elena, as she heard the news. Henk pulled a chair over for her and Caro accepted, burying her face in her hands, like Helga.

"We have to be strong for Gretchen," Helga spoke calmly and firmly. "When she gets here, I want everyone to be as optimistic as possible and make her last days good for her."

Carolina nodded silently. Henk, sitting beside Carolina, took her hand in his and held it to his chest.

Karin continued. "Paul is going to make arrangements for them to leave sometime in the next few days, as soon as everything can be arranged."

"We'll help get things ready for her," Caro spoke in a firm voice. "Whatever she needs, just tell me and I'll get it. I want them to fly first class. I want her comfortable on the plane. Henk, call over there and tell Paul to get first-class tickets for all of them. Put it all on my card. Oh, and tell Dieter he can shut the bakery. He can just shut it down or leave it with Mike, but he can make the trip. He must not let work hold him back."

"Yes, I'll call Paul as soon as possible." Henk's expression matched everyone's. He felt a strong kinship with the woman who was more a sister than a friend to Carolina.

Carolina had to call her family in El Paso. She spoke first with Michelle, who cried at the news.

"I don't want anything to happen to you, Mommy. Promise me."

"Oh, my sweetheart, your mommy's as healthy as can be. I pray every day that God will keep me safe for you."

"I am so terribly sad about Aunt Greta."

"Yes, my love, we all are."

Thirty-Two

The entourage landed in Munich several days later. The entire Neuberg clan was on hand to welcome back their loved one. Greta's brothers and their families had taken time off to spend at least some precious time with all of them together. Both brothers, Frank and Martin, arrived for the weekend to bid their sister goodbye. The few days with her would have to be their last with her, for now.

"Gruss Gott" everyone said to each other as Greta was wheeled off the plane. She stood up determinedly, stating she was able to walk.

"It was a necessary precaution, hon. You can walk if you like, but the wheelchair is here in case you get tired," Paul told her.

"I'm having one of my good days, so I'll walk—slowly, of course. How nice of all of you to be here to meet me," she said in German to her brothers and their wives, Anna and Hilda.

Karin and Lotte took turns hugging Greta. Helga stood back, willing herself to hold back her tears. Greta looked well, though unusually thin.

"I know what all of you are thinking," Greta said with her usual hearty laugh. "I've never been this slender, so I know I look pretty good, huh?"

Everyone laughed, though not as heartily as Greta.

"I want everyone to cheer up. For as long as possible, I want to be treated like my old self. I'll do as much as I can, okay?"

Carolina also held back, waiting for Greta's family to have their time with her. Greta reached for Caro's arm and walked down the terminal, leaning a little as she needed to, chatting with her friend as if it were a usual occurrence.

"See, I'm fine today. There are many days like these, where I am so strong I can do just about anything. And I don't feel weak at all. Now, take me home to Grunwald, to my room facing the garden. I want to see the trees and feel the breeze coming in through the window."

Monika and Dieter admitted they felt strange to be back so soon. "We thought we'd stay in Los Angeles longer. It's still our desire to return. We love it there and Dieter loves the bakery," Monika stated firmly. She was afraid they'd never get back to LA.

Paul made himself at home among Greta's family. They put their arms around him and chatted as they waited for their luggage. Helga and Carolina had taken Greta to one of the cars. Henk would drive them on ahead of the others.

The days passed slowly. Greta was glad of that. She wanted to relish every single day, stretch every minute and hour as much as possible. Often she would walk slowly down the stairs to take breakfast and lunch with her mother. Helga had started cooking all of Greta's favorite dishes as soon as she knew Greta was on her way. Whoever was in the house would complete the circle for breakfast, often just tea or coffe and bread with butter and cheese. The aromas in Helga's kitchen were most enticing at any time, for she always had something either on the stove or in the oven, or both. Helga was determined Greta would have anything she desired and her nutrition would at least be at its best.

On many days Greta was strong enough to take a ride with Paul, who took either Henk's or Carolina's car. The two would set out for an hour or so to sightsee. Greta would point out the different attractions she wanted Paul to see.

Every afternoon Greta would rest in her bedroom, the sheer white curtains billowing in the breeze. She would doze off after reading a few lines of her old favorite German authors, books she had read as a teenager and were now most welcome to her. She would tell Carolina the story as she read bits of it, sometimes reading a few lines in German to her friend. Caro was at Greta's side every day.

"Mom is tiring a lot more," Monika reported after they had been there about three weeks. "Karin and Mutti took her to the doctor yesterday and he said it looks like she is getting nearer to the end. He suggested we call the family in."

Paul asked to be alone with Greta the day after they had been to the doctor.

"Greta, I've asked you before and I understand you had to say 'No,' but I'm asking you now to marry me. I'd like for you to be my wife before you—I'd be honored to have you be my wife now."

"Oh, Paul, I don't know why I was so stubborn. Of course I'll marry you. I'll be happy to be your wife, if only for a short time."

It took a few phone calls before the family priest, who was a friend of Karin's, was able to get everything arranged. Greta and Paul would be married with her sisters and Carolina as the witnesses.

Helga, her daughters, and Carolina helped Greta get dressed and sat her in a comfortable stuffed chair. They brought in another one for Paul to sit beside her. The family gathered in the hallway outside the room as the priest, Pater Ludwig, pronounced the couple husband and wife. Greta's bouquet of freesias and white roses had been picked from the garden, as she wished, and they lay in her lap.

"You are a beautiful bride, *meine schatz*, and I will treasure the memory of this day forever," Paul said almost in a whisper, holding back tears. He pinched himself as he said the words, telling himself it would be unmanly for him to break down. He leaned toward her to kiss her lips as she leaned in to him.

She smiled as big a smile as she could, and took a deep breath as she looked at him. I should have married him a long time ago, she told herself, nodding at him. I will tell him later how much I love him, she thought. I have to conserve my energy for now.

The group applauded softly and stepped down to the dining room, where Greta was going to attempt to join everyone, at least for a few minutes. Her sisters helped her out of the chair and down the stairs.

"No miserably unhappy faces," she had demanded. "You are all to celebrate my life. I've been blessed with wonderful people all around me all my life. My parents, especially my beloved Mutti, *mein Papa, meine schwestern*, my William, Carolina, *meine Monika und Dieter, meine bruder,* all my nieces and nephews. My dearest husband, Paul. I hope I have included every-one so dear to me."

She rested several minutes before she continued.

"I want a grand lunch or dinner, you can decide that, here in my *garten*, oh, dear, the German keeps coming up," she laughed at herself. "But the main thing is, everyone," she had raised her arm and slowly moved it side to side, "you all must celebrate." She said the word "celebrate" slowly, stressing every syllable, and nodding as she spoke, pointing her index finger at everyone. She laughed heartily, with the others slowly joining in her laughter.

Carolina nodded along with her friend as she stood beside Henk, saying in a soft voice to him, "That may be the last time we all hear her wonderful, strong laughter." Henk nodded solemnly.

A few days later, with a priest, Paul, Helga, and Carolina holding her hands, her sisters at the foot of the bed, Greta breathed her last. After the services, the feast was held in the garden as she had wished.

Paul refused to return to Los Angeles and at first rented a hotel room.

"What do you mean, 'stay in a hotel'? No, dear Paul, you must stay with one of us," Helga insisted. "I have several bedrooms upstairs that are empty most of the time. Only when I get company from my sons and their families, or now that Monika is here with Dieter, are those rooms used at all. No, Paul, you must stay here. At least for now—please accept my home as yours."

Monika was to stay on for a week and then return to "my new home in Los Angeles with my husband." Dieter had already made the trip back. Elena had returned to El Paso shortly after Greta's passing.

Thirty-Three

"Hello!"

"This is Carolina Morten. Is this Carol?"

"Yes. Thank you so much for calling." Carol was elated to hear Carolina's voice, but was nervous something would ruin her plan to meet with her privately.

"I'm looking forward to helping you," Caro said, smiling into the phone.

The guilt overcame Carol. She had used the ruse of Carolina's business and would have to follow through for her grandfather's sake.

Carolina continued, "When would you be able to meet me at the store?"

"At the store?"

"That's where the art pieces are. I don't have a warehouse here. The bulk is in Munich."

"I can meet you wherever you say, but I have a difficult schedule. I'm not available until after seven in the evening. I—have a full-time job. I'm a nurse, and I must continue working until I get this other business going."

"Oh, I see. We can meet here at my house, I guess."

Carol considered the offer an excellent omen.

"That would be so nice of you. I also need to see about getting a business partner." This is getting messy, Carol thought. I better cut it short.

"I have time tomorrow evening, anytime after seven. Let me give you the address and I'll see you here."

Carol hung up before she said too much. Her heart was pounding and she was so excited. She'd wait to tell her grandfather after she met with Carolina and followed through with her plan to give her the recording. Poor woman, she thought, she has no idea what a shocking secret I have to disclose to her.

Carolina had flown directly to Texas to spend time with Michelle and her family. Henk had offered to accompany her, but Carolina had told him she would easily be gone longer than the four or five weeks he could take off from work. Carolina was always amazed at how much vacation time the European countries gave their employees. She would shake her head at the thought of that happening in the US.

I dread going back to LA, Caro thought. I can't imagine going into the Couture Shoppe. She felt Greta's absence every day. How many times had Caro started to pick up the phone to chat with her friend?

Michelle was content with her grandparents. Caro knew she had made the right decision, allowing Michelle to stay in El Paso. This is her life now, she thought, this is where she belongs. I miss her so much. I'm glad I can fly in to spend time with her almost on the spur of the moment.

When Carolina finally flew to LA, she looked through her appointment book and the notation to call Carol. She was glad to have something pressing to do, if the promised phone call could be considered that. She would not go to the Couture Shoppe, she decided, not yet. It's running well with Connie's leadership. That meant not going to the shops she had created, her other business and bakery. I'll put it off as long as I can, she smiled wryly to herself.

As soon as Carol got off her shift she dashed home to get ready. She was too nervous to eat and was ready to leave in a few minutes. She set out well before the time she needed and found the address in ample time.

What a beautiful house, she thought. The trees give it a serene setting. She was several minutes early, but didn't want to wait any longer.

"Hello," Carolina said cheerfully at the door. "I'm happy we were able to meet at last. May I offer you something to drink?"

"Thanks, some tea or lemonade will be fine. What a beautiful home you have, Mrs. Morten."

"Thank you. Please, call me Carolina. Our names are similar, mine is the Spanish version of yours."

"Yes. I love the way you say it, the way you roll the *r*."

"I never got your last name."

"It's Russell."

Carolina's smile froze. That last name, what an odd coincidence, she thought. She showed her guest into the living room. "Please, make yourself comfortable while I get the lemonade."

After pouring lemonade, she placed the tray on the

table. "You're considering opening up a shop—there's a lot involved. Where had you thought about setting up? Do you have experience in business?"

Carol felt terrible. I can't go on with this story, she thought, almost in desperation. For a while she did not reply. Carolina looked at her questioningly.

"I—I have to be—truthful with you, Carolina." She sipped her drink. What if she throws me out? she wondered. "You're from El Paso, aren't you?" She spoke quickly, stalling for time.

"Yes, I am. Are you familiar with that part of Texas?"

"In a way, yes. My grandfather and his parents were from there, a long time ago. I've heard quite a bit about it."

"My family has been there as long as anyone can remember, before it was a city, actually. What a small world, Carol."

"I hope you don't get upset with me, Carolina. I—I have something for you to listen to—something that will strike you as not being true. But it is all true, and it's very important that you listen to it. You'll be glad I brought it to you." Now I'm rambling, she thought. She must think I'm a lunatic.

Carolina's face went pale and her eyes opened wide. Russell. No, surely it can't be . . . She was silent, staring at the young woman seated in front of her, looking at her features, wondering . . .

"My grandfather knew your family quite well. That's why I'm here—the real reason I'm here. Please don't be angry with me, and please promise me you will listen to the tape recording I'm going to give you."

Carol opened her purse to take out the tape, not daring to look up.

Carolina was silent, her mind reeling. She sat back in the chair and heard the words the woman was saying and she knew. It's him—and this is his granddaughter. I guess she's my niece.

Carol was frightened by the look on Carolina's face as she raised her eyes. She was trying to read what she saw. As a nurse, she was trained to look for nonverbal signs, and this was definitely one of those. She couldn't tell if Carolina was stunned because she was angry or because of disbelief. It looked like a bit of both to Carol. She wished the woman would say something.

Finally Carolina spoke. In a very low, sweet voice she asked, "What is your grandfather's name?" Her polite tone was a good sign for Carol. She's not angry! she thought. She cleared her throat, afraid her voice would crack.

"It's . . . it's Robert Russell." She said the name slowly and waited to see the effect on Carolina.

Carolina immediately let out a small gasp. Her face showed several reactions at once: shock, pleasure, displeasure, confusion, and again shock. What confused Carol the most was a look of relief as the lovely woman shook her head slowly.

"How—how did you find me?" Her voice was low, gentle, almost childlike. She sat back in the comfortable chair and touched the armrest covers, smoothing first one and then the other, almost without being aware of what she was doing. Her face was pale. The smile on Carolina's face was oddly forced. Carol felt an urge to go over and embrace Carolina and console her. She resisted for the moment.

"Gramps has been looking for you, Carolina. He has been in agony and heartbroken for so long. I knew I had to do something. This was the only way I could get to you. Please—listen to this tape. He's poured his heart into it. It will be a shock to you. Will you listen to it?"

After a long silence, Carolina answered in a strong voice. "Yes, I will. Tonight. After you leave, I'll listen to it."

"And you'll call me? It's important. He desperately wants to meet you. If you'll allow it. At least think about it before you decide either way." Carol was holding back tears.

"Yes, I know. We will meet. I promise you." Her voice was soft and kind and gentle. Carol could not believe her good fortune. Oh, Gramps will be so happy, she thought. Her tears were flowing now.

Carolina sat by the young woman and put her arms around her, calming her. Carol placed her head on Caro's shoulder and cried like a child, the way she had cried on Gramps' shoulder when her mother had left.

"You said you know. What do you mean you know?" she sniffled.

"I knew he was looking for me."

"How? When? How did you know about him?"

"I've known a long time."

"You have? How?"

"It's a long story, my dear. No one knows I've known all these years. I heard them talking—my mother and Robert. I'll tell you the story another time, after I've heard the tape."

"All this time, you knew?" The younger woman's

voice was shrill in disbelief. "He doesn't know that you knew. He thinks you have no idea. Oh, my God, this will be a shock to him. He's my dearest Gramps. He's the sweetest man you'd ever want to know. He is the best dad and grandpa."

"Carol, you and I have the same name. I was named after his mother. That's what I heard that—that awful day. I was in the bedroom, but no one knew I was there. I heard bits and pieces, not everything, but enough to know he was my real father. It would have torn the families apart if the truth had been known. My mother doesn't know I know. No one has any idea how I've kept the secret and guarded it with my life."

"Oh, you poor thing—what a terrible thing to go through." Carol was crying again. "I've heard from Gramps that your family is wonderful, that your dad is such a highly respected man. He told me after my grandma passed away. He couldn't hold it back any longer how he's kept track of you all these years. He always knew where you were. He's afraid he'll die without meeting you at least once."

"I'll listen to the recording. It means a lot to me to finally know the story behind—me. How I came to be. My sisters don't know. One of them, Lisa, the snoopy one, has been after me to find out what happened that summer, the summer I found out. I've always managed to keep it from her. This would devastate her. She thinks—we all think—our parents are perfection itself. I've made a life for myself away from home, and even though my daughter lives with them, at times it's still hard for me when I'm with them and see how close everyone is."

"I better go now so you can listen to the tape. He asked me to listen, but I only heard the first minute or so. It's too personal. I want you to be the first to hear it. Do you think you will consider coming to meet him? It would mean the world to him. He would be so happy, you can't imagine. It can stay our secret, just the three of us. We'll be our own little family here in LA."

"You're such a sweet young woman. Yes, we'll meet. I'll call you tomorrow and set up a day and time to meet very soon."

"You're wonderful. I love you already. You're my Auntie Carolina, in Spanish, like Gramps says it. I can't roll the *r* but I try."

"It's fine the way you pronounce it. Are you okay to drive?"

"I'm fine. I'll be waiting for your phone call. Thank you, Carolina."

Though the evening had been emotionally draining, Caro was eager to listen to the tape. She went to her room to her comfortable chaise, a box of tissues by her side along with a tall glass of lemonade. She turned the machine on.

The raspy voice was the same she had heard so many years ago, but much older now. The tenderness came through as she heard his words.

"This is Robert Russell speaking on June twenty-third. I am in full capacity of mind and body and wish to tell the story of how I came to be the father of a wonderful woman, Carolina Sanchez Morten." A shuffling of papers could be heard, followed by a few seconds of silence. "I hope to tell this in chronological order so it will make sense to my daughter. I wish no harm to any of the persons mentioned by me and ask God to help me through this story I have carried with me all these years."

Carolina leaned back and closed her eyes as she listened to his voice. She knew she would cry, but she was prepared to hear their story. She had waited for this moment since that day she first heard his voice. Calmness settled over her as she listened.

"It was the summer of 1942. I was twenty-nine years old, married with two children. My mother had been sick so I went to visit and help out at the grocery store in El Paso. My wife and I had been living in Los Angeles seven years by then. I would take a break from the little grocery store each evening around eight, after I'd closed it, walking around the neighborhood, remembering where my brothers and I had gone to school and all the good times we had.

I saw a pretty lady working on her front garden and said a simple hello. She smiled at me. A few evenings went by where I'd see her sitting on the porch, watching her little girls playing and tending to her flowers.

One evening I stopped to talk a bit. She was the prettiest lady I had ever seen, with big dark eyes and beautiful dark curly hair, her skin a light tan. I told her now nice her garden was, and she told me how much she loved her flowers. 'They are my passion,' she said, 'after my family.' I asked about her, where she was from, as she had a slight accent, and she told me her story. I told her my family was in California, that my mother had the grocery store a couple of blocks down. It was all innocent talk. We didn't mean for anything to happen. I figured her husband was gone to war. I accepted a glass of lemonade and sat on the porch with her. She said her husband was at work, he was on the early evening shift. Another night I asked after the children. They had all gone to their grandmother's house, she said. We talked and talked. I knew I was falling in love with her, her sweetness, her soft voice, her slender body. Her hands touched mine as she handed me a glass and we just looked at each other a long time.

Finally one evening she told me it would be best if I did not stop to visit with her anymore. I asked her why and she looked away. I reached for her hand. She let me hold it. I left, vowing to myself not to return. But I'd walk by, not daring to go near. One night I saw her on the porch. I stood looking at her. I walked up to her and took both her hands in mine and kissed them. She was standing so close I could smell the sweetness of her hair. I touched her shoulder. We walked in the house and kissed passionately. I told her how I had fallen in love the first day I saw her. We both cried when she nodded. 'It's wrong,' she kept saying. I told her I didn't care—our love was more important than anything else. We saw each other every night when she was alone after that. The children stayed with family most of those nights. I knew she sent them so we could be alone. We were passionately in love and lived for those moments together. Maybe it was the war or the heat of the summer or knowing we had only those few hours. We told each other everything about our lives. I wanted desperately for us to be together forever. I knew we would hurt our families, but that did not matter to me at the time."

Carolina heard his sobs for several seconds before hearing him clicking off his recording.

He cleared his throat and continued, "Sorry, it's still very hard for me to think about those days. She had only known her husband and had never had other boyfriends. I begged Esther to come away with me to start a new life. I told her I would support both families. I would never shirk my duty to my children. Esther wouldn't hear of it. She cried when I told her I had to return home. She said she could never leave Miguel, he's a wonderful husband and father and she loved him. She was so young when they met and married.

It was a terrible time for both of us. We knew we were wrong and we said goodbye, swearing never to get in touch with each other again.

When I visited again sixteen years later and saw her at the store—I had to talk to her. We arranged to meet one day when no one else would be at her home. That was when I found out about my daughter—our daughter. I felt the rush of love for Esther all over again. She had to tell me, she said. She had been devastated when she found she was pregnant—she knew the child could only be mine. She did not go into details, but that was not necessary. I knew it was the truth. I had fathered a child despite the precautions we had taken."

A few clicks were heard. His voice continued in a firm tone.

"From that day, my life changed. I wanted to see and meet this daughter of mine. She had named the child Carolina, after my mother. I was able to get a few photographs that first day. I saw a beautiful girl, very much like her mother, but with dark auburn hair, like mine—a sweet, innocent child who was growing up believing her father to be the man who raised her. I loved the child from the moment I heard about her. Not one day went by that I did not look at her pictures and think about her. I started to keep an album, hidden away in my shop, in a safe. I learned she married and went to live in Salinas. I have the newspaper clipping of that wedding. Before the paper became yellowed and aged, I made copies and had them encased in plastic. Esther would occasionally call me to let me know how she was and where.

I made a trip to Salinas and found where she lived—a pretty little house with flowers all around. I saw her one day tending to her flowers, just like Esther. I didn't want to call attention to myself so I only drove by a few times. I gave myself a week off from the shop and managed to get away by myself. At Mass on Sunday I saw her with her husband. I walked by her, even smiled at her, and she smiled back. Of course, she did not have any idea who I was, but I still remember her smile. There was something about her husband that wasn't right, I remember thinking, and it turns out I figured correctly. She left him. And the reason was a good one.

I got the news she moved to Los Angeles. I learned from Esther she was staying at her aunt's house. I saw her a few times. I didn't dare go to the sewing shop where she worked, but I saw her from my car. She was prettier than ever. She looked the way Esther did at that age. I have a few pictures I took at that time."

Carolina stopped the recorder and let her tears of joy, sadness, relief, and happiness flow freely. "He has loved me so much," she said aloud. Caro was tired and sleepy but wanted to finish the entire tape.

"The wedding photograph from the second marriage is here in front of me. The man is older, he has a distinguished air. She is truly happy in this photo, especially when I compare the two wedding pictures. Here's the announcement of the birth of their daughter—my granddaughter, Karen Michelle. I noticed the child has his name—Miguel's. I was shocked to read the obituary of her husband, Jack. Esther called me with the terrible news the same day I read about it. The whole family was in mourning. She told me what a fine man Jack was and what a good life he, Caro, and the little girl had together. I had never heard Esther sound so sad. She also made a comment that stayed in my heart. She said, 'I love Carolina—but she reminds me of my sin. It's so hard for me to be close to her.'"

Carolina shut the recorder off. She clenched her fists and sobbed. "That's why," she said aloud, over and over, angry, bitter, yet relieved. That's why she has such a hard time showing me her love. She lay on the bed and cried until she fell asleep. She awoke at dawn, showered, and prepared her coffee. She took the recorder to the kitchen and turned on the tape where she had stopped it.

"I've been in Carolina's house, the house she lived in with Jack. I felt their presence. No one was around so I touched the furniture and walls. When the workmen returned I said I was interested in buying the house."

He laughed, saying, "As if I could afford such a grand place. But it's her house and I love it. I thought she was selling it and I wanted to be in it before it went to someone else. Then I finally heard from Esther—Carolina's moved to Munich! Well, there goes my dream of seeing her again and maybe meeting her.

I remember telling Esther that my paternal grandmother was from Munich! I cannot imagine a more fitting city for my daughter to live in. Grandmother would sing to me and tell me about her beloved Alps. I can hear her voice with the German accent saying Alpen, how much she missed Munchen, pronouncing it in German. How my grandmother loved that city and the forest. And now Carolina lives there and loves it, too."

Carolina held her hand to her mouth in surprise as she heard this and stopped the tape recorder to take in the thoughts going round in her head. "That would explain my feelings for the city and Bavaria in general, wouldn't it?" she asked herself out loud. She sipped her coffee as she lost herself in her thoughts, remembering the first two days in that city, her adopted home, and how unusually comfortable she felt there without knowing anyone other than Greta's family and not having seen more of the city.

She clicked the recorder on again. Robert's voice was strong at this point. "Caro is doing very well in business. I wanted to think she took after me in that respect, but I can't take the credit. She's a sharp-minded woman, independent, kind, generous to family and friends. I feel like I do know her, hearing about her and seeing pictures of her.

I pray—I beg God to give me the blessing of living long enough to get to meet her in person, talk to her, maybe even spend time with her. I don't ask her to deny her other father, for he is an excellent man. I'd just like a few moments with her, for her to know how much I've loved her all these years."

There were a few seconds where she could hear his breathing, and then he said, "That's all."

She shut the recorder off.

She picked up the phone and called Carol, who answered on the third ring.

"I'm sorry to call so early."

"No, Carolina. I need to get up and get going. Did you . . ."

"Yes, I heard it all. It was beautiful. I can't tell you how touched I am. I want to tell him in person. It's short notice, but would you and Robert—my father—be able to come over for an early Thanksgiving dinner tomorrow?"

Carol's huge smile accompanied her resounding "Yes, we would love that. You have no idea how happy he will be to hear this. What time would you like us to come over?"

"I have the whole day free for you. Come as early as you can. If possible, spend the day with me. Is there anything he can't or shouldn't eat?"

"Oh, he's a hearty eater. I guess just cut back on salt. That is wonderful of you."

"It's my pleasure. I'm looking forward to our meeting. Come as early as you can. I'll prepare a special breakfast. We can sit around and talk while I prepare a big meal."

"He'll love that, Carolina. Bless you."

"Bless you, my dear."

Carolina placed the phone back on its receiver.

I'll have to go to the store to get groceries, she thought, getting her notepad to make a list. How I wish

I could talk to Greta and tell her all that's happened. I can hear her voice telling me, Schatzie, this is your chance to have peace now that you know what happened all those years ago. Yes, I can hear her as if she were standing here in my kitchen. She would be happy and excited for me.

She brushed a tear aside. I miss Greta so much, she realized. I don't think I'll ever get over losing my friend. Enough! she thought. No more tears. All these years I've wondered so much about what happened and what made my mother so "indifferent" to me. I could never understand her. Now maybe I can. It must have been so terrible for her to have me. I can only imagine what went through her mind when she found out she was to have a child with this man. It had to be the worst day of her life. And yet, here I am, a happy woman, for the most part, and I, too, have had my share of pain and suffering along with the beautiful days I had with Jack, and now with Henk. I would not change one day of my life despite all that I've been through, first with Joseph and then meeting my wonderful Jack, having my precious Michelle, and now the kindness and warmth I have with Henk.

Carolina wanted to set aside time for Robert—she could not yet call him father—and give themselves time for what would be emotional moments together. From what Robert said, and Carol's keen interest in having the two meet, their time together could be limited.

I hope he's in good health. We have to make up for all the time that's passed, she thought. I'll have to keep this secret side of my life to myself—Michelle won't be able to take the truth. I'll have to keep it from her. She mustn't know now, and especially while my parents are so much a part of her life. Awkward and odd as it sounds, I'm looking forward to the meeting and finally knowing what he's like.

I wonder if . . .

She took her car keys and went out the door to buy the groceries.

Thirty-Four

Esther was putting dishes away after breakfast. She hummed as she placed the last cups and saucers in the cupboard. It was so nice to have all her family at home over the Christmas holiday. She sensed something different about Carolina, but could not put her finger on it. Her youngest daughter and Michelle had left right after breakfast to visit Ana, Esther's mother, who was doing quite well for her eighty-nine years, and Esther's sisters. The three women had moved out to a ranch, as they called it, by the New Mexico border, almost an hour outside of town.

Thoughts ran through Esther's head. Carolina loves living in Munich and visits her daughter frequently, living the best of both worlds. She's a free spirit, independent, strong, much like me, though I have given in to please the most wonderful husband in Texas. It won't be long before Michelle will choose to go live with her mother, Esther thought. We'll have to let her go. My granddaughter needs her mother.

Her pleasant thoughts were interrupted by the phone ringing.

Her heart skipped a beat as she heard Robert's voice after she said a soft "Hello."

"Can you talk, Esther?"

"Si, Roberto, what a surprise to hear your voice. I hope all is well."

"Yes, Esther." He was quiet a long time before he continued. Neither of them said anything for a while.

"I took a chance calling you. If anyone else had answered I would have hung up. It's so good to hear your voice. Say something, just so I can hear your voice."

"Well, I hope you had a nice Christmas, Roberto. We've been busy, all of us, getting ready for the big day with all our grandchildren here. They are all mostly grown up now. We had a big dinner that day, on the twenty-fifth. What about you, how is everything going with you?"

Robert was silent such a long time Esther wondered if he was still there.

"Hello?"

"Yes, I'm here, Esther. I want to tell you the most wonderful thing has happened to me. I almost didn't want to tell you but it's too special for me. I—I met her. I've spent time with her. The first day was about a month ago. She cooked for me and for Carol, my granddaughter. It was a delicious meal but it wouldn't have mattered what she cooked. Being with her was a dream come true. We talked all day. She told me all about her youth, how she sewed all the time, when she started working at her shop here in LA. She told me about her friend, Greta, and how she misses her. The next time we met we went to a park she said reminded her of the open-air zoo in Munich. I told her about my grandmother and her Alpen. She cried when I told her about her great-grandmother. She's such a joy to know. I had to tell you. It seemed like something I had to share with you, Esther. She'll never tell anyone, she promised me. She could never hurt anyone in her family so she'll keep the secret."

He waited for a response. He thought he could hear her breathing. Maybe she's crying with happiness for me, he thought.

"Esther? Are you there?"

He had no way of knowing Esther was in shock. She kept shaking her head and mouthing the words over and over. "No. No. It can't be. It can't be. *No puede ser. No puede ser.*" Her mind switched back and forth from English to Spanish. She thought she was saying the words out loud. Her mouth was open and she wondered why no sound was coming out. She finally replaced the receiver and sat at the kitchen table, staring straight ahead. Now and again she would say the words again, this time aloud. "No. No. It can't be."

She had no idea how much time passed before Miguel walked in and found her.

"Esther—my God, Esther, what's happened? What's wrong, mi amor?" He called Anita and thankfully she was home and rushed over.

"She's not talking. She's been sitting there, not answering me since I got home a few minutes ago."

"Mom!" Anita shook Esther but there was no response, though Esther's eyes were open.

"We have to get her to a doctor—no, to the hospital. Let's put her in my car. I'll drive, Dad, you're too upset," Anita said.

The hospital was a few minutes away and the

emergency room was almost empty. Esther was taken into an exam room almost at once. A doctor ordered tests and was looking at the results as fluids were being put into Esther's veins. It seemed that in no time at all the doctor told Miguel and Anita the news.

"Mrs. Sanchez has suffered a heart attack, and she's responding well to the medication we're giving her. What concerns me, though, is she seems to be in a state of shock that does not often accompany her illness. Do you know if she went through anything traumatic recently?"

Both Miguel and Anita shook their heads, looking at each other in wonder. Miguel spoke, "She was fine when I left this morning and a few hours later I found her staring, not speaking; she wouldn't answer me." He broke down and could not continue. Anita put her arms around her father as best she could, as he easily stood a head taller.

"I know you're worried, Mr. Sanchez. We're going to do everything to help her come out of this. She'll rest and hopefully whatever caused the shock will be eased as the hours pass. She'll be in the cardiac unit for a while until she is over the worst of this." The kind physician smiled wanly, sensing the family's warmth and closeness, hoping to give both husband and daughter an optimal prognosis. "I do believe she'll come out of this as strong as she seems to be."

Miguel and Anita stepped out. They sat next to each other silently.

"We need to start calling the others to come in to visit Esther," Miguel said.

"Yes, I know, but we also need to let her rest. When they all start coming in—you know how hectic our family can be. Let's give her a little more time, at least until she gets up to the unit." Anita sounded clearheaded.

"As you know, we decided to move to this ranch, on the west side of the city, about a year ago. We have everything we need, thank God, and all of the family is minutes away," Grandmother Ana reported. She was as strong as ever, it seemed, as were Esther's sisters, who were both widowed. "All I take is an aspirin every other day. I use my glasses only for reading. Look at Amelia and Mariana—they still sew almost every day. They don't really need any more dresses or skirts, so most of the items they sew are donated to a ladies' group in the village."

"I'm so happy to have you and my aunts, Abuelita, you have always been my inspiration. Now I hope Michelle will also have you as her models."

Michelle hugged her great-grandmother and her own mother. Amelia and Mariana were in the kitchen preparing lunch for the small group.

"The women in our family do seem to be healthy and strong," Michelle voiced. "I hope I'll be like that, too."

After lunch they all sat around and talked, Grandmother Ana dozing off now and then. Michelle cuddled into her mother's side, looking up at her in admiration, thinking the obvious.

I have to go live with my mom, Michelle thought. I have to leave the home I've known the most. I can come visit every time my mom comes in, which is pretty often, so it won't be like I'm gone forever.

As they were saying their goodbyes later in the day,

the phone rang. It was Anita. She said to Carolina, who answered the phone, "Mom's not feeling well so Dad took her into the hospital. She's doing okay but we thought you should go to the hospital instead of going home and not finding anyone there. Don't say anything to Grandma or our aunts yet."

"Oh! What happened? She was fine this morning."

"We'll tell you when you get here. She is fine, though, but she'll be kept in the hospital a day or so." Anita sounded calm so Carolina went along with not telling the others, not wanting to cause them unnecessary distress.

Carolina made an effort to sound less nervous than she felt. How ironic, she thought, we were just talking about how healthy the women are, and now this. What could be wrong? She felt a chill.

"Well, thank you all for a lovely day. I'll call you tomorrow to see what your plans are for New Year's," Carolina said to her aunts and grandmother. She hoped she sounded like her usual self. It was understood that she would keep alarming news from her grandmother and aunts until she had something definite to tell.

After more hugs, Carolina and Michelle were on their way.

"We're stopping by the hospital to see Grandma. Anita wouldn't say exactly what happened, but it seems Grandma's not feeling well." Carolina clasped Michelle's hand with her free hand.

"Grandma's strong—she'll be fine. You'll see." Michelle's young voice had an expected maturity. She had lived through sorrow in her young life. "She's never sick, so it's probably some bug she picked up."

Miguel and Anita were outside the cardiac unit waiting by the elevator as Carolina and Michelle arrived. They all wrapped their arms around each other in a four-person hug. Michelle wiped away a tear, turning her face from the group.

"She's better, hija. The doctor just told us she's out of danger, thank God. She's sleeping, so we mustn't wake her. One of us can go in for a minute or so, not more." Miguel's voice was strong and firm. "I know she's going to be fine."

Carolina went in to be by her mother's side and reached for her hand as Esther blinked her eyes open and smiled as straight a smile as she could muster. She grabbed Carolina's hand, grasping it tightly. A tear rolled down Esther's face, falling to the pillow. Carolina stood silently, and then sat by the bed. Their eyes did not waver from each other's. Esther opened her mouth and swallowed, wetting her lips to speak.

"Hija, I'm glad you're here." She waited, gaining her strength. "Forgive me. Please forgive me." Her tears rolled down each side.

Carolina wiped her mother's tears with her hands. "Mom—don't stress yourself." She choked back her own tears. "Rest for now. We can talk later." She kissed her mother's forehead as she continued to wipe Esther's tears. "I love you, Mom. Just get well. You don't have to say anything to me. Your love is all I need or want."

"Si, hija. You have all my love." Esther closed her eyes with a tranquil smile on her face. She whispered, "Miguel."

Miguel walked in and held his wife's hands. He leaned over to kiss her lips lightly. "I'm here, Esther.

I'm always by your side."

Esther nodded as she dozed off.

"She's doing very well. The shock seems to have dissipated. We may never know what caused it. When the neurologist spoke with Mrs. Sanchez, she had no memory of what transpired immediately before she suffered the myocardial infarction, the heart attack. She's being checked out to see what damage there is to her heart. We'll let you know as the tests come in." The doctor shook Miguel's proffered hand as he spoke.

"Thank you. You've been everything I had hoped for. My family thanks you, doctor."

As the days passed and Esther recuperated, she realized she had no memory of the hours prior to her heart attack, just as the doctors told her. She had a vague feeling of discomfort related to the day it happened, but she could not state what it was. I may never know, she thought.

She thought of Robert—my Roberto, as she always thought of him—and wondered why he was so present in her mind these days. I have not spoken to him for over a year, not since that time we talked about Carolina living in Munich and how touched he was then, knowing his own history, she remembered.

As she continued to recuperate while still in the hospital, she made up her mind. She would spend time with Carolina, making up for all the years her youngest daughter was gone. Yes, even though Carolina would leave again, Esther would dedicate whatever time Carolina afforded her own family in El Paso to do anything Carolina wanted.

Once at home the days went by peacefully, with Carolina by her mother's side most of the time. Michelle was in school, of course, so the two had most of the days together. They cooked. Occasionally Carolina would sew and Esther would be nearby, commenting on her daughter's creations. How talented she is, Esther thought, just like my sisters. Too bad I did not inherit this talent, at least not as good as the others.

She noticed a sadness in Carolina a few weeks later. Carolina went off by herself and would not tell anyone what had occurred. Esther could not have guessed the sorrow Carolina was hiding, nor how much it would have affected her, Esther.

It is just as well, Carolina thought, that Mom does not know Robert passed away, days after her recovery from her illness. The fact gnawed at Carolina. Should I tell Mom? But how can I justify knowing Robert and that he passed away so suddenly, so unexpectedly?

Esther had been in the hospital a few days when Carolina received a call from Los Angeles, with Carol using the pretext of the art business. The first phone call had taken Carolina by surprise.

"He asked me to call and ask how you and your family are, Carolina."

"Mom's suffered a heart attack, two days after Christmas. She was alone in the house, so we're not sure exactly what happened. Dad found her in shock."

Then a week later Carol had called with her horrific news. Robert had also suffered a heart attack, a couple of days after learning of Esther's sudden illness. Carol was coping but having a hard time, considering how close she had been to her gramps, she said.

"I can't help feeling there's a connection with Esther's illness. He was so insistent the first time I called you about news on Esther. When I told him she was in the hospital, he almost fainted. I probably shouldn't have told him straight out, but it's hard for me to keep news like that a secret. People have a right to know what's happening to their loved ones. I can't help but feel he knew, somehow, that Esther was not doing well before I called you, and then he had his own heart attack days later."

"It is odd, and even touching, that he insisted on knowing how mom was. She was in shock the first twenty-four hours, Carol. Nobody could explain what happened to cause that. When the doctors examined her, she had no memory of the morning of the heart attack. It all seems strange, frankly."

"Yes, it does. I'm trying to settle everything to do with his estate. He left a lot more, financially, than I'd expected. There's the house and all the furniture my grandmother collected—antiques, and such. I'm having everything appraised. I guess I'll inherit all of it, but I sure wish I still had him. He was everything I had. I don't even know where my mother is, if she's alive, and I've never kept in touch with her side of the family."

"Well, you do have me. I am your aunt," Carolina said as she laughed softly, trying to lighten the mood. "We can talk whenever you want, or need to, Carol. I'm a phone call away. When you get vacation time, come stay with me in Munich."

"Oh, Carolina, that is so sweet of you. Thank you, my dear aunt. I may take you up on that beautiful offer. I feel like I've known you a long time and yet, think about it, it's been only a few months. You're a special person, you know that? You're kind, and forgiving. I'm so glad we were able to get together, and you made

Gramps' last few months so happy."

"I was glad to do it, Carol. This is a sad day for me, though I can't mourn Robert openly. I will mourn his passing in my own way. I have no idea how Mom will take it if she finds out. I don't think I can tell her. There's no one from his family left in town, so she won't know that way, either. We'll see—she may find out some other way on her own. I don't think it's a good time for her to hear such news, with her just getting over her own illness."

Days later, as Carol was going through her grandfather's final papers, settling his estate and paying off what he had left pending, she realized she was looking at the reason for all that had happened, just days after Christmas. She stared open-mouthed at the telephone bill. Should I tell Carolina? she wondered, or will she see, as I'm seeing with my own eyes, that Robert did indeed cause Esther's illness, and eventually his own death? Carol put the bill down on the table and wept bitterly.

Thirty-Five

"Everyone is fine, thank you, Helga. I had a quick phone call from Karin just yesterday with the same questions. 'When am I coming home to Munich?' she wanted to know. I probably won't leave until the school break so I can take Michelle to stay. How are you doing?"

"I've been doing the same as usual," Helga said with a sigh. "I realize I have to watch my own health after the scare with your mother. I had a full check-up last week and everything came back normal. How are you spending your time? You're used to gardening and taking care of your business."

"I never dreamed I'd enjoy playing cards almost every day with my mom, sisters, and also my aunts and grandmother on occasion. I've spent time with Marta, my oldest sister, sort of getting to know her now as an adult. I forgot how much they all enjoy the innocent fun of card games. I've gotten pretty good at all of them. Michelle joins in when she doesn't have too much homework. All in all, it's been a pleasant time, getting together just about any time without the pressure of my leaving. When I come back I'll teach you the games so all of us can play."

"I can't wait for you to come back. I realize how much I miss you and how close I've become to you. You're a link to my Greta, you see that, don't you, Caro? Though I love you for yourself, too."

"Yes, I know, Helga," Caro smiled and laughed. "I'm eager to get back, too, but for now, spending time with my mom has been at the top of my priorities. It's been a miracle for me to have her like she is now. I'll tell you more about it when I get back. Oh, thank you for keeping up with the gardener and whatever needs to be done to my house."

"I'm glad to help in any way I can. Oh, of course I heard from Monika with the news of their business."

"It was natural for Monika and Dieter to take over the bakery, and it's fair that he gets to be the owner. He's putting in all the work and running it quite well from the reports I get. I let the two ladies, Maria and Edna, who were assisting Greta in the shop, purchase the business for a few dollars. I know that's what Greta would have wanted. The one who ran the shop, Connie, helped out so much, but in the end I decided the other two women deserve a break, like the one I got. Though I own the building, the women will keep all the profits. Their rent will be minimal, though; they need the tax break."

"What happened to Connie?"

"The last I heard she's dancing with a group and doing fairly well with that. That was always her first love. I don't know what happened with her family though."

"I've redone the bedrooms now that Paul has moved out. Except for Greta's. That will stay the same. I'm not ready for any change in her room yet. My sons want me to come visit them so I may go soon."

"That's good. The trip will be great for all of you. I also hear from Henk almost every week."

"Were you surprised when you found out about your niece and Frank?"

"No, not really, not after the way he behaved around Elena when they met in Munich."

Caro and Helga said their goodbyes and Caro thought back to the week before, when Elena's news came out. Esther and Caro were visiting in Anita's home when Elena walked in with a smile that rivaled the sun's rays. They all looked expectantly at Elena.

"Stay seated, the three of you. Though you can see how happy I am, it will be a bit of a surprise when I tell you." Elena waited to have their attention. "Aunt Carolina, I know you won't be completely surprised to hear my news. I will have a visitor quite soon. He's coming all the way from Germany to spend time with me, to get to know me, to meet our family. He'll stay in a room I've found for him nearby, or he might stay at my brother's apartment, and then we'll see what happens."

She waited for everything to fall into place. Carolina stared at her niece. Anita started to stand up, reaching her arms out to Elena, but Carolina held her down. The three older women were seated on the sofa and Elena took the easy chair facing them.

"Yes, it's Frank. He's been calling me and we've talked so much and I can't wait to see him. He's the most wonderful man I've ever met."

"He may be that," Carolina interrupted, "but he's also engaged to a lovely woman and they have been together for years. They were planning a wedding for next summer. Elena, that doesn't sound to me like the 'most wonderful man' for you."

"Hija, how can you do this, when you know how painful it is to have a relationship destroyed? Think about your own feelings—how would you feel if this happened to you? I don't know how I can face this young man. When is he supposed to get here?" Anita asked.

"Next week. He was going to wait until summer, but he's taken a leave of absence from his job and will spend a month here. That may be enough for us to know if we are meant to be together. I wanted him to stay longer, but he doesn't want to risk losing his job. He's also told Agnes about us. Their engagement is off."

They sat silently, taking in the news. The older women, who had life experiences they held in their hearts, looked at the cheerful, young woman with the dark, curly hair bobbing as she spoke so lightheartedly about a future with a young man. They were lost in their thoughts. The oldest, thinking of the perfidy of her life that had resulted in the birth of the daughter seated next to her and all the pain endured from that indiscretion, asked herself if she would do it again if she could. Would she have had the affair, loved that other man who was not her husband, had a beautiful daughter who was now giving her such pure joy? Would she? She nodded to herself yes, a thousand times, yes.

Anita thought of the pain she had gone through, discovering her "true love" had not been true after all. How she had grown after facing a future without her husband—that was what she now thought about. Not the pain, but the strength she had found in the challenge of fending for herself, at least in getting the education she had always denied herself, or thought she could not obtain. Yet, here she was, doing well in the adult classes she was taking, excelling, in fact, and serving as a role model to the younger women who were just getting started.

Carolina thought of her own existence. She would not be here if it had not been for her mother's love affair with a man who haunted them both, all these years. She could not now look in judgment upon her mother and accuse her of anything. Who am I to judge? she thought. Who are any of us to judge?

All three started speaking at once.

"Do what is right for you, hija."

"Follow your heart, Elena."

"If he's the right one for you, you'll know."

They all laughed as they drowned out each other's voices.

Elena spoke somberly.

"You first, Mom."

"I said, 'Do what is right for you.' If he loves you enough to change the direction of his life, then take the chance. You're young, you have a right to give someone a chance you might not get again."

"Okay. Now you, Grandma."

"I said, 'He might be the right one for you.' If he is, your heart will tell you. I know it's hard to have things going against you, but he hasn't made the final commitment to the other young woman. It's best to know now if he is the one for you."

"Auntie Carolina?"

"I say, 'Follow your heart.' That's all. If you love him and he loves you, don't let anyone keep you apart."

Elena smiled at the three women sitting in front of her, three women she loved with all her heart. Her curls bobbed as she nodded happily at them.

About the Author

I am a registered nurse, work full time. Enjoy time with my family and friends, travel around the United States and Europe.